THE VAMPIRE OF SIAM
THE SIAMESE CONNECTION

JIM NEWPORT

Encyclopocalypse Publications
www.encyclopocalypse.com

ISBN: 978-1-960721-33-4

The author acknowledges the use of lyrics
from the following songs:

"Ain't Nobody's Business"
Porter Grainger & Everett Robbins
MCA Music Publishing.

"The Sleepers"
Kurt Elling
B.M.I.

Cover formatting and design by Sean Duregger
Vampire of Siam logo and branding designed by Ben Howard of Eqco.one
Internal formatting by Sean Duregger
Author photograph: Anthony Edwards

www.vampireofsiam.com

BOOKS BY JIM NEWPORT

The Vampire of Siam

Ramonne: The Return of The Vampire of Siam

The Reckoning: A Tale of The Vampire of Siam

Chasing Jimi

Tinsel Town

The Siamese Connection

A Dark Christmas

PRAISE FOR JIM NEWPORT

THE VAMPIRE OF SIAM

"Grand Guignol entertainment...good for nibbling on the beach."

— JAMES ECKARDT, THE NATION.

"Chilling and morbidly hilarious. Newport's intimate knowledge of the Far East makes this an ultra-realistic journey into terror."

— PULITZER PRIZE NOMINATED AUTHOR
CHRIS BUNCH.

"Well-researched, engrossing, smart and sexy. A graveyard smash."

— BOBBY 'BORIS' PICKETT, SINGER-
SONGWRITER: THE MONSTER MASH.

Rating: 5 stars

— JOHN WALSH, MANGO SAUCE.

"Newport has gone from the vault of the dead to the electrifying life of Jimi Hendrix. If you can remember Woodstock, you will enjoy this book."

— LANG REID, PATTAYA MAIL.

TINSEL TOWN

"It moves like a runaway asteroid."

— TIM HALLINAN, BESTSELLING AUTHOR OF THE POKE RAFFERTY SERIES (SET IN BANGKOK).

"Tinsel Town is the best introduction-to-Hollywood novel I've ever read."

— DAVID GILER, PRODUCER/WRITER OF THE FILMS ALIEN, UNDISPUTED, MYRA BRECKINRIDGE AND MANY MORE.

THE SIAMESE CONNECTION

"Jim Newport is a writer with great skills. Non-stop, hold your breath action. A true thriller. "

— LANG REID, PATTAYA MAIL

"Newport clearly knows Bangkok...An easy read."

— BERNARD TRINK, BANGKOK POST.

THE VAMPIRE OF SIAM

THE SIAMESE CONNECTION

INTRODUCTION

It's been a little over four years since the last *Vampire Of Siam* tale—*The Reckoning*. In the interim I wrote two books—*Chasing Jimi* and *Tinsel Town*. Both of these were 'factoids'—mixtures of fact and fiction. I had first tried my hand at this with *The Reckoning*. In that tale the modern-day narrative is crossed with flashbacks to 1860 and the young Frenchman Ramonne Delacroix's journeys with the explorer Henri Mouhot up the Mekong River and into the ruins of Angkor Wat.

I used the vampire's own journal from 1860 as the vehicle to introduce this part of the story. It was great fun to delve into Mouhot's own well published journals (*Travels In Siam, Cambodia, Laos and Annam* [White Lotus]—highly recommended) and inject a Chinese vampire that had been haunting the temples for 1,000 years (thus solving the mystery of what happened to the original inhabitants—driven out by a bloodthirsty vampire).

In *Chasing Jimi* I got to write about a real legend—the great Jimi Hendrix. Great fun. Imagining conversations between Jimi and the likes of a young Brian Jones. It flowed from the keyboard like the blues from Jimi's stainless-steel guitar strings.

When it came time to write the new vampire book, I knew I

was headed down the historical trail again. In the earlier books I had alluded to my vampire having spent some time at the original Bamboo Bar in the Oriental Hotel, as an impresario. If you've read any of the books, you know that Ramonne is a jazz aficionado. He often ends his evenings by putting a Chet Baker or Miles Davis disk on the turntable (none of this digital crap), and slipping into the silk folds of his coffin. Compère at the Bamboo Bar would have been his idea of a dream job. And you couldn't ask for better hours for a vampire.

So I started with that. A simple premise. A dapper French vampire running the Bamboo Bar. Now on to the research. When did the Bamboo open? In 1947. An interesting time. The Second World War was just over. Thailand had a curious position in the war. And then I found a very intriguing fact: Jim Thompson was one of the original partners in the restoration of the Oriental Hotel. Jim Thompson—the mysterious Silk King. OSS agent. In the Oriental. With a French vampire. Thus began the tale that you now hold in your hand. I trust that you enjoy reading it as much as I enjoyed writing it.

Jim Newport
Bangkok
2011

This book is dedicated to the memory of

William 'Billy' Hutnick
(1945-2010)
a great friend…and a fan of Ramonne.

AUTHOR'S NOTE

The US Army estimated that by the end of the Second World War there were at least 75,000 members of the Kempeitai, the Japanese intelligence agency. Many of these continued their work after the war by joining the Black Dragons, a secret society with political aims.

1

―――――

Bangkok, 1948

> *"If me and my baby fuss 'n' fight,*
> *And the next day everything's all right,*
> *Ain't nobody's business if we do."*

The singer was tall, black and handsome. His hair was lightly 'conked' and combed back from his high brow. His thick mustache was neatly trimmed, and he wore a double-breasted charcoal suit with fine silk pin stripes. Jimmy Witherspoon was *suave* personified, and he held the small room in the palm of his large left hand.

It was Spoon's style to grip the microphone close to his chest with his right hand while punctuating the lyrics with his left. Ramonne Delacroix, resplendent in a Hermes tuxedo, smiled at the confidence Spoon exuded, as he closed his first set with his signature hit. No theatrics, no histrionics—just clear enunciation and phrasing surprisingly delicate for a man of such magnificent stature.

Moins c'est plus. Less is more. Ramonne led the generous applause.

The intimate confines of the Bamboo Bar were conducive to this music. Ramonne marveled again, as he did every night, at the stroke of fortune that had led to his being the impresario of this fine establishment. Night after night he was able to indulge his own musical tastes as he convinced the management to bring in the stellar stars of the international jazz scene for residencies. Jimmy Witherspoon and the Jay McShann Trio were booked for just two weeks, a relatively short engagement, as they had the good fortune (and bad timing) to have "Ain't Nobody's Business" reach the top of the American charts while they were in the midst of a nine-month world tour. They were cutting all their engagements short as they attempted to return to the States and reap the benefits of the chart-topping hit. Concert halls and lucrative bookings awaited them if they could get back while the record was still in the stores. They had just cut short a two-month engagement at the Grand Hotel in Calcutta, where Spoon had made his first appearance as a guest vocalist with Teddy Weatherford's band in 1942 while he was serving in the merchant marine. The gig at the Oriental Hotel in Bangkok was originally commissioned for the fall, but Ramonne had acquiesced to the two-week summer booking rather than lose the opportunity to have the suave Mr. Witherspoon appear at his club. For that was how Ramonne viewed the Bamboo Bar —*his club.*

He'd been talent coordinator for the room since its opening nine months ago. He'd already had the good luck (and keen instinct) to book jazz violinist Stephane Grappelli and clarinet player supreme Tony Scott. Madame Germaine Krull, the hotel's manager and one of the owners, seemed impressed with the relatively young Frenchman's knowledge and instincts. Ramonne was 35 then. The other partners in the hotel, particularly the American adventurer Jim Thompson, also seemed more than satisfied with his performance.

Thompson—or 'Lord Jim' as Ramonne liked to call him— was a regular in the late evenings at the club. Tonight, as usual, he was seated in his favorite of a group of wing-backed chairs along the room's south-facing glass wall. The stately gentleman with the deep tan and shock of dirty blond hair motioned and Ramonne crossed the room.

"*Bon soir*, Lord Jim. *Comment allez vous?*" Ramonne bowed low, his hands pressed together and held to his chest.

Thompson returned the *wai*, the Thai-style greeting, a warm smile spreading across his handsome face. "*Maestro. Et tu?*"

Ramonne smiled back. "Never better. I trust you have been enjoying the evening's entertainment?"

"Enjoying it? How the hell did you pull this off? Jimmy Witherspoon. With a number one hit in America."

"Yes. But fortunately this is not America. Here one can see this fine performance for the mere purchase of two of our renowned cocktails."

Thompson smoothed his beige linen suit, raised his glass—a gin sling—and saluted Ramonne. The impresario made but the slightest nod of his head to a comely waitress, and in a moment he was holding a glass of red wine.

"*Chok dii.*" They clinked glasses and each took a sip. Rather, Ramonne sipped. Jim Thompson downed his drink in one gulp and signaled for another.

Thompson turned to the man seated to his left. "Monsieur Delacroix, allow me to introduce Yoshiro Nakimira. A Japanese attaché."

The man was dressed to the nines. Top hat, tuxedo, vest, cummerbund, silk cravat, white gloves and white spats on his shoes. He stood, doffed his hat, and bowed deeply while clutching a pearl-handled walking stick.

Ramonne returned the bow, bending at the waist, but not extending himself the way the man before him did. Ramonne was automatically on alert. *Un Japonais.* It had been just four years since they were driven in defeat from this land. With their leaders now branded as war criminals and facing daily trips to the gallows, movements of any and all Japanese in Thailand were closely monitored by the American Office of Strategic Services, the OSS.

C'est va, Ramonne thought. *That was it.* It was well known that Thompson had been sent to Bangkok to help the Seri Thai underground resistance movement to the Japanese occupation during the war. Thompson must still belong to the OSS. He was escorting this Nakimira while keeping him under surveillance.

"Monsieur Delacroix, may I refer to you as Ramonne-*san*?" the man asked, as he motioned to a chair.

"I would prefer Monsieur Delacroix, if you don't mind," Ramonne replied as he sat. He didn't lean back in the chair, but maintained a perpendicular posture, leaning slightly forward, in anticipation of the conversation to come.

"Of course. I speak nine languages and find it quite the nuisance to shift one's cordialities to suit the environment *du jour*, as it were."

Ramonne detected a smirk and felt that somehow he had just been insulted. He decided he didn't like this *Japonais*.

"What brings you to our fair establishment?"

Nakimira extracted an etched silver cigarette case and took out a dark cigarillo. He tamped the case with the thin cigarillo as he replied, "Business, of course." He leaned forward and took a light from a waitress who knelt before him.

"Yes?"

"Antiquities. I am on a search for a specific and rare artifact."

"You have come to the right place. Thailand is well known for its wealth of artifacts. Khmer, Chinese, Indian…all are in abundance. The shops, just three blocks to the east, are over-laden. One needs but to bring one's checkbook and, dare I say, anyone can partake, like the great Lord Jim here, and reside in a domicile embellished with a wealth of antiquities. That is, if the presence of severed Buddha heads and pilfered treasures do not weigh too heavily on one's conscience."

Ramonne leaned back in the chair and waited for Thompson

to reply to his joust.

As expected, he took the bait. "Legally acquired Buddha heads are a blessing, my French heathen friend. They provide sanctuary and calm in a turbulent world." He leaned back and shared with Ramonne a smile that said *touché* without speaking the word. He drank his fresh gin sling and Ramonne sipped his wine.

"However, it is not the treasures of the Orient that I seek," Nakimira continued. "Rather I seek something more urbane. A family treasure."

"Oh?" Ramonne arched an eyebrow. "A Japanese family heirloom?"

"In a manner of speaking, yes."

"Mr. Nakimira was with the occupying forces." Thompson crossed his arms and raised his own eyebrow as he delivered this announcement.

"In a *civilian* capacity, I hasten to assure you. I was formerly with the management of the Imperial Hotel in Tokyo, and was entrusted to oversee this grand establishment's conversion to a housing and communications facility in 1942."

Housing and communications facility. Ramonne frowned. At the start of the war in the Pacific in December 1941, Thailand was a sedate outpost surrounded by the Asian colonies of the European empires. This buffer zone, so to speak, had a foreign civilian population numbering in the thousands. Bankers, missionaries, traders, engineers, miners, foresters, mariners, civil servants, judges, hoteliers, entertainers, government advisors, and diplomats. They had been a carefree lot, convinced of their safety by the combined British, Dutch, French and American military prowess in the Pacific. That illusion was shattered in the winter of 1941 with the lightening attacks by the Japanese land, air and sea forces. In a matter of weeks they had conquered all of Southeast Asia from Hong Kong to the Indian border, south to New Guinea, threatening Australia, and east to Midway. Thousands of British, Australians, New

Zealanders, Canadians, Dutch and American civilians—men, women and children—were interned by the Japanese army in Bangkok alone.

Ramonne, being French, was relatively free to move about during the war years as he—along with the Germans, Austrians, Italians, Czechs, Danes, Belgians, Swedes and Swiss —came from the Axis or occupied and neutral countries.

The stately Oriental Hotel was seized and employed as an officer's club. After the war, it was used to house recovering American veterans. The vets, under the misconception that it was a Japanese hotel, thoroughly trashed it. This was the condition of the hotel in 1946 when a partnership, including Jim Thompson, purchased the ruined establishment and gave it its rebirth.

"Exactly what kind of family treasure is it that you seek, monsieur?"

"I am not at liberty to discuss this in detail, Monsieur Delacroix."

"*Non?*" Ramonne set down his glass. "Then I'm afraid I may not be of much assistance."

"Actually, I'm certain you can." Nakimira crushed out the cigarillo. "Although I cannot go into detail, I can tell you that the treasure I seek was hidden on these very premises."

Ramonne leaned towards the man. "The hotel?"

"This room, to be exact."

Now both Ramonne and Thompson were leaning in. Nakimira had their full attention.

"This room?"

"Yes. It was not as you see it today." He swept his hand over the elegant nightclub. Leopard-spotted upholstery covered the furniture, while tropical plants and shafts of bamboo completed the exotic décor.

"No. It most certainly was not," Thompson interjected. "This side of the property was mainly for staff and support. It included the livery and stables, carriage houses, and pantries."

"As it was when our Imperial forces…occupied it. Enlisted men and munitions took over this side of the hotel. The officers had the run of the hotel proper."

A fresh round of drinks was brought by a waitress dressed in a traditional Thai dress known as a *chakkri*. Formal and elegant, the full-length, wrap-around skirt was woven with silver and golden threads and left one shoulder bare. She knelt before the men and gently placed down their drinks. The conversation stopped as she bowed low to the floor and retreated on her knees. The *Japonais* was obviously entranced by the graceful young woman.

"Thailand is a country steeped in tradition. It gives it charm, *ne c'est pas?*" Ramonne picked up his wine glass as he spoke. "As I hear the same is true of your country, Monsieur Nakimira, though I confess that I have never visited the ubiquitous land of the rising sun."

"*Hai*. Both countries share the blessing of centuries of civilization, which gives the people their strength of character. This was the basis for our great emperor's plan to unite the Asian races in grand world domination. We would crush the West."

Nakimira had his right hand balled into a tight fist and was about to raise it over his head. Ramonne and Thompson now had their arms folded and were leaning back in their chairs glaring at him. He quickly recovered his composure.

"*Sumimasen*. I'm afraid that my patriotic fervor is still smoldering."

"Mine too, I assure you," Thompson said through pursed lips. "May I remind you that you have been granted an unusual and extraordinary waiver to conduct your search, under the condition that your movements are by no means counter-productive to or interfere with the peace. To that end, I am your escort. But I will have no problem in escorting you back to your homeland or to a judicial seat for that matter, should I suspect that you intend to usurp those terms."

Nakimira was sweating now. He loosened his cravat and

took a long pull from his water glass. "Of course not. I am indebted to you, Jim-*san*. You need not fear, for I know and respect the courtesies that have been extended to me. Now, if I may, I'll continue with my tale."

"Please do. We wait with baited breath, I can assure you." Ramonne smiled.

"This room was indeed a cook's pantry. However, as we depleted its meat and packaged goods within a few months, it was quickly converted to common storage, for the implements of the hotel that were not deemed necessary to our..." He made a slight bow of apology as he said the word: "Occupation. It was crammed with sewing machines, pianos, office items, and business machines. Please, follow me, *dozo*."

He rose and crossed in front of the small stage. Ramonne and Lord Jim followed. Witherspoon and the band were just returning to the stage, and Ramonne shook the singer's hand and patted his broad shoulders. Ramonne nodded politely to the customers seated in front, before moving up the two short steps to join Thompson and Nakimira in the alcove at stage right. The room was completely full. They stood against the rear wall and Nakimira spoke in a whispered tone, "Here, gentlemen." He used his stick to point to a spot on the polished teak floor, roughly two meters from the wall. "There was a cellar entrance in the floor there. I suspect the cellar still exists."

"It does," Thompson stated. "However, it was sealed when Madame Krull and I laid out the construction of this club and the gardens in 1946. There is another entrance, through the subterranean garage, but I assure you that whatever you are seeking has long been removed if it was of any value."

"It was not left in common view, I assure you. The relic I speak of was sealed within the very walls of the structure."

Thompson frowned. "Forgive me, Nakimira-*san*, but I'm afraid I cannot allow you to go thrashing about the foundation of the hotel in an attempt to redeem some family bauble."

"Family bauble? Pray tell what has given you the illusion

that I am after a family 'bauble?' I assure you that nothing could be farther from the truth." He was turning crimson. His voice had risen above a whisper and people had turned their attention to him.

"Monsieur Nakimira, I must insist that you lower your voice." Ramonne's tone was stern, in direct contrast to the smile that he presented to the curious patrons.

"*Sumimasen.* I apologize. My tone is passionate now that I am so close to that which I seek. If I could be permitted to enter below, I assure you there will be no *thrashing* involved in my securing that which is rightly mine. Give me a small hammer and pick, and I will quickly delineate the exact location of the item I seek."

The band began to play. Witherspoon stood at the bar, chatting amiably to a group of Americans. Ramonne knew that the trio would play one or two songs before the singer joined them. "Messieurs, I suggest you return to your seats...if you wish to keep them."

Nakimira laid a gloved hand on Thompson's arm. "Jim-*san*. Assure me that you will allow me to complete the mission that I was entrusted into your care for. It will simply require your guiding me to the cellar entry, and no more than an hour's exploration within."

Thompson studied the Japanese. He hadn't liked the man from the moment the American consular officer introduced them. Thailand had suffered enough diplomatic humiliations to the Japanese when they were in Bangkok as 'trustees,' while they committed atrocities a scant few hundred kilometers away at the infamous River Kwai labor camps and the subsequent POW's 'death march.' Many of Thompson's own friends and comrades fell to their deaths on that hell road. His original inclination was to declare Nakimira a war criminal immediately when he learned of his role in the occupation of his beloved hotel, but he succumbed to curiosity. Curious to the true nature of Nakimira's quest, and to the amount and source of the *baksheesh*—the tea money paid under the table to open virtually any door in the East—that had, of necessity, been exchanged to grant the countermanding circumstances that permitted Nakimira's return to Thailand after his repatriation to Japan.

Lord Jim lifted the gloved hand off his arm. "I will make enquiries in the morning to secure access to that which you seek. Let's meet in the salon at midday."

"*Domo arigato*, Jim-*san*." He bowed from the waist. Thompson nodded in acknowledgement.

"Gentlemen. With this portion of my purpose fulfilled, I will take my leave. The excitement of being so close to what I seek is giving me some gastronomical distress, I'm afraid. I have medication in my chambers, and will retire there forthwith."

He bowed again, this time to both Thompson and Ramonne. Ramonne returned the bow while Thompson remained erect.

"I trust your accommodations are to your liking?"

"*Hai*, Monsieur Delacroix. The suites are resplendent enough for royalty. Far too luxurious for a common hotelier as myself."

"Royalty often takes advantage of our accommodations, Nakimira-*san*," Thompson commented as Ramonne held the door for the departing *Japonais*. "Be careful not to soil the sheets."

They watched the bow-legged man meander through the stately hallway and disappear into the hotel's grand lobby.

"Curious man, *non*?"

"Curious, yes. Arrogant, deceptive and dishonest, as are all Japs. I have a mind to send him back to his hallowed shores...in a casket."

At this Ramonne arched an eyebrow again. "*Un cercueil eh*? Tell me, Lord Jim, you are not of the disposition that insists the only good *Japonais* is—"

"A *dead* Jap. Yes, my friend. I do subscribe to that theory. You would too, had you not been immune to the indignities of their crimes."

Ramonne decided not to pursue this conversation. "Lord Jim, I must attend to my guests."

"Regrettably, I too must leave. I have an appointment with a young *demimondaine* who frequents the Silver Palm."

Ramonne smiled knowingly, and the two friends politely *waied* each other.

Ramonne re-entered his club. He surveyed the rapt audience and smiled as Jimmy Witherspoon took the stage for his third and final set of the evening.

> *"How long, baby, how long?*
> *Has that evenin' train been gone?*
> *How long, baby baby, how long?"*

Ramonne took his customary spot at the bar. In spite of his thorough enjoyment of the music, his mind and his eye continued to wander to the alcove and the spot that had been pointed to by the *Japonais* with his cane.

———

Motion.

Something moves. You don't know what it is. A breeze blows the leaf of a plant. It rustles a paper on the desk.

You don't know what it is...but it wakes you.

So it was with Nakimira. A flutter awakened him. He craned his neck to see what had disturbed his sleep. The shutters, which he knew he had secured before his slumber, were open. The warm night breeze of the tropics blew into his chamber and roused him. Groggily, he arose and went to shut the windows.

A blood red moon hung in the black sky.

A figure stood in the garden below, silhouetted in the moon's glow behind it. But even without delineation, whoever it was seemed to beckon to Yoshiro Nakimira and call him out.

Out into the night.

Without knowing why, he slowly dressed and left his room.

As he approached the figure, a mist rose and enveloped his feet. He faltered in his steps, but the shroud of fog seemed to propel him forward, whether he willed it or not. He was being drawn through the mist by some mysterious force.

"Monsieur Nakimira. Good evening"

"Delacroix?"

The features were revealed to him now. The long hair. The wide shoulders. It must have been a trick of the moonlight, but the *Furansu-jin's* eyes appeared yellow. Similar to those he had seen who suffered from dengue fever or malaria.

"What is this? Why are you here?"

"I am here for you, Monsieur Nakimira."

"For me?"

The *Furansu-jin* smiled.

"To help you."

Ramonne stretched out his left arm and pointed away from the river towards the darkened hall across the garden.

"To find what you seek, simply follow me."

———

The next evening found the American OSS agent and the French impresario sharing a table in the beer garden of the Cathay on Rajadamnern Avenue.

"How was your adventure today with Monsieur Nakimira? I trust you limited his desecration of the foundation of my establishment?"

"*Our* establishment, Delacroix."

Ramonne smiled at the American's jest and saluted him with his wine goblet. "*Touché.*"

"He didn't show."

"No?"

"No. The little twerp stood me up."

Thompson sliced his steak and slid it onto his fork. He was

having an early meal and Ramonne was sipping at a bottle of Château Haut-Bailly.

"I'm surprised, given his unrequited passion last evening."

"So am I. I was ready for him, I'll tell you that."

"Oh?"

"Oh yes." He leaned in and lowered his voice. "You see, according to the terms of the Cooperation with the Allied Authorities, signed in Ceylon, all properties of the Japanese and the enemies of the Allied Forces are to be, quote, 'confiscated and surrendered.'

"I had my keys to the cellar chambers, and I had a hammer and chisel. But I also had a staff sergeant and two privates in the lobby waiting for my instruction. If and when Nakimira-*san* uncovered whatever it is that he deems so valuable, it would have been seized and remanded to their custody."

"Really? This seems a bit, shall I say...overzealous?"

"Call it what you want, but he came onto my radar the day he applied in Tokyo for safe passage and diplomatic immunity, and I've been under direct orders from MacArthur himself to monitor his activities, behavior and all changing of information."

"Perhaps Monsieur Nakimira got word of your intentions, Lord Jim, and...how do you say...flew the coop?"

"Perhaps he did, Mr. Delacroix, perhaps he did."

A horn honked, signaling the arrival of a motor car, a relatively recent luxury. Bangkok had few paved roads, still relying heavily on its glorious network of *klongs*—canals—for transportation. This was changing, however. All eyes turned to the dark-green Peugeot 402 Éclipse Décapotable. It was, simply put, a work of art. The two-seater had its retractable soft-top down. Its futuristic design featured headlights set back behind the grille. A well-heeled couple slipped the keys to the Burmese valet, who stared in wonder at the exotic vehicle.

Ramonne and Thompson followed the woman's prominent

derrière as she negotiated the short flight of stairs at the club's entrance.

Momentarily diverted, Ramonne returned to the conversation.

"Perhaps he will show up tonight with an explanation."

"Perhaps."

Thompson finished his steak and slid the plate away. "Just curious, Delacroix...When *do* you dine?"

"Very late, I'm afraid. It's hard to break the continental habits."

"Hmm." Thompson wiped his mouth with a large linen cloth, folded it and set it aside. "Strange."

"My dining habits?"

"No. The Jap. I had the housekeeper let me into his room. He wasn't there. His trunk was open as if he'd just arrived and barely unpacked. Everything was in attendance except for Nakimira-*san*."

"Perhaps he went out for a stroll and lost track of time."

"Perhaps. But I kept an eye on his room all day and he never returned.

"Odd," Ramonne mused.

"Odd indeed. He wasn't seen leaving the hotel or his room by any of the staff."

"Perhaps he's back now."

"I think not. I left strict instructions that I should be paged here upon his appearance. I don't see that that has occurred, do you my French friend?"

"No, Lord Jim...but perhaps it will."

Ramonne knew that there would be no further appearances from Yoshiro Nakimira. Ramonne had seen to that.

He had led the *Japonais* to the north portico of the hotel's outbuilding that housed the bar, and down a stone staircase to a bolted cellar door. Ramonne didn't possess a key to this portal, as Thompson would twelve hours later, but opening it wasn't a problem. Ramonne had powers, and locked doors presented no challenge. The door unlocked at his touch.

As the cellar door slowly creaked open, cobwebs and dust surrendered and formed small, wispy clouds. Ramonne had a torch, and he thrust the metal-cased light before them.

Nakimira had seemed reluctant to enter the cellar.

"Monsieur?"

"Are you sure we should be doing this?"

"Of course. After all, you are a guest of the hotel."

Cautiously he stepped over the threshold. The vaulted room was dank, possessing odors both ancient and current. Its stock was similar. Ancient commodes and wooden bathtubs vied for space with assorted shipping trunks, lighting fixtures and files of yellowed documents. Racks and racks of empty bottles occupied most of the walls.

"Monsieur. Which way?"

Ramonne swung the torch in an arc

"It's so...dark."

Ramonne tried a light switch. He flicked it twice to no avail.

"It seems there is no current. Ah..."

On a table were a half-dozen squat beeswax candles He lit them with a gold lighter. A warm glow permeated the dark, casting mixed shadows on the block walls.

"*Voila*. We have light. Now, monsieur...which way?"

"It looks so different."

"Come now. It's a cellar. What could be different, other than the contents?" Again, Ramonne swept his torch around the perimeter. "But I assume we are not looking for a particular case or bit of luggage. Are we, Monsieur Nakimira?"

Nakimira seemed to be gaining confidence as the room became more illuminated.

"There. Through that arch."

He stepped forward and straight into a stack of crated wine bottles. The stack began to topple, but Ramonne deftly caught and righted it.

"Careful, monsieur."

The small chamber they entered was less congested, and Nakimira moved directly towards the south wall.

"There was a stamp on a machine. A metal plate. 'KOHL...'"

"Kohler?"

"Yes, Kohler."

"You mean *that*, monsieur?"

Ramonne pointed his torch six meters to the left of Nakimira. A metal plaque was riveted to the cylinder of a small gas engine, attached to an ancient electrical generator. It bore the name 'Kohler.'

"*Hai*. Yes...Oh yes. Yes."

Nakimira was rapt with joy, and quickly followed the beam of the torch. He put his candle down on a small monotype printing press. Its set of fonts were neatly stacked in several cartons alongside. It seemed to have been lovingly prepared for its trip into this final resting place.

"It's here, yes." He pulled on the bottom of the crates of type fonts.

"Monsieur, please."

Too late. The type, spacers, dingbats and leading crashed to the stone floor.

Ramonne shook his head at the mess.

Nakimira seemed not to notice. "Tools? Do you have the tools?" He pressed his hands to the stones. The rough-hewn stone scratched him as he caressed it.

"It is here, Monsieur Delacrioix. Just beyond this façade. Thinner than all the other concrete walls, I assure you. One single brick in thickness." He swept his hand over a two-meter-wide area. "I supervised the construction of this façade, myself."

He took up his candle and held it to the low ceiling. "Do you see, Monsieur Delacroix? This is a false wall. Set out ever so slightly in front of the room's buttress."

Ramonne followed the man's maniacal gaze. Indeed, the room had definitely been encroached upon.

"Very curious, monsieur."

"This is it." He looked at Ramonne. "The tools, monsieur...You have the tools, yes?"

Whatever had awakened Nakimira from a sound sleep and sent him down to the moonlit garden seeped through him again and he felt a cold aura pass over him. He shivered.

"Tools? I don't need any tools, my *Japonais* friend."

With that, Ramonne punched through the wall with the back of his closed fist. His eyes had never left Nakimira.

"My God." Nakimira went to the hole that Ramonne's fist had made and pried at the edges. He managed to loosen another brick.

Without warning Ramonne punched the wall again with his bare hands. Once...twice. A half-meter hole opened in the façade.

"Monsieur." He held out his hand in escort.

Nakimira took out his handkerchief to stave off the putrefied dust that had arisen as a result of Ramonne's pummeling. He strained to see through the gap.

"Here." Ramonne gave him the torch and he shone it inside.

"This is not possible."

"Monsieur?"

"It's not there." He desperately swung the torch from corner to corner.

"Are you sure?"

Before the *Japonais* knew he had done it, Ramonne had smashed two more holes in the wall.

"How can you do that? It's impossible." He backed away. His free hand went into his coat.

"Many things that seem impossible can be done by those of us who are, shall we say...different."

The *Japanois* raised the torch toward Ramonne. In his other hand he now held a small pistol. "My God. Who *are* you?"

In the flickering light Ramonne appeared bizarre. His pale skin seemed stretched across his skull so tight that his features were chiseled in marble. The yellow eyes glowed as twin orbs channeling Nakimira to come forward.

With the pistol brandished in front of him, Nakimira tried to step back.

He could not.

He was held by an invisible force.

"Nakimira-*san*. Do you not know me?"

"I don't know *what* you are, let alone who you are."

Ignoring the pistol, Ramonne took the torch from the trembling hand of the *Japonais*. He held it aloft so that the light fell on both of them.

"Ramonne-*san*. When we were introduced, you requested that you use that familiarity with me. And yet, you had not been told my given name. How is *that* possible, monsieur?"

"I don't know what you mean." Frozen as he was, Nakimira could only shrink back in his mind. He tried to escape. *This can't be happening.*

'*Oh, but it is.*'

Ramonne's lips hadn't moved. The voice was in Nakimira's head.

Terrified, he tried to squeeze the trigger.

But his finger would not move.

"Let me refresh your memory," Ramonne said. "April 1942. You arrive in Bangkok. Your destination..." He swept his free arm to the ceiling. "The Oriental Hotel. You did not travel light. You brought everything but the proverbial kitchen sink.

"Hence you attracted a lot of attention. Your caravan was watched in wonder by dozens of hungry eyes as it was offloaded to a barge and transported to the hotel's dock. One pair of those eyes belonged to me, monsieur."

Perhaps it was gravity, but somehow, entranced as he was, Nakimira was able to dislodge the stack of monotype crates behind him. They crashed to the floor. The sound of the thousands of characters falling to the floor was like a thunder-clap, yet it did not faze the Frenchman.

"I became curious, monsieur, curious at your civilian posture amid the occupation of the city. You see, at that point I had already resided in Krung Thep for close to a century."

Nakimira's eyes widened. *What is this horror?*

"I watched with more than curiosity as you performed your duties as hotelier. Your commanders considered the French to be neutral, but you chose to close the hotel to all except those allied to the flag of the Rising Sun."

Ramonne moved closer. His breath fogged Nakimira's spectacles.

"But, as I now believe you suspect: That didn't bother me. I work under a veil of secrecy and go where I please. I stalked you, monsieur. And I watched as you secreted your treasure."

Nakimira's eyes widened. "You have it?"

"Yes. I have it. I've had it since I came here under the guise of jazz concierge. Removing it was one of the first things I did."

"Then you know that it must be protected at all costs."

"It is, I assure you."

With the realization that he had lost what he sought, Nakimira sighed.

The atmosphere seemed to settle. The dust slowly fell onto the broken mortar, the scattered type stopped clattering and finally the torch flickered out.

Darkness fell across the *Japonais* as Ramonne lowered the light. Trembling, Nakimira looked into the dark. The Frenchman was but a shadow again.

"Monsieur?"

The end was merciful. Ramonne—the ultimate hunter—struck in a swift arc of death. His razor-sharp teeth penetrated the pale *Japonais'* throat with surgical precision. Nakimira gasped and immediately fell faint.

Soon, his life was no more.

2

Bangkok, Present Day

Nothing's changed.

Everthing's changed.

Time marches forward to its own incessant, unyielding drumbeat. The moon sets, the sun rises. You could crawl into a box and sleep the day away, it wouldn't matter. Another dawn would come tomorrow.

So you try and accomplish something. Rational people make nests. Raise families. Make contributions to society.

Martin Larue considered himself a rational being. Therefore he was making a nest for his family. His wife, Areeya, was in the family way. Three months pregnant. Their nine-year-old adopted son Hon had journeyed with them when they made the decision to leave Cambodia and return to Bangkok.

Irrepressible Hon had enjoyed the plane ride. He stared wide-eyed at the clouds and was never scared, even when a monsoon storm buffeted the small craft on its descent into Suvarnabhumi Airport.

He was a country boy. He'd fended for himself the first five years of his life, scavenging through the giant Stung Mean Chey trash heap outside Phnom Penh. Martin had brought him and eleven others to his orphanage school in Siem Reap, at the gateway to the temples of Angkor.

The limo ride in Bangkok was as eye-opening for Hon as the plane ride. Martin himself, though it had only been six months since his last journey to the 'City Of Angels,' marveled too at how far the urban sprawl stretched. There seemed to be no end to it. East towards Pattaya, south to Hua Hin, or north to Khon Kaen, it just went on and on. Bangkok was a city of, officially, 12 million, and unofficially 64 million when you included the untold millions of upcountry workers, undocumented Burmese construction workers, refugees and plain shadow-people. The whole country, it seemed, converged on the capital.

The rain had stopped and the sky was as clear as it ever gets over the city. Though they traveled on the new Chonburi expressway, above the congested streets, they had eventually to join the stop-and-go—mainly stop—of the city's main cross-town thoroughfare, Sukhumvit Road. They came to a halt as the off-ramp descended. Fifty meters took fifty minutes. When they were finally able to turn onto the six-lane city street, little Hon was fast asleep. Even he had exhausted his tolerance for watching other drivers and passengers chat endlessly on cell-phones and contemplate their acne in rear-view mirrors.

Another forty-minute crawl and the limo finally turned onto Soi Langsuan, and Martin could actually see the thirty-story apartment building that had been his sanctuary in Bangkok for nearly fifteen years.

It hadn't been an easy decision to leave Siem Reap. The school and orphanage had been Martin and Areeya's passion for five years. Walking away from it was probably the most difficult thing he had ever done. But when Areeya became pregnant, they both realized that to concentrate on raising their child, as well as the others in the orphanage, would mean compromising too much. They refused to do that. Having their own child had been their dream for as long as they had been together. The brood, as they referred to the initial dozen refugees they'd taken in, was a substitute for their own failed attempts at conception. That she was finally pregnant was seen by both of them as a miracle.

Areeya took to remodeling Martin's apartment with a vengeance. Out with the old. In with the new.

She was lucky she didn't marry the typical Bangkok expat bachelor, Martin thought. A cluttered studio apartment and a postman's pension. Martin was wealthy beyond imagination. Family money. It had allowed him to live a stress-free existence in sumptuous surroundings. The 500-square-meter, three-bedroom, four-bath apartment boasted its own horizon pool. It was the penthouse unit, occupying the entire top floor. He'd bought it when it became available and moved up from the seventh floor. He owned perhaps the finest private art collection in Southeast Asia, although at present the Kandinsky, Renoir and Degas pieces resided in a vault.

Ayeeya watched as the dust covers were removed from the furniture and the recessed lights turned up. She frowned.

"It's so…"

"Yes?" Martin anticipated praise. He was puzzled.

"So…Zen."

"Yes. Isn't it."

"It's cold, Martin. It's not a home."

"But I thought you liked it?"

"I did." She twisted her hair as she surveyed the overly spacious room. "But we're a family now, Martin."

"I know." He went to her and put his arms around her, cradling her stomach. She put her hands over his.

"I'll just make a few changes."

Good, thought Martin. Anything to please her. He truly loved this woman with all his heart.

"Ma ma!" The air was pierced by the special phrase Hon used to address either Martin or Areeya. He came running, barefoot, into the room, clutching a squirming, clawing, hissing, ragged old cat.

"Hon, let it go," Martin shouted.

"No, ma ma. No."

"Where in the world did you find that?" Areeya scolded as she reached to remove the creature.

"Areeya, no!" Martin warned. "I know this cat. He bites."

And so Small Talk, as the hissing cat came to be known—for it only made one sound, a prolonged hiss—also became a member of the family.

Ultrasounds, hormone injections—this was Martin and Areeya's regular routine. They had tried and tried to conceive. They went through three miscarriages. Each time the doctors held Areeya's hand and told Martin that it was God's way of eliminating a child that was not meant to be born. A less than perfect child. The toll it took on both of them was almost unbearable. They had—if they wanted to look at them—their own little library of sonogram photographs of unborn children —each one lost before the end of the first trimester. Each of them loved, anticipated…and wanted.

And each of them gone.

Lost.

Forever.

Martin was sure he could never put Areeya through that again, when, lo and behold—she was pregnant again.

Okay. This time he confined her to complete bed rest. She felt foolish. Abandoning all her chores, her responsibilities. The running of the orphanage. But Martin insisted. Feet up. That's it.

And miracle of miracles—they passed the first trimester mark.

She began to show. Her belly swelled. The clock ticked. Fourteen weeks, sixteen—then they were looking at sonograms of a healthy, beautiful little baby.

And so Martin had made the decision to move back to

Bangkok. He left the orphanage school in the capable hands of Justin and Julianne. They were as responsible as any young people he knew, and they truly loved the children. Martin promised that he and Areeya would be back on their child's second birthday and would put off any decisions on the long-term running of the orphanage until then.

Martin could afford the best medical treatment for his wife, and that was what he wanted. It wasn't available in Siem Reap. It was available in Bangkok. The city's hospitals had a world-class reputation exceeded by only a very few. The doctor that would now be guiding them through this next phase of the pregnancy was well regarded as one of the pre-eminent obstetricians in the world.

Martin's child was special. This he knew.

Martin trusted that the astronomical fees his new doctor was charging meant that he also knew that Martin's child was special.

3

———————

Roluos, Cambodia, Present Day

Ramonne thought that vampires knew nothing of God.

He was wrong.

The connection was as black is to white. One is the absence of all color. One is the presence of all color.

From *that* night, everything changed. In the temple—the finest sacred architecture in the world, the absolute center of the universe—he had battled the great Satan, with a child, an innocent, at his side. Together they had brought the devil to his knees. Defeated and driven him back to hell.

And now?

What?

Ramonne raised the goblet to his nose and inhaled. The syrupy Shiraz had a strong, smoky scent, with perhaps a hint of persimmon. He swirled the ruby liquid once more. It left good trailings on the side of the glass. He took a sip.

The grapes had been cultivated to match the terrain, climate and soil of the rolling Roluos Hills, where Villa des Oiseaux—the rambling country home that he had restored—was located. Instead of the traditional pergola—a trellis supporting and sheltering the vines—these vines were grown in vertical rows that allowed them to catch as much sunlight as possible. This meant that only one crop of grapes could be harvested each year, as opposed to the vineyards in France that harvested two, sometimes three crops a year.

The wine he was tasting was almost four years old. Not old —but enough to determine whether it had a future.

"Master?"

The white-haired man stood patiently awaiting Ramonne's decision.

"Professor. How many times must I tell you."

"I'm sorry…monsieur."

He swallowed.

"It's not…bad."

The old man smiled, relieved.

"Good." He reached to pour from the decanter and fill the goblet. Ramonne put his hand over the glass.

"That's all right."

"As you please." The old man bowed slightly and then turned and went back to the house.

As soon as he'd left, Ramonne tossed the remainder of the wine onto the trunk of the huge banyan tree that he sat under, and wiped his mouth.

"*Phaw.*" And spat.

He shook his head, then reached into a soft leather bag that sat on an ottoman next to his wicker chair, and extracted a bottle of Petrus Pomerol 1945. He opened his pocket knife and used the corkscrew blade to open the bottle. He poured it without ceremony and gulped down the rich liquid.

The difference was immediate. Like night to day.

He sighed and stretched out. The sun was on the wane, sinking low on the horizon. He treasured this time of day. Truly treasured it.

For over 150 years he had been denied the simple pleasure

of a sunset. Or for that matter, a sunrise. That was the curse of the vampire.

Sleep the sleep of the living dead.

But, when he had fought the beast and won…somehow he had changed. Somehow he had been given a reprieve. The curse —the veil—had been lifted. Ever so slightly, but it had definitely been lifted.

The first clue had been the boy. He'd been dead. Surely.

But somehow Ramonne had managed to revive him.

Ramonne had possessed strange powers for nearly a century and a half. He had taken countless lives and had been struck down by bullets, garrotes and knives. He'd been decapitated and incinerated. A five-megaton bomb had wiped him out. His study of the arts of necromancy and black magic had increased his powers to the level needed to best the thousand-year-old devil Zhoupeng. But the dead child had presented his greatest challenge ever.

He had never resuscitated a soul before. There had been that matter with the female vampire Kanchana, but she had not been fully transformed, and he had merely followed the ancient rites to reverse her condition.

But he had brought the boy back to life. And that was when things began to change. Slowly. Ever so slowly.

The first thing he noticed was his lack of appetite.

One week. Two weeks.

He did not hunt. He did not feed.

Dr. Gerhardt Kaestle, his assistant—showing a remarkable recovery from his own debilitating disease—was prepared to offer any help Ramonne might need in his procurement of sustenance, but the vampire soon realized that the desire for human blood that sustained him had abated.

———

Roluos, 2007

"Master? Are you all right?"

Ramonne didn't know the answer to that question.

"How long have I been…asleep?"

"Two weeks, master."

Two weeks. It had been that long since the battle. He had crawled into his silk-lined coffin and shut the lid.

Now he was thirsty. He was hungry.

"Bring me some wine, please."

Kaestle brought the first bottle that presented itself in the ample supply that they'd brought from Bangkok. He pried out the cork and poured a glass. Ramonne ignored the glass and took the bottle. He swallowed long and hard.

"What time is it?"

Kaestle was taken by surprise. "Master?"

"The time. What is it?"

He checked his pocket watch. "Nearly 5:45."

"The dawn? When is it?"

"A half-hour, maybe less."

Ramonne walked to the door. He unlatched it.

"Master, don't."

Ramonne pulled the door open and stepped into the grayness. The morning dew shimmered in the beautiful little garden. He breathed in deep.

Kaestle stared in wonder from the doorway.

A wrought-iron table and two chairs were set in the garden. Ramonne sat down and called out, "Professor, come…bring your glass."

Kaestle did as he was bid. He marveled at his master's calm demeanor.

"Master, please. You should go in."

Ramonne smiled. He stretched out and poured wine in Kaestle's glass. He took another long drink, then leaned back in his chair—face turned to the rising sun.

"Brilliant, isn't it?"

"Master…please. You must go inside."

A pink glow penetrated the gray stillness of the dawn, and backlit the array of flowers and greenery. The calathea with its handsome leaf patterns was contrasted with the distinctive pinkish-orange flowers of the flamboyant birds-of-paradise. Dark-red banana leaves provided ground cover while yellow orleanda shrubs provided privacy. Ramonne threw back his head and smiled. He closed his eyes. The first rays of the new morning sun fell across his perpetually youthful face.

Kaestle shrunk back, expecting the worst.

But…nothing happened.

Everything happened.

———

"The story is the same the world over. You and I, and all the devils that plague the world—we are the product of the elimination of indigenous peoples. Their connection—the native Indians of America; the aborigines of Asia; the hilltribes of Southeast Asia—they lived predominantly by the forces of Nature and lived off the land. They all lived in connection with the 'Great Spirit.' They knew their place in the cosmos.

"Angkor Wat was the 'axis mundi,'—the absolute center of the universe. Architecture whose measurements and cosmological interpretations were based on ancient Vedic scriptures. Sorcerers and mathematicians were given free reign to analyze the powers that they knew they were in touch with. When they learned how to align themselves with the stars, they began their ascent to the realms of the gods and beyond.

"Their ancient scriptures hold the keys to these powers."

The demon Zhoupeng's words still rang in his ears.

From that day forward it was not just Ramonne who underwent a transformation. He ordered the complete restoration of Villa des Oiseaux. Scores of workers clamored over the estate while he spent the days locked in his study. His forays into the sun were limited to the early morning and late afternoon, for as invigorating as the sun felt, it seemed to weaken him. His innate fear kept him in the shadows.

He was drawn to this new life and wanted to make whatever he could of it. He sent the professor on regular runs to the Royal Angkor Foundation to trace the location of certain ancient scriptures. When these proved fruitless, the good doctor was dispatched to Paris. He carried a very rare daguerreotype metal plate and a letter from a 'Monsieur Ennomar.' When the professor arrived, he was met by a bookish little man, Charles Serviette, who took immediate possession of the daguerreotype. He took Dr. Kaestle to the huge library and museum, L'Ecole Française D'Extrême Orient. There, in the world's largest institution devoted to the study of Asian societies, Dr. Kaestle was allowed to handle and copy literally hundreds of the rarest of rare ancient manuscripts. Ramonne's letter was a virtual shopping list, and it took more than two days to secure all that he desired.

When the doctor returned, he found that not only was his master now able to go in and out of the sunlight safely, but he had begun the consumption of solid food. Although Ramonne's taste ran to blood-red meats barely seared, Dr. Kaestle was aghast at the transformation he was witnessing. Upon producing the research from his trip, Ramonne snatched the thick parcel from the doctor and retired to his chambers for a fortnight.

4

———

Bangkok, 1948

Jim Thompson used his key to open the bolted door to the cellar. He went inside but emerged moments later and charged upstairs.

"It's been ransacked."

Ramonne, in the midst of counting a large stack of money, held up a hand while he finished. He snapped a rubber band around the bills and dropped them back in the cash box and closed it.

"*Bon soir*, Lord Jim. What, exactly, has been ransacked?"

"The cellar." Agitated, Thompson pointed to the floor in the middle of the bar.

Ramonne frowned for a moment and then smiled. "Ah, yes. The treasure. Correct?"

"Whatever it was, it's gone. There are bloody holes punched in the cellar walls."

Ramonne stood up. He took Thompson by the arm and escorted him back to the colonnade hallway and locked the door to the club. They talked as they walked to the riverside.

"And Monsieur Nakimira? Where is he?"

Thompson ran his hand through his hair. "No one knows. He hasn't returned to his room for two nights."

"So, it seems he has…flown the coop?"

"He broke into the cellar and got what he was after. And now he's gone." Thompson seemed distraught.

Ramonne led him down the path to the river. "Perhaps he will return."

Thompson turned to the Frenchman. "You don't seem to understand the seriousness of this. I'm an OSS officer and I was assigned to take custody of a dubious and mysterious attaché who presented himself with credentials allowing courtesies that would not be extended to the fucking emperor himself…and I blew it." Thompson threw his cigarette into the river and watched as fish the size of bulldogs fought over it.

"Lord Jim. How can I help?"

"His belongings are still in his room. We need to keep him there."

"Excuse me?"

"If he continues to absently occupy a suite in our…*my* hotel, then he continues to exist."

"*Je ne comprends pa.* I don't understand."

"This only becomes a problem when Nakimira-*san* officially disappears. Until then—he's still under my watch."

"Again, I'm afraid I don't—"

"Come on, man…I need you to provide a bit of substance to my story."

"Your story?"

"Look, as far as we're concerned Nakimira has been having the time of his life—right here. In our hotel. In this bar."

"He has?"

"Yes. Damn it."

Ramonne looked across the river. Thonburi, on the opposite bank, was virtually black—as if electricity had yet to find its way to its shore.

"And what has Monsieur Nakimira been doing for these past two days that has not allowed him to return to his own hotel room?"

"I don't know, man. Use your imagination. This is Bangkok for Christ's sake."

Ramonne Delacroix, mass murderer, serial killer extraordinaire, had never heard these words before. *Use your imagination.*

"I like it."

Relieved, Thompson lit another cigarette. "I thought you would."

"So what do you need from me?"

"Not much. A few phoney chits. He spent the last two evenings entranced by the music. Intoxicated."

"You flatter me. But I must warn you that the famous Mr. Witherspoon took an unannounced departure from the stage last night for a dalliance of a rather indelicate nature. The band made apologies and performed without him—to an empty room. He is, it seems, quite the cocksman."

Thompson frowned. "I don't care if there was a naked dwarf in here diddling three-legged frogs—Nakimira was here. You understand?"

"Of course, Lord Jim." Ramonne smiled. "You seem to have a flair for exactly what I do. Can you actually pull off such an act?"

Lord Jim turned and scowled. "What I need is time. I have to find this little Jap bastard."

"Of course." Ramonne smiled to himself, for he knew that try as he might, Lord Jim Thompson would never find the mysterious Nakimira.

Yoshiro Nakimira was now resting as the newest inductee to Hernando's Cemetery on Silom Road.

As the mid-century approached, Ramonne Delacroix, with the absence of plague, pestilence and war, had proved to be one of the principal decimators of Bangkok's population, and as such, had recently entered into a relationship with the cemetery that would prove invaluable to him and profitable to a generation or more of Thai policemen.

———

Jimmy Witherspoon returned to the Bamboo Bar the next night. Ramonne attempted to chastise him but decided that he didn't want to risk a public row with the six-foot-four American negro, and so he discreetly passed a note to Jay McShann that informed him their wages would be reduced to compensate for Spoon's disappearing act.

Ramonne was on the terrace enjoying the night breeze when the lounge's door burst open and Jimmy Witherspoon emerged, note in hand.

"What the hell is this bullshit?"

He thrust the note at Ramonne, who took it from his massive fist.

"You failed to appear last night. A violation of your contract."

"Bullshit. I did the early set."

"And then you disappeared."

"There was no one here. It was raining. Besides, McShann played until one a.m. You got your show."

"We were full when you left, in spite of the weather. The house emptied out because they came to see you."

Spoon's thick brow was furled into a deep crevice. He reached out and grabbed the lapels of Ramonne's dinner jacket. He seemed on the verge of throttling the upstart Frenchman. Ramonne hoped that would not occur. Decorum would force him to allow such a beating—to a point. And then, no doubt, he would cross a line and the consequences to Monsieur Witherspoon would be most serious, if not fatal. He knew this would be disastrous.

Ramonne was the administrator of the Bamboo Bar. He

considered himself a patron of the arts. But more than that, he was a fan.

"Monsieur Witherspoon. Please."

Spoon smiled and released his grip. "I was sick. You can't punish a man for being sick."

Ramonne arched an eyebrow. "Sick, monsieur?"

"Something I ate. This fucking Chinese food is killing me."

"You are in Thailand, monsieur."

"Thai-nese, Chinese, whatever. This spicy shit is killing me. My mama always told me I have a cast-iron stomach, but I swear one week of this fucking red-hot goo goo gai pan or whatever the fuck you call it, and my formidable black ass is burning a hole right through my lily-whites."

Ramonne was impressed. "I have never heard the local cuisine described quite so colorfully, monsieur. However, I was here when you made your departure last night. And you were not alone."

"What? That little ol' gal? She was just helping me to my room. I could barely make it."

"Yes, that is true. You could barely walk. You were...how did Monsieur McShann put it...? Legless."

"I was sick."

"You were drunk."

Jimmy Witherspoon studied the Frenchman. Something about him presented a threat. He wasn't sure what it was. He couldn't put his finger on it. He towered over the man and could have easily tossed him into the river. But he just knew that would be unwise.

Instead he did something he rarely did. He apologized.

"Mr. Delacroix. You're right. I was drunk last night. I took a sweet thing to my room and we chased each other around to the sound of Johnnie Walker tinkling on the rocks until the cows came home. That was unfair and unprofessional. It won't happen again."

Ramonne smiled. "As I said before, you are a unique performer, Monsieur Witherspoon. The Oriental Hotel has been most honored with your presence and we look forward to the rest of your brief stay with us. But please, no more dalliances during your performance, and try to keep your imbibing to a minimum while on the premises."

"I know that was English, but what did you just say?"

"Keep it in your pants when you're supposed to be on stage, and lay off the sauce."

Jimmy Witherspoon smiled and put an arm around Ramonne's shoulder. "You're all right, Frenchy...you're all right."

The air was alive. A firework exploded and the full moon backlit the gunpowder trailings.

Ramonne strolled along Yaowarat Road in Bangkok's Chinatown. Alive with revelers, it was the Moon Festival, and the parapets and balconies were draped in red and green. Ramonne enjoyed the feeling of vitality that the Chinese brought to the city, with their street stalls, rickshaws and general love of mayhem.

He passed through the China Gate, crossed the broad avenue of Charoen Krung Road and was soon facing the massive stained-glass windows of the neo-Renaissance train station, Hualamphong. Behind him was the tallest building in the area—nine floors—which was topped with the Hoei Ten Lao nightclub. Ramonne chuckled to himself as he mused on the two façades. One took people on a physical journey, the other took them on a flight of fancy. The Hoei Ten Lao dispensed elixirs of contentment and its hostesses' charms gave its patrons a sense—perhaps false, perhaps not—of allurement. The promise of an encounter with ladies whose charms were known throughout the kingdom lured many a wayfarer just recently arrived at the grand train station. Just such an occurrence had led to Ramonne's present position at the Oriental. On a night such as this, Joseph Elias Bautista had arrived in Bangkok. His appointment at the Oriental wasn't until the following afternoon, and he had the intention, as so many men do when they arrive in the evening hours in an exotic location, to sample the local nightlife.

Unfortunately for the young Frenchman, he asked Ramonne Delacroix for directions.

The rest, as they say, is history.

Ramonne reported to the Oriental in the young man's place, explained that an unfortunate illness had necessitated a change at the last minute, and apologized profusely for the inferior postal system that had failed to announce this prior to his arrival. It mattered not what the management of the Oriental thought, as Ramonne controlled their very minds and they all agreed that he would be a splendid addition to the staff.

The moon that had been red and full a few nights before was only slightly less so, and it illuminated the streets like a torch. It would be a full year before the moon was this close to the planet again.

A silhouetted figure approached.

A woman. Alone.

She carried a bag. Not large, but not small. She was a traveler.

This was good.

She had dark features. Spanish perhaps. She had a small pamphlet. A map.

He approached.

"Madame. Can I be of assistance?"

"Hablas Espanol?"

He switched languages. *"Como puedo ayudarte?"*

"I'm looking for Saint Theresa's."

Ramonne knew the convent well. It was a starting point for young women of the Catholic faith on various missions in the City of Angels. The good sisters took in the girls and gave them a rudimentary education in the whys and wherefores of life in the Orient. For most it was but a way station, a stopping-off point. They would soon move on to the life to which destiny had assigned them—nursemaids to diplomats' children, school teachers, wives and mothers.

"It is not far. I can show you…Please."

He reached for her bag.

"Thank you, you are very kind."

"Not at all. It is my pleasure."

He hefted the travel case onto his shoulder and motioned to a nearby alley.

"This way, madame."

She hesitated. "Are you sure? My guidebook seems to indicate that direction. She pointed towards Yaowarat.

"No, madamoiselle. I assure you. This is the way. Trust me."

Trust me.

These were the last words the *señorita* from Barcelona ever heard.

She followed him into the darkness of the alley. Within moments Ramonne turned on her and sunk his teeth deep into her neck and took her away from all the little souls she thought she'd been put on this earth to save. Away from the dreams of love and a lover—*there could be only one*—and of the life she had yet to live.

Took her.

Took her for his own selfish pleasure and need.

Took her.

Away.

Far, far away.

———

Diego Hernando heard the shrill whistle. He wasn't sure if he actually heard it or if he merely felt it. Whatever, it was a sound so high-pitched that hounds across Bangrak howled in unison.

Otro? Another? *Tan pronto?* So soon? *How could this be possible?*

The man rose from his bed and quickly dressed in the dark. His wife cursed him for disturbing her slumber. He cursed her back and went into the hall, where he turned on a light.

He checked his watch.

"Two-thirty. Does this man never sleep?"

He took a bottle of rum down from a cupboard in the kitchen and poured about four inches into a heavy glass. He took a sip, savored it, and then threw the rest down his gullet. Thus fortified, he took up a Coleman lantern, lit it and unbolted the door.

He stepped out onto his porch and surveyed his 'garden.'

Stone angels spread their wings, some caressed by cherubs. They looked out upon a sea of crosses, canted urns, marble vases and statuary, for Diego Hernando's garden was in fact a cemetery. A working graveyard of tombs, crypts, stones and a huge mausoleum.

He stepped off the porch and his boots crunched the light gravel that had been laid atop the paths that linked the various sections of the sprawling graveyard. As he made his way with the lantern held before him, it cast eerie shadows over the entanglement of tombs. Again the silence was pierced by the shrill whistle of that who commanded his presence.

"All right, all right. I'm coming."

Señor Hernando took a left turn and headed to the west wall. It fronted onto the newly paved Silom Road. A gate that had previously been used mainly by the diggers and masons, and opened onto nothing but rice paddies from the cemetery to the river, was now a portal onto a new boulevard in the ever-expanding city of Krung Thep. As he inserted a heavy brass key into the tumbler in the gate, Señor Hernando pondered the necessary renovation of this now prominent entry to his establishment.

Slowly the wrought-iron gate creaked open. The *porte-cochère* appeared empty.

But Diego Hernando knew better.

"Monsieur?"

He was answered by a gust of wind. It blew with enough force to pin him against the gate while the Frenchman, who he knew was there, emerged and walked effortlessly into the cemetery, in spite of the cumbersome burden that he bore on his shoulders.

"*Buenas tardes,* Señor Hernando."

"Monsieur."

He swept into the graveyard as if he belonged. In fact, Señor Hernando admitted to himself, he did belong. He was a purveyor of the dead. Much like the funeral homes that conveyed the deceased to his garden, this mysterious Frenchman also bore corpses that needed the attention of Señor Hernando.

The difference was that when the funeral homes came calling, and when the caskets arrived, it was Señor Hernando's task to arrange their internment. This was the very reason for the parceling out of seven and a half acres of this former rice paddy. It served a very ancient and renowned purpose—the internment of loved ones, the contentment of the bereaved. The final rights were performed here. Dignity was bestowed. Families grieved together. Old wounds were healed. Closure was sought.

All this took place within the confines of Hernando's Cemetery. As it had for a century or more.

But this Frenchman, whoever he was—he came for none of this. His appearance was unwelcome. Unwelcome and unwarranted.

This matter was beyond Señor Hernando's control. He had been told by the brigadier-general of the Bangkok police that this mysterious Frenchman would periodically be bringing bodies—actually the office referred to them as "deposits"—that should be held in abeyance for the police to dispose of.

For his role in this clandestine affair, Señor Hernando would receive a tidy monthly sum and a favorable standing with the constabulary—which, as anyone who did business in the Orient knew, was everything.

5
___

Bangkok, Present Day

Martin's bachelor pad was transformed. Ethan Allen had entered his world. The Boxetti minimalist set with leather that felt like butter on your skin, was replaced with a cream-colored Pratt sofa with Aubussen crewel floral pillows. A nineteenth-century Roma chair and trillium ottoman completed the look. His sixty-inch Samsung plasma screen was housed in a neo-Grecian modular bookcase. His bedroom now had a Tuscany sleigh bed with a Vinci quilted sham coverlet, gold embroidered sheets and enough caramel and avocado pillows to float the Titanic. "A grand but approachable style with a seamless blend of rich fabrics, traditional patterns and Continental accessories." That was how Banana, Areeya's *tres chic* designer, had described it. Martin was convinced he had merely hired a two-ton truck and waved money at the fruitiest merchants on Soi Thonglor, Bangkok's trendy design center, until it was full.

He sat in the leather Marcelle desk chair with its scrolled arms, and stared at the Louis XV desk with its Versaille-inspired diamond-patterned inlay top. It would be at home in the White House. His 27-inch iMac work station seemed like it had been transported through a black hole and back to the eighteenth century. He put on his Bose headphones just as Areeya entered his pre-revolutionary French sanctuary.

"Martin. Look at these."

He removed the headphones and obediently looked her way. She had a swatch book in her hand. Martin dreaded this. She had succeeded in covering his once egg-white satin veneer walls in all manner of finishes and papers. There was only one room left for her to tackle—the guest room with its en-suite bathroom. She had saved it for last, as it would now be the baby's room. Hon was comfortably ensconced in Martin's former media room. Small Talk had learned to sleep in an English willow basket.

Pink or blue had been made an easy decision by the latest sonogram that told them they were having a girl.

"I can't decide between the swirls or the ballerinas." She handed the book to Martin. Two pages were clipped. He stared in shock. The choices were an abstract pattern of pink and yellow or vintage ballerinas pirouetting on a pink background. Though the thought of either one adorning the walls of his home mortified him, the idea of encountering ballerinas every time he entered his daughter's domain bothered him more than the pseudo-psychedelic swirls.

"The swirls. Definitely the swirls." He handed her the swatch book.

"I don't know." She moved to Martin and sat on the corner of the eighteenth-century replica desk. "The ballerinas might inspire her."

To what? All Martin could think of was comedian Chris Rock's warning that a responsible father's job these days was to keep his daughter *off the pole.* "They don't grade fathers," Rock warned. "But if your daughter is a stripper, you fucked up." Surrounding her with ballerinas just seemed like a nudge in the wrong direction to Martin.

"What does Banana think?"

So far Khun Banana had managed to spend over six million baht.

"I fired Banana."

Good.

"You did? Why?" *I can think of six million reasons.*

"I don't know. I think he was off on a couple of his choices. That's why I'm doing the baby's room myself." She instinctively put her hand on her stomach when she said the 'b' word. "She's doing her two o'clock dance."

Martin got up and went to his wife. He put his hand next to hers. He felt the tiny vibrations. "Well, maybe the ballerinas are the way to go."

Areeya reached up and gently stroked his hair. "You were right the first time."

For perhaps the thousandth time since he'd been in this relationship Martin marveled at how a woman would ask your opinion and then do whatever was the opposite of your judgment. But still, he'd be spared the dancing ballerina wallpaper.

For a while.

Areeya got up, kissed him on the cheek and left him alone in his Ethan Allen sanctuary.

Siem Reap, 2007

The gnarled hands carved the slender carrot into a flower. Next they cut a banana leaf into circles and softened it over a gas flame, before folding it into pleats and fastening them with toothpicks. This formed a banana-leaf cup to hold the fish *amok* —the Cambodian national dish. It was made by pounding fish and spices in a stone mortar into a *greung* paste. This was poured into the banana-leaf cup and garnished with the carrot flower. Ramonne took a bite. It was absolutely delicious.

He continued his late-afternoon stroll through the vast

bazaar. Though the sun was on the wane, he wore dark, round sunglasses. He entered the wet market. Live fish, live chickens, dead fish, dead chickens, row after row of headless chickens with their legs splayed, chickens being chopped, fish being chopped, piles of skinned and diced chicken, piles of pork cutlets, baskets full of raw meat, pig heads—some of the vendors, mainly women, seemed to stroke the snouts of the pigs affectionately—sausages, jars full of unknown delicacies, and then…the spices. Stall after stall of colorful spices. Chilies of all sizes and colors, ginger, shallots, cinnamon, cardamom, lemongrass, turmeric, limes, sweet basil, peppercorns, cloves, mint and mountains of garlic.

Next were the fruits. Papayas, mangoes, bananas, mangosteen, rambutan. All arranged in pyramids. Each one singularly declaring dominance over its particular hue in the rainbow.

Ramonne walked with purpose. This wasn't a casual stroll. In his pocket was an heirloom that he cherished like no other thing on earth. His intent was to give it away.

Across the crowded market, Martin strolled with his beloved Areeya on one side and Hon on the other. Ramonne smiled as he paused and let the trio meander, unaware of his observance.

He loved the boy. The boy had saved his life. And he in turn had saved the boy. They were bound. He knew that. And he was sure the boy knew it too.

But neither Martin nor the boy was his target. With them and walking hand in hand behind was the young French couple —the handsome Justin and the delicately beautiful Julianne.

Julianne. He remembered the first time he saw her. She had been frightened out of her wits by the horrific battle that was going on outside the orphanage. Prior to Ramonne and the devil Zhoupeng's arrival, a ragtag band of demented former Khmer Rouge cadres had stormed the little stone building. Martin had a cache of weapons, and he and his small group had managed to hold their ground.

It had just been a glimpse through a window, but it had

registered with Ramonne. Beauty he hadn't known in almost 150 years. He reached into his pocket and withdrew the sterling silver watch. He stroked the slender fob before opening it. He removed his sunglasses and studied the sepia-tinted portrait within. A soft, fair-skinned girl.

Giselle.

His beloved.

He closed the case and returned the watch to his pocket. Julianne glanced his way just then and, for the moment, he was frozen. Their eyes met. If he was capable, he would blush. She smiled and nodded, just slightly. He did the same. He remained frozen, savoring this forbidden moment, wanting it…and more. So much more. He wanted to sweep her up in his arms, carry her away. But that had been tried once—in the disastrous encounter in Pattaya with the young American woman whose resemblance to his beloved had driven him mad, and the subsequent bloodlust had led to her demise and the creation of an enemy that it took years to be rid of.

No. He would not make the same mistake again. This was the new Ramonne. He was different now. He was…*changed*. He was capable of standing here in the waning afternoon sun, going about amongst mere mortals as if he were one of them. He could not jeopardize his new freedom for this woman—though he knew…he knew she really was Giselle reincarnated.

An instant after it happened, the girl turned away and it was over.

Over.

Ramonne sighed and moved forward through the crowd. He approached an old woman selling betel nuts. She flashed a stained-tooth smile and he told her what he desired. He handed her the watch. She wrapped it in the wax paper she used to dispense her wares. He handed her some bills and the transaction was done. He turned to go.

The boy was standing in front of him.

"Da da," he shouted with glee.

Ramonne had never heard the word before. 'Da da.' Papa. It was one of the first words one desired to hear from a child. He felt unworthy.

"Boy. Do you know me?"

"Da da," he said the word again.

Ramonne bent down. He looked into the sweet boy's eyes. His innocent eyes.

"Yes. I am your *jao por*. Your godfather.

The boy beamed, as if a spaceship had come down to take him away.

Ramonne smoothed his silken hair and the boy reached for his hand. Ramonne felt like lightning was passing through him when the little fingers wrapped around his thumb. He stood up, still allowing the boy to grasp him. He smiled and gently worked his thumb loose from the child's grip.

"I must go."

And with that, Ramonne disappeared.

The boy stared. He couldn't understand what had just happened. His emotions, always a heartbeat away from going haywire, began to overload. He cried. A primal, mortal scream.

Martin heard it and rushed to his son's side.

"Hon. What is it, son?"

"Da da." He said that word again. Martin reached out to smooth his tousled hair. But the boy's gaze was not directed at him. He was looking across the market, and his little finger was pointing.

Martin followed his gaze.

"Impossible."

At the edge of the market square, a tall man with long hair studied an object in a vendor's cart. Slowly he turned away and the unmistakable shock of white in the hair caught the morning sun. His bright blue eyes glowed and he smiled.

The man nodded at Martin just as a group of Japanese tourists, cameras clicking, passed between them. When the tourists were gone, the man had vanished.

"Martin. What is it? You look like you've seen a ghost." Areeya took his hand.

Martin's face wore a look of shock and wonder. *In the daylight? How can that be?*

"Martin?"

He looked to the boy. He was still looking across the market. He took the boy and held him close, but the child's gaze remained fixed on where the man had been.

"It's nothing. Let's go."

They started to leave when an old woman approached Julianne. She had a small paper-wrapped parcel in her rough hands. She gave a betel-stained smile and extended the package to Julianne.

Julianne stared at it, puzzled.

"The *barang* told me to give this to you."

Julianne unwrapped the brown paper. A thin cloth was folded around the object. She carefully removed it.

"Oh! How beautiful!" Areeya exclaimed.

It was a pocket watch, in an ornate silver case with a short gold chain attached.

Martin held his breath. He had seen the watch before.

It was Ramonne's. It had been his only remaining possession from his mortal life. Martin had kept it for over a year and had personally given it back to Ramonne when the vampire re-entered his life.

"Open it," Areeya said excitedly.

Julianne fumbled a moment and then managed to spring the latch that allowed the case to open. Inside was a sepia-toned portrait of a beautiful young woman.

"Oh my God," Julianne gasped. "It's my grandmother."

6

———————

Bangkok, 1948

The boys were naked and small, like cherubs, but being Thai, there was hardly an ounce of fat on any of them. They dove off the wooden pier and splashed into the river. Again and again. Each dive or jump was accompanied by squeals of laughter. At any given moment, one was in the air, descending to the river, one was splashing to the shore, and another was climbing the rickety ladder to repeat the process. It was a scene played out dozens, if not hundreds, of times each afternoon as the mighty Chao Phraya shifted course and flowed southwards.

The boat travelled downriver, passing fishermen casting wide nets, men and women bathing or doing laundry. Harmony was demonstrated as both banks were lined by temples, mosques and churches. As the craft left Bangkok, verdant rice fields stretched as far as the eye could see.

The name of the country had just the day before been officially changed back to Prathet Thai, or Thailand—the 'Land of the Free.' It had been changed from Siam to Thailand in 1939, but in 1945 the new regime had made 'Siam' fashionable again.

Jim Thompson was still recovering from the hangover—any occasion called for a celebration; renaming the country called for merrymaking of grand proportions—when he got the call to report to the new customs house at Klong Toey port. The reason was still quite sketchy, but he groggily climbed aboard the forty-foot police boat and was on the river before he had a chance to question where they were going.

Lulled by the serenity of the passing scenery, he decided to ask no questions and merely enjoy the ride, as the fresh sea breezes were slowly unfogging his sleep-deprived and inebriated brain. He fell fast asleep.

It was a leisurely ride of more than an hour and a half. Thompson awoke when the twin motors suddenly ceased their roar. He took a few swallows from the canteen that a young police officer had kindly provided him with, and watched as they glided towards their destination. He felt almost human. *Nothing like a boat trip to clear the head.* As the engines were reversed, Thompson ventured to the bow.

They were in a thick mangrove swamp. Two smaller craft were tied to pylons by a rickety pier. A small crowd was gathered there. What appeared to be a large fish was at their feet

Christ. As they got closer, it was plain to Thompson that the object lying prone on the pier was a corpse.

But that wasn't what upset him. Standing on the pier, sporting a tan shirt with epaulets, and a pair of breeches tucked uncomfortably taut into riding boots that extended her diminutive height by six inches—obviously part of the military look she was affecting—was former OSS officer Jane Farmer. The dragon lady of the OSS. It had been two years since he had last seen her. She was still one of the sexiest creatures he'd ever met, and today she was dressed like a military dominatrix.

She must have left the riding crop in her boudoir, Thompson thought, as the craft gently nosed the pier. Two policemen grabbed the side of the boat while the mate handed off the lines.

One of the cops offered Thompson a hand, and he was hauled onto the pier.

"Hello, Jane. I heard you were in town." Thompson smiled and then, as an afterthought, snapped off a salute. She ignored the salute and looked to the body sprawled at their feet.

"Recognize him?"

He bent down to get a closer look and immediately stood back up. He took out his handkerchief and placed it over his nose. "Christ. How long has he been in the river?"

"How the hell would I know? Do you *recognize* him?"

"Yes. It's Yoshiro Nakimira."

"The Japanese that you were assigned to escort?"

"Yes."

"Are you certain?"

Thompson looked again at the bloated corpse. Great chunks had been bitten away. Rats, he supposed. The eyes were just twin black sockets. The mouth was also gnawed at, and the tongue appeared gone. But the stature and dress were similar to that of the missing Japanese. *But could he be sure?* Covering his mouth and nose, Thompson bent down once more. The body was resting slightly on its right side and the arm was pinned beneath the corpse. Thompson motioned, and a cop rolled the body onto its back, freeing the arm.

Clutched in a death grip was Nakimira's ornate walking stick.

"It's him."

"He didn't drown, did he?"

They were both staring down at the bloated body. There was a three-centimeter-wide tear across his neck.

"No. His throat was cut."

"Who was he, Big Jim?"

"A Japanese hotelier. He ran the Oriental during the occupation. Works for the Imperial in Tokyo."

Jane Farmer frowned. "I know that. Who was he really?"

"Same as us, I imagine. He was Kempeitai. Japanese intelligence. That's what MacDonald told me. He returned to Bangkok on a diplomatic passport issued by the Thais. As such, he was under consular observation."

Jane Farmer crossed her arms. "What else did Alex MacDonald tell you?"

"MacDonald runs a newspaper now, Jane."

"Bullshit. He's still OSS. You're still OSS."

"I believe they call it the CIA now, Jane."

"They can call it what they want. If it looks like a duck, it's a duck…what did MacDonald tell you?"

"Supposedly Nakimira was here to retrieve some family heirloom stored at the Oriental."

"Family heirloom…? A samurai sword? Wedding kimono?"

"I have no idea. Whatever it was, I was supposed to confiscate it as spoils of war. On direct orders from Douglas MacArthur."

"And?"

"And…he disappeared."

"Really? The great Lord Jim couldn't keep track of one lonely little Jap? My, my, my. Not the man I knew." She took out an ivory holder and fitted it with a cigarette.

Thompson gave her a light.

When she exhaled, she blew the smoke in his face.

"And this heirloom. Where is it?"

"I have no idea. The basement of the Oriental was ransacked. Whatever was stored there is gone."

"He got it and ran."

"Apparently. But he left his belongings. His bags, all his clothes. Everything was still in his room. It seemed that he was coming back."

"Not anymore it doesn't." Jane Farmer flicked her ash on the corpse.

"So, Big Jim. Who killed him?"

Thompson shook his head. "I have no idea."

She stared at him. Beads of perspiration on his brow turned to sweat and ran down his face. He took out a handkerchief and wiped his head and neck.

The police crew had given the foreigners lots of room, staying a discreet distance away and watching in silence.

"This is not good, Big Jim. Not good at all."

He started to say something but she cut him off. She motioned and one of the policemen came to her. "Roll him over again."

The bloated body was now back on its right side again.

"Lift the hand."

The officer gently lifted the left wrist by the sleeve. The hand had lost its silk glove.

And was missing two fingers.

"He lost those before he took the big swim. Yakuza."

Thompson knew the term for the Japanese crime syndicate that employed mutilation as a rite of atonement.

Jane took the cigarette from her holder and flicked it into the river.

"This Jap was supposed to lead us to a secret that has eluded the Allies for ten years."

"A secret weapon?"

"Not a ray gun. Not another nuclear bomb…but a source of power."

"I've heard nothing of this."

"That's why it's called a 'secret,' Big Jim. You're not supposed to have heard of it."

"Then how do you know?"

"Because I'm *supposed* to know."

———

Jim Thompson and Jane Farmer had first crossed paths after the war ended in Europe.

As the 1930s wound down, Thompson was a practicing

architect in New York. With the escalation of the next war in Europe in the early 1940s, Thompson volunteered for service in the United States Army, enlisting as a private in the Delaware National Guard. Shortly after Pearl Harbor was attacked, he received his first commission and was assigned to a coastal artillery unit in North Carolina.

A year after the outbreak of the war in the Pacific, he was urged to become a member of the recently formed Office of Strategic Services. The OSS specialized in subversive propaganda, intelligence gathering and clandestine warfare behind enemy lines. It had a knack for attracting upper-class types like Thompson, with its alluring promise of world travel, adventure and intrigue.

After his training, Thompson was assigned to work with the French in North Africa. Shortly after VE Day, he volunteered to go to the Pacific. He was sent to Catalina Island, off the California coast, for a rigorous training program to prepare him for service in Thailand. It was here that he first met the ubiquitous Miss Farmer.

Thompson was transported from Long Beach, along with hundreds of new Marines on the steamship SS *Avalon*. The former SS *Virginia* was bought in 1920 by the chewing gum magnate and virtual owner of Catalina Island, William Wrigley Jr. It was re-commissioned when the Second World War broke out.

The US Maritime Services, Coast Guard, Army Signal Corps and OSS occupied the city of Avalon. Thompson stowed his gear at the Hotel Atwater, where he would spend the night before heading off to remote Toyon Bay and survival training.

The US military occupation of Catalina hadn't kept the citizens from turning a profit. The second-floor ballroom of the casino, the gorgeous round pleasure palace that sat at the north end of Avalon harbor, was being used as an officers' club. The movie theater was still in operation, each show sold out.

But by far the most successful entrepreneurs on the island were the owners of the saloons. There were at least a dozen bars on the waterfront and in the lanes that snaked up the hill from the harbor. Thompson wandered the little town and settled on a bar that had no name. The only sign that it existed was an old fishing net stretched over a blue neon crab.

He saw her as soon as he entered the smoke-filled room.

OSS officer Jane Farmer was the focus of attention. Seated atop the old wooden bar, she was surrounded by officers in a variety of uniforms. She wore the distinctive arrowhead crest pinned to her lapel that identified her as OSS. Her skirt was hiked up on her thigh, exposing her gorgeous gams.

Thompson was a married man, having tied the knot in 1942 when he first joined the OSS. He'd enjoyed a scant six months of married life before being shipped off to North Africa.

Jane Farmer was, in the vernacular of the day, a knockout. And married or not, Thompson was immediately smitten. He ordered a whisky neat and took one of the many empty chairs. Drink in hand, he studied the alluring Jane Farmer. Her hair was brunette and of medium length. It had waves that reminded Thompson of Rita Hayworth, the number one love goddess of the time.

Soon, Thompson noticed that officer Jane Farmer was looking his way. She was now studying him. Basically a shy man, he found himself feeling uncomfortable. Shortly she offered her hand and two stalwart Marines lifted her off the bar. She clicked glasses with her admirers and then walked straight towards him.

"OSS?"

Thompson was puzzled. "Yes. How did you know?"

She nodded to his collar and the OSS crest.

"Oh. Of course."

"Please." He motioned to an empty chair.

She thanked him and sat, again revealing her gorgeous legs.

"Jim Thompson. I'm being deployed to the Pacific theater."
He extended his hand.

"Jane Farmer. Pacific, as well." She took his hand and gave it
a firm shake. "Know what you're in for?"

"I think so."

"I doubt you do," she said with a wicked smile.

Thompson motioned to the bartender, and a boy brought
them two fresh drinks.

"I've been thrown out of an airplane, and spent three days
and nights alone in the woods with only a knife and a canteen.
Learned to throw a grenade, fire a sub-machine gun, and a
hundred ways to kill a man without firing a shot."

"Really?"

"Really. And I was taught to never hesitate to go for the…"

Jane Farmer leaned in very close to Thompson.

"Balls."

She wore a light perfume that he found intoxicating. He
hung on her every word.

"Do you know what the last item is that they give you
before you're deployed?"

"No. What?"

"A little metal canister. It contains three pills. One for energy,
one to wake you up. And the third, cyanide—to kill yourself in
case you're captured. You even learn how to crack the hard shell
in your mouth."

She demonstrated on the olive from her martini.

Thompson was spellbound. "You really were taught that?"

"Oh yeah."

Thompson was definitely smitten. He blushed.

She smiled. "Here's a survival tip for you. You know those
little Hershey's Kisses? Wrapped in foil?"

"Yes?"

"Well, when they left me alone for three days in the interior
—did you know they actually have buffalo in there?"

"No. I didn't."

"They were used in a movie and then just left behind. Anyway, I filled my bra with those little chocolates."

"You got away with that?"

She looked at him like he was a Mormon hick from Salt Lake.

"Got away with it? Of course I got away with it."

They spent the night in Thompson's room at the Atwater. She shipped out the next day, and Thompson never saw her again.

Until she appeared on the rickety pier with a bloated Japanese corpse.

OSS agent Jane Farmer became notorious in OSS lore when she obtained a large supply of condoms from a doctor in Ceylon. Farmer and her team then stuffed the condoms with messages urging the citizens of Indonesia to resist the Japanese invaders. They then blew the condoms up and tied the ends shut. Submarines then released them off the Indonesian coast— thus earning OSS officer Jane Farmer the infamous nickname of 'Rubber Johnny' Jane.

———

Ramonne sat at the bar, alone.

He liked to be alone.

Alone was natural. He was a solitary man. Well, not actually a man, but solitary anyway. Hunters usually were solitary, unless they hunted in packs. Even then, the pack relied on the solitary alpha male.

Alpha male. Ramonne wasn't quite sure where he'd heard that term. It seemed to be catching on now, as he noticed things did in the twentieth century. They became trends. Somebody said something new, and then it was repeated, endlessly.

Fads, they were called in the 1920s. Ramonne had little to do with fads or fashion. He looked pretty much the same as he did in 1858 when he first arrived in Siam. His hair was long and curled over his collar. He supposed he'd worn it that way as an artist in Marseilles. It was fashionable then, and it never grew after he was *changed*, and thus he had never changed its style. One more difference, one more freedom from the routines of the mortals who surrounded him. Ramonne felt blessed.

And cursed.

The current object of his wrath came through the door and entered the bar. Brigadier-General Natiwat Pongchan. *A pompous ass. Poseurs* such as this ghastly policeman insulted him. However, the brigadier-general had to be endured. For the moment.

Ramonne raised a hand and the general spotted him through the thick smoke in the bar.

"Khun Natiwat. Good evening. *Sabai dee mai?*" Ramonne courteously inquired.

"*Sawat dee khrap. Sabai dee.*" The general took a seat.

Ramonne motioned and a girl came over. General Natiwat ordered his bottle of The Macallan single malt. Ramonne had a bottle of burgundy in front of him and indicated to the girl that he was fine.

"Let's dispense with the formalities, shall we Khun Ennomar?" Ramonne desired for the general to know as little as possible about him, so he used the inverted alias Ennomar with him. "Do you have my payment?"

Ramonne smiled. "But of course." He produced a sealed manila envelope. General Natiwat's beady eyes lit up at the sight of it. He reached out his hand, but Ramonne withdrew the envelope.

"One moment, please. I have a question."

The general frowned.

"I pay you to make my victims disappear, yes?"

"Yes. Your point?"

Ramonne hefted the envelope. "This is full of 1,000-baht notes. It is not insignificant, is it?"

The girl arrived with the whisky. The general waved her off

and poured his own tumbler. He downed it and poured another. He was obviously agitated.

"Khun Ennomar, please say what is on your mind."

Ramonne put the envelope down, in front of him.

"Today a body floated into the *klong* at Nonthaburi. Two fishermen pulled it out of the water."

The general feigned indifference and poured himself another whisky.

Ramonne leaned in. "Do you know who this corpse was?"

"Of course I do. I am brigadier-general of the Bangkok police. It was that annoying little Japanese prick. Nakimira."

"Precisely. Yoshiro Nakimira. Who…if my memory serves me, I dispatched three nights prior and went to a lot—"

He leaned in even closer. "A *lot*…" He was in General Natiwat's face. "…of trouble to deliver to Hernando's Cemetery."

Seemingly unfazed, the general sipped his whisky.

"And yet, three days later, this same little Japanese prick washes up in Nonthaburi. Can you explain this for me please?"

General Natiwat lit a cigarette. He drew the smoke deep into his lungs and let it out the side of his mouth through tightly clenched teeth.

"We have an arrangement. You pay me to dispose of your trash. You told me your victims would be 'nobodies.' Derelicts, prostitutes, life's dregs, as it were." He drew in more smoke and hissed it out. "But you did not say that you would be asking me to dispose of a foreign attaché. A significant enough individual as to have appeared on both the United States' and the government's watch list."

Ramonne grabbed the general's cigarette and snuffed it into the ashtray. "Understand me, Khun Natiwat. I don't give a fuck who I ask you to dispose of. This—"

He slid the envelope back under the general's nose. "This buys me immunity. Do you understand?"

Suddenly, General Natiwat felt fear such as he had never

known. He knew what it was like to be in a tiger's jaws. In the coils of a python.

"If I wanted him to end up in the river, I could have saved myself a lot of fucking trouble and just thrown him off the Oriental pier."

7

Siem Reap, Fall 2007

*The solar and lunar alignments at Angkor Wat were alignments with
the gods, alignments that tied the nation to the heavens above, and
alignments that imbued the king with the power to rule by divine
association.*

Ramonne pondered this.

He had entered the holy arena to do battle with the devil.
No matter who he was—God was on his side.

*To extract the elixir of immortality, one needs an intimate knowledge
of the stars. If we know how to align ourselves with the stars, we can
begin our ascent to the realm of the gods and beyond.*

Ramonne. The immortal. The necromancer was clearly
absolved of his sins when he challenged Zhoupeng.

*A mandala of time and divinity, and its center or creator, was built
into the periphery and heart of the temple, making it an image of the
universe and its source. Only the truly innocent shall be able to pass*

the four outer circles: the purifying fire of wisdom, the vajra circle, the circle with the eight tombs and the lotus circle.

The truly *innocent*. Ramonne had known of the power of the innocent. He had experienced it firsthand when he entered the mind of the child of his victim in Paris. The boy was so pure of thought, so innocent that it was like being in a stark white room.

Thus it was that he summoned Martin to bring his favorite orphan—his son—to the battle. He was drained, utterly depleted of energy, and was succumbing to Zhoupeng's slow and painful dissection—when the boy appeared. Instantly the tide was turned. Through Ramonne's bond with Martin, he was able to channel the child's pure white energy. He defeated the devil—drew him out of his protective cloak and destroyed him.

But it took the life from the boy.

The confluence of events coincides with the churning of the Milky Ocean in seeking to extract the elixir of immortality. The elixir has the ability to perfect any substance. When applied to the human body, the elixir cures diseases and restores youth. A blessing beyond all blessings upon earth…given to very few, and to those few rather by revelation.

The words, written in Khmer by a strong hand, resonated on the page. Though it was only a copy of the ancient parchment, Ramonne felt the author's power as he caressed the paper.

He marveled at the wisdom of these ancient sorcerers. These illumined seers. Surely they foretold of his battle and the subsequent phenomenon.

It was he who restored the boy. He possessed the elixir of immortality. He was granted the power. Consequently he'd been redeemed. The blessing of all blessings.

Gradually he was returning to human form.

It had all been foretold in the ancient scriptures.

He continued to marvel at the change that allowed him his short forays into the sunlight. And his slaked killing instinct.

Ramonne had been in his den for the best part of two weeks. He'd been totally, utterly absorbed in reading the documents that Professor Kaestle had obtained in Paris. He'd ventured into the garden in the days' waning light for a meal and a bottle of wine. Then he'd returned to his den until the wee hours when, exhausted but mentally infused, he crawled into his coffin for a fitful sleep.

When he finally closed the last of the volumes that Professor Kaestle had bound the documents in, he felt an emotion in him that he had long suppressed.

He was lonely. He wanted companionship.

This was, he realized, a basic *human* need. He thought of Giselle every night. The sketches he had made when they were together in Marseilles were in the journals he retrieved four years ago. He opened and studied them constantly. The resemblance to the girl Julianne was remarkable. He knew the girl was still in Siem Reap. But he had deliberately avoided her. Approaching her, abducting her, was unthinkable.

And then he had the dream.

It was strange. In the dream he was with the only woman since Giselle who had meant anything to him.

He was with Kanchana. The woman who had ventured into a cave in Cambodia and resurrected him. The woman he turned into a vampire to save her from an incurable disease.

She had been magnificent. Strong and powerful, her bloodlust had rivaled his. They had been hunters...and lovers. But then she had rejected the embrace of darkness and pined for her mortal soul. Her mournful cries filled the Bangkok night and he took pity on her and delivered her back into the light.

As she had not fully transformed, her condition was

reversible. He released her from his spell and she returned, cleansed of her illness, to the world of the living.

He awoke. He was full of old romantic feelings.

He climbed out of the coffin, took pen and paper and composed a note. He went into the hall. Professor Kaestle was having a snack.

He looked at the telephone on the table in the hall. "Does that thing work?"

"Yes. It was considered a necessity by the former owners. The line was left open," Professor Kaestle replied.

"Give me the number."

He added the number to the letter he had composed, sealed the envelope and dispatched Professor Kaestle to the post office.

One week passed, then the phone finally rang. Ramonne picked up the receiver. "Yes?"

"Ramonne."

He heard his own name and knew instantly who it was. His blue eyes widened and he smiled.

Bangkok, Present Day

If you are pregnant or are supporting someone through pregnancy, you probably have had some experience with mood swings. You are not alone; mood swings are common during pregnancy.

Well, they got that right.

Martin stared at the computer screen. He had Googled 'pregnancy' and 'mood swings' and gotten a half-million results.

Starting about two weeks ago Areeya had become irrational, irritable, emotional and paranoid. Usually all at the same time.

Martin now knew why men had jobs. To get away from their wives.

Blessed with an inheritance initially worth ten million, Martin's hobby of studying and investing in emerging technologies had now quadrupled his worth. Unless he developed a serious gambling habit, there was no way that Martin Larue would ever have to get a job. But right now he wished he had one. Eight hours of peace and quiet every day. Even nine-year-old Hon left each day for six hours of school, when they weren't on one of Thailand's innumerable public holidays.

Maybe I could go with him?

"Martin." The cry split the air in the Ethan Allen apartment. Martin left his computer and walked to the bedroom. He didn't hurry, as there never was any urgency to her calls. It was a cry for attention. Nothing else.

She was in bed. Feet up. That had been the advice, and she'd followed it. Now she was milking it.

The mountain of cushions and pillows piled behind and around her gave her the appearance of royalty—the bed being her throne.

"Martin. Why don't we have a family?"

Huh? "I don't understand."

"You have parents. I've never met them. You have a brother I've never met."

"You know my relationship with my parents is complicated. They're separated. Have been for over ten years. And they live half a world apart."

"What about my family?"

What about it? Your father tried to have me killed, threw me in jail, and died by Ramonne's hand. Good riddance. "We see your mother, don't we? She's nice." *She's a shrew.*

"You've met her once."

Once was enough. "Yes…Is there a point to this?"

Areeya had taken to wearing reading glasses. He was convinced she didn't need them. She just liked the power it gave her to peer over the rims at him. Like a judge. She had bought the strange kind that snapped apart in the middle and then hung on each side of her neck.

"Family, Martin. I want a *family*."

"What are you talking about? You're pregnant, for God's sake."

"That's not what I mean. When the baby's born, I want her to have grandparents, aunts, uncles…family."

"Honey. We are a family. You, me, the baby, Hon…we're a family."

"Aren't you listening to me?" she suddenly screamed.

Here it comes.

"You never listen to me. You don't care about me. You've *never* cared about me. All you think of is yourself…What about me? Huh? Have you ever thought about what I might want?"

She started crying. Big wet, deep sobs.

"Honey, please don't cry."

He went to the bed, tried to put his arms around her. To comfort and console her. Even though he knew exactly what was coming.

The minute he touched her, she turned to him—in a perfect impression of Linda Blair's head-turning trick in *The Exorcist*. She shrieked, "Don't touch me!" She flung his arm from her shoulder and snarled, "Get out!"

Why am I doing this? "Look, honey. You're upset. You're depressed. It's a phase. You'll be—"

"Get out!"

She buried her head in the pillows and continued the deep wet sobbing.

Fuck it. The maid's here. She doesn't need or want me. "I'm going out," he announced.

This news brought a momentary break in the sobbing. A muffled voice spoke through the pillows, "Where are you going?"

He didn't know. "Out…Just out."

"Why?"

"Because I need to. I'm suffocating here."

"Fine. Go. Leave me here alone."

"You're not alone. Nee is here."

———

He wandered Sukhumvit Road, the great avenue of opportunity for foreigners of all colors and ages—as long as they were male. His mind was so far removed from the present that he saw nothing and no one. The endless street vendors and food stalls. The hookers—ladies and ladyboys. He didn't see them. He didn't see anything until he saw a sign. 'Soi 7.'

He returned to reality. It was here, he remembered, that his forays to the dark side began with Ramonne.

He turned into the dim little street. It was like hundreds of small streets all over Bangkok. A pizza joint, an Indian restaurant...

And a sex club.

The Gardens of Babylon.

Its neon beckoned to him. He entered. Nothing had changed.

"Ah. Herr Martin. Long time, no see. How are you?" Fritz, the affable German owner greeted him. "You are all alone?"

"Yes. Quite alone."

"Good. The last time, you caused quite a ruckus."

The last time, Martin thought. Eight years ago, when he came here with Jonathan Peyton, the vampire hunter, and they attacked and carried the unconscious vampire to a waiting cab. That was a night to remember.

"*Mai pen rai.* Never mind. Please choose your girls."

There were two groups of young girls sitting around, separated by a yellow line. As Fritz would proudly tell the uninitiated: "Those on the left take it up the ass. Those on the right do not. I suggest you take one of each." Martin glanced around briefly at the vacant-eyed young women. They smiled at him.

He turned back to the bar. "I think I'll have a drink first."

"Suit yourself. Just don't drink too long. This place is for ze fucking, not for ze drinking."

This is where it began.

Well, not exactly. It began when he saw a dead woman in Hernando's Cemetery appear in the local press as a drowning victim. That had provoked Martin's search that uncovered a decade or more of police cover-ups. He wrote an article that appeared on the *Bangkok Times'* front page as 'Bangrak serial killer.' Within 48 hours the vampire Ramonne was on his doorstep—seeking vengeance.

But Martin's limitless wealth intrigued the vampire, and instead of killing him, he made Martin his friend. He literally seduced Martin by transmitting his thoughts. Martin was able to witness historical events—like the coronation of King Chulalongkorn, Rama V. He was there. Martin stood amongst the crowds as the torches illuminated a great procession of mounted elephants and horses through the gates of the Grand Palace. For this he handed over money, and Ramonne took him on excursions. Excursions that led him down a path of sexual decadence and sensual pleasure. The brothel bar that he sat in now was one of Ramonne's portals of earthly delights. These women, these whores, tolerated Ramonne's abuses, both physical and verbal, for it was their job. He took three or four at a time. Under Ramonne's spell, Martin was also able to perform vigorously. His sexual prowess was unlimited when he was with Ramonne. They prowled like jaguars. No doors were closed to Ramonne. Nothing was off limits. All women would succumb to Ramonne's charisma. He was irresistible. And this power was transferred to Martin when they dallied together.

Martin's head spun and he felt dizzy as the memories flooded over him.

"Are you all right, mate?"

He realized he had actually passed out. He lifted his head off the bar. *Where am I? What happened?*

Then his focus returned and he knew. The Gardens of Babylon. He looked at the ruddy-faced stranger at his side.

"You all right?"

"I think so."

He looked around at the girls, the men, the seedy atmosphere. He picked three 1,000-baht notes out of his billfold and placed them on the bar.

And he bolted for the door.

Back on Sukhumvit he walked aimlessly, passing Arab tourists, Asian tourists, Russians, Africans, Europeans. Mostly men on the prowl. Black men, white men, fat men, skinny men —all on the prowl.

He passed their prey. University girls looking to supplement their allowances, lurking in doorways. Older women in their mid-twenties who didn't want to pay the commission that go-go bars demanded. Freelancers that had been secretaries, nurses, anything, before the economy collapsed and turned them into nothing more than streetwalkers.

He passed them all, but he saw very few. In fact, he saw no one. For his mind was focused on one thing. *Ramonne.*

From Ramonne a force emanated. A force he had encountered before.

Many times.

It drove him to it. Beckoned to him.

And then—just like that. It happened. Suddenly—in the middle of the Nana intersection. Some would call it a flashback.

He knew that his options, his ability to resist and continue his normal life no longer existed.

Horns honked. Lights flashed.

He was frozen in the middle of the street. He blinked and then shuffled to the curb. The cop in the traffic box glared at him.

8
____

Roluos, Present Day

She arrived in the middle of the night. Professor Kaestle met her car at the border. Kanchana had a fear of flying. So she was driven the 225 kilometers to Poipet on the Thai-Cambodian border. Her driver escorted her to immigration. She passed through, suitcases in hand, and Dr. Kaestle drove her to Roluos.

Ramonne stood in the doorway as the van pulled up. He watched her as she stepped from the vehicle. The same long legs. The thick, dark hair cascading down her back. The easy grace with which she carried herself.

He took her in his arms, pressing her close to his chest. He buried his face in her hair. Her arms encircled his neck. Her fingers gripped his hair.

She emitted a sigh—long, low and guttural. He felt a release of tension that cascaded through her body and escaped into the ether.

They stayed this way for several silent minutes. Embarrassed, Professor Kaestle deposited the bags and retreated.

Ramonne broke his embrace and held her at arm's length.

He smiled and stared at her pale face. A tear had escaped from each of her eyes. He took a thumb and gently traced them.

"My darling. How I have yearned for you."

She looked up at him. Her face bore an expression of both joy and puzzlement.

"I didn't think we would ever see each other again."

Gently he cupped her chin.

"I know. It was too dangerous."

She blinked.

"It *is* too dangerous."

He smiled.

"No. It is not."

She buried her head on his chest. She crushed him to her.

"I don't care. Take me. Destroy me. Kill me…I cannot live without you. Even if we have just one night."

Ramonne stroked her hair. Petting it, he gently kissed the top of her head.

"Do not fear my darling."

She was sobbing softly now, the sound muffled as her face was buried in the folds of his jacket. Gently he pried loose her arms.

"Listen to me, my darling." He held her arms at her side. "You truly have nothing to fear."

Slowly she raised her head.

"I have no fear. I want you. I must have you. I *need* you. I have no life without you."

Ramonne felt another of the strange feelings he'd been experiencing lately. *Human emotion.* It coursed through his body. He didn't know what it was, but he enjoyed it. It made him feel…warm.

She put her head back. "Take me. I am yours."

Ramonne bent to her neck. He pushed her hair aside and placed his lips on her throat. He felt the tension in her body. Her muscles tightened. The veins in her neck stood out.

He kissed them.

And then he withdrew, holding her again at arm's length. Her eyes were closed.

"I told you there is nothing to fear."

She opened her eyes.

"I have changed."

Her eyes widened. "How is this possible?"

He smiled again. "It's complicated. But it seems that in battling a great evil, a transferrence occurred and I am gradually being freed from the force that I've been under."

Her eyes were as wide as saucers now. "Like I was, yes? The spell has been broken?"

"You were not fully transformed. I was able to reverse your curse. But I've been a demon for over a century and a half. I've transposed countless souls. This is a most astonishing occurrence."

He brought her closer to him.

"It means that we can be together without fear. Without harm to you…or others."

She looked into his eyes. "You no longer hunt?"

"No. I feed like a human."

"You can go out in the sun?"

"Yes."

"Lord Buddha." She brought her mouth to his. She licked his lips and then they kissed.

As mortals kiss.

Long, hard and passionately. As though they were the only lovers in the world.

———

Bangkok, Present Day

The darkened hotel room was lit only by the pulsing city skyline visible through the open curtains, and the flickering of a silent television screen. In the dim light, a figure stirred, tossing in the bed. Martin slept the fitful sleep of the somnambulant. He had passed out a few hours before. He was tangled in the bed sheets. He turned on his side and drew the sheet up to his chin. As he did this, his hand touched something sticky.

He opened his eyes. A brief explosion of light on the TV illuminated the bed for just a moment.

Martin saw the blood and awoke with a start.

The sheet was drenched in it. His hand was covered with it. He threw off the offending sheet. He was naked. The bottom sheet was clean.

His body was clean.

The blood wasn't his.

As he frantically attempted to escape the bed, his own blood pulsed and raced to his brain. He cringed under a massive migraine. *What the hell did I do?*

His head throbbing, he attempted to sit upright. He had to brace himself against the wall. With his left foot he kicked the bloodstained sheet to the floor. As he watched it fall, he saw the room for the first time. *Citadines.*

He realized where he was. He was in a hotel on Soi 11. Although he'd never stayed there, he had a friend who was a long-term resident, and he'd visited it a few times. *Okay. I'm in a hotel. But why?*

Then he saw the shoes. Red stilettos. Parked demurely by the door. His own cordovan loafers were strewn in a corner, as were the rest of his clothes. Draped on a chair was a white blouse. And what looked like a black skirt.

My God.

He attempted to stand, fearful of what he would find as he searched the room.

The room was divided by a sliding *shoji*-screen, separating the entry and sitting area from the bed. Slowly he slid the screen back, fearing the worst. *What have I done?*

Nothing. The room was empty. No bloody corpse.

No torn and ravaged, nameless female. Nothing.

Just a few Heineken cans and a half-full bottle of Smirnoff.

The blood? Thinking perhaps he had imagined it, he unraveled the sheet from the floor. The sheet was indeed soaked in the viscous red fluid.

His head throbbed. His mind raced. He tried to reconstruct the evening.

Nothing. Apart from the clanging and banging of a dozen hammers, his mind was blank.

And then the bathroom door opened.

"Sorry. Did I wake you?" A voice speaking Thai.

She was in her twenties. Very pretty and very much alive.

Martin breathed an audible sigh of relief.

The girl, wearing nothing but a white towel, walked to the bed. She stooped, holding the towel in place with one hand, and picked up the bloody sheet with the other. She held it out and inspected it.

"I made quite a mess, didn't I?"

Martin pulled the sheet up to his stomach and smiled. His head started to clear. The throbbing began to slow down.

"*Men?*" He used the Thai slang for menstruation.

She nodded. "*Ka.* I'm very sorry. Let me wash it."

"*Mai pen rai.*" Martin shook his head. "Don't bother. It's not important."

He studied her. She was dark-skinned, very young, he could now discern. Probably nineteen or twenty. Her feet were a bit large. Isaan, he surmised. This meant she was from the rural northeast. From a farming family. Until recently she'd been a farmer. Martin wondered what bar he had taken her out of. As he was on Soi 11, she could have come from either Nana Plaza or Soi Cowboy. Both were equal distance from the Citadines and each had a dozen or more go-go bars full of former farm girls tarted up and ready for a roll in the hay with a paying customer.

"What's your name?" he asked.

"Noi. Don't you remember?"

"Of course," he lied.

She climbed into bed, still clutching the towel. "Khun Martin, how is your head?" She put a cool hand on his forehead.

"It's okay," he lied again.

She put her head on his shoulder, like a puppy looking to be petted. Martin took her by the shoulder and looked her in the eye.

"Noi. Did we...?"

She cocked her head, not understanding. Martin took his hands from her shoulders, made a circle with thumb and forefinger on one, and inserted the forefinger of the other.

She got the idea.

"No. We started to...but you were too drunk."

He smiled, slightly embarrassed.

"You fell asleep...and then..." She pointed to the bloody sheet, her eyes downcast. "I'm sorry."

Martin was relieved, again. "Don't be sorry. It's all right."

He was twice blessed. For one, he hadn't killed anyone. And two, he hadn't technically cheated on his wife.

He picked up his Rolex from the nightstand. Four o'clock. If he hustled, he could be home in half an hour. He'd be in trouble. He'd have some explaining to do, but he thought that the marriage would survive.

"Noi. I'm going home."

She stiffened. Her eyes went wide. "You don't like me?"

He stood, pulling the clean sheet with him. "No. It's not that. Of course I like you. You are *suay maak.* Very beautiful. It's just that..."

He held up his left hand. The one with the wedding band. "I'm married."

She smiled. "I know."

He started to pick up his clothes—with one hand. The other clutched the sheet. When he had his pants, he put the pile on the dresser and extracted his wallet. He opened it and took out a wad of 1,000-baht notes. Five thousand would be more than double what she was expecting. He handed it to her.

"Here. You can stay if you like. I'll pay for the room when I go downstairs."

She cocked her head again, wondering what was going on with this curious *farang*. But having the money in her hand made her feel ambivalent, and she smiled. "*Ka*. Thank you." She took the money in both hands and raised the notes to her forehead and bowed. In doing so, the towel fell open, revealing two very pert little breasts.

Martin beat a hasty retreat.

———

Roluos, Present Day

Ramonne lowered the woman onto the bed.

It was a four-poster, an antique that someone had widened to accommodate a modern mattress. It had come with the villa but had never been used in the four years that Ramonne had leased the place. However, in anticipation of the lady's arrival, Ramonne had dispatched the professor to town to purchase a new mattress and all the accoutrements that made the four-poster a real bed—an endless stream of duvets, sheets, pillows and cushions.

For a century and a half, he had slept contentedly in a very comfortable wooden coffin. In more recent times he'd put a jazz record on the turntable—Chet Baker or perhaps Miles Davis—and he'd drift off to a blissful sleep, the days passing without notice.

"*Mon cherie*," Ramonne whispered in her ear as he parted her legs. She gasped as he entered her.

In an instant he was transformed. He became primeval. Carnivorous. Bestial. He was an animal devouring his mate. Taking her. He plunged deeper and deeper, each thrust drawing moans from the astonished woman. His grip on her arms was like steel traps. She was pinned beneath him. His eyes were closed tight, his head arched back.

For Kanchana, the pleasure was mixed with pain. She had never felt such force. Such fury. Ramonne had once been her lover, during her transformation. She had marveled then at his fortitude. He could make love three or four times in succession, but then he had been tame compared to the beast she was hosting now. He shuddered as he exploded within her. She climaxed simultaneously with him. His hot breath was upon her as he smothered her gasping with his mouth.

He released her arms and she felt numbness where he had held her. As he continued to kiss her, she came again, digging her nails into his muscular back.

When he finally ended the kiss, she saw his eyes clearly for the first time.

"Blue."

"What?"

"Blue...Your eyes are blue."

———

Bangkok, Present Day

Martin showered in the guest bathroom. He padded down the hall as lightly as a fox. He lifted the door as he opened it, so that the hinges would not squeak.

The bedcover was still tucked on his side of the bed, and he gently tugged it free. He made not a sound as he slipped beneath the sheets.

"Where have you been?"

The voice that rose from the other side of the bed was as cold as ice.

"Nowhere."

Bad answer.

A light came on.

"Four-thirty in the morning? And you've been *nowhere*?"

He didn't want to, but he turned and faced her. She was sitting up, her arms folded across her ripened breasts.

"I told you, I went out." He tried to roll back but knew it wouldn't work.

"Out? Where is *out*? *What* is out?"

What's the use?

"I left here and I walked. I had a drink. I walked some more. I ended up on Sukhumvit. I had a few more drinks."

"A few drinks and a walk and you'd be in by midnight. Coming in at half past four is more than a walk and a few drinks."

"Okay…I had a lot of drinks."

"Alone?"

"There were other people there. I was in a bar."

"What bar?"

Okay. Time to lie. He'd never lied to Areeya before, but he couldn't tell her he had been in the Gardens of Babylon or whatever go-go bar he'd bought Noi out of.

"Brown Sugar."

"Brown Sugar closes at one."

"I told you. I walked. I wanted to clear my head."

His head started to throb again. *Probably the lying.*

"My head aches. Can we talk about this in the morning?"

"Fine."

She switched off the light and turned her back to him. He lay in the dark wondering what the hell was going on?

9

Bangkok, 1949

In the middle of the twentieth century, when a person of the status of the late Yoshiro Nakimira traveled abroad, he did so with luggage. Not baggage—luggage. Two Louis Vuitton steamer trunks occupied the center of his suite at the Oriental Hotel.

Jim Thompson watched as the young policeman fitted the latches on the wardrobes. He had already emptied the contents of the dresser drawers, making careful note of each item.

Two bell carts were now bulging with the belongings of Nakimira-*san*, and Lord Jim did a final survey before closing and locking room number twelve. He pocketed the key and watched as the police helped the porters drag the luggage downstairs and into the waiting police van.

In his hand was a small leather-bound journal. It was inscribed with the initials *Y.N.* He slipped it into his pocket and took the stairs up to his suite on the top floor.

"Lord Jim. What are you reading?"

Ramonne had been watching his friend for several minutes. The American was so engrossed in his reading that he hadn't noticed Ramonne. He looked up, surprised.

"I'm not actually reading."

He handed the little journal to Ramonne, who opened it.

"It's Japanese."

The *kanji* characters marched up and down the pages. He handed it back to Thompson.

"But occasionally there is an English word or phrase."

"I assume that it belonged to the late Japanese?"

"Yeah, Nakimira's. I need to get it translated. Trouble is, no one knows I've got it."

Ramonne arched an eyebrow. "Ah…espionage."

"Of course espionage." Thompson looked around surreptitiously and leaned in to the table. "I was with the OSS you know."

Ramonne feigned surprise. "You were?"

"Yes."

Ramonne, of course, knew everything about his friend. He had always found the clandestine nature of his military service most intriguing."

"I assume you still have connections in the spy game. Why don't you tell your colleagues and have them get it translated?"

"I don't trust them, Delacroix. This damned 'lady' from my past is heading up the investigation."

"A lady?"

"Rubber Johnny Jane. You've heard of her?"

"Intriguing name, but no, I'm afraid I've not had the pleasure."

"Pleasure's hardly the word. She's a bitch…pardon my French."

Ramonne had heard this latter expression before, but still its meaning eluded him.

"What secrets does this hold?" Thompson held up the journal.

"I have no idea." Ramonne had his suspicions, and if he was right, his friend would be better off not knowing. He thought for a moment. "Give it to me."

"You? Why?"

"There's a girl. In a teahouse. She says she's *Chinoise*, but I don't believe her. I speak more Mandarin than she does. I suspect she's really *Japonais*."

"Why would she want to help?"

"Why does anyone here do anything? For money of course."

Thompson hesitated for a moment, then slid the journal across the table.

"This has to be on the QT, my friend. Very confidential. Very hush hush."

"Of course." Ramonne would be most certain that the girl never spoke a word of what she transcribed. Most certain.

He slipped the book into his jacket pocket and gave it a reaffirming pat. "I will seek out the young lady later this evening."

"Thank you, my friend. Just remember—"

"I know." Ramonne put a finger to his lips. "Hush hush."

———

Throughout the evening Ramonne's hand slipped into his pocket and felt the soft leather cover of the journal. Had the *Japonais* had this on his person the night of his demise, then Ramonne would have been the only one aware of its existence. Now he had a dilemma. He must possess the knowledge secreted within it, and he must report some of that back to Lord Jim. Thompson was a powerful ally, and in the quicksilver political climate of Bangkok, it was good to possess friends in positions of strength. Ramonne could not afford to offend or disenchant him in any way. Yet he could not be allowed to know the secret that the *Japonais* was after. This must continue to rest in the possession of Ramonne alone. He would seek out the faux *Chinoise*, pay her for her services, secure her in safe lodging and give her the journal to translate.

———

The smoke was as thick as fog. It could literally be cut with a knife. With only candle or oil light for illumination, visibility was limited to a few feet around each lattice-work cubicle. Ramonne, however, had the eyes of a cat, and saw through the haze and darkness. Inert and slow-moving shapes occupied most of the stalls. Opium-smokers and their attendants. Some of the female servants were in various degrees of undress, and they performed other more erotic tasks than keeping the pipe lit and the bowl full.

He soon found the girl he sought, Miaow—like the cry of a cat. She was alone, expecting him. He'd sent a messenger with a note earlier. At this hour, when the bars and teashops were closed, she would normally be occupied, and Ramonne didn't want to chance that.

She nodded when she saw him, and started to prepare the pipe. He waved his hand and she stopped. She looked at him curiously, not knowing what to expect. His gaze bore deep into her and she knew, within seconds, what it was he required. There was no question of her compliance.

"Gather your things," he said to her in Japanese. She took a small bag off a shelf and a light sweater from it. Ramonne handed a wad of 1,000-baht notes to the *mamasan* as he and the girl exited into the night.

———

Soon the girl was safely ensconced in a small hotel in Yaowarat. Immediately she began to transcribe the journal. She would work at it throughout the night, stopping only for meals he had arranged to be delivered. This was the spell he had cast upon her, and it could not be broken. She was no longer in control of her own mind.

Ramonne returned to his lair of more than twenty years beneath the Bangkok Nursing Home on Convent Road. The handsome two-story colonial building had been under construction in the mid-1920s when he bribed the contractor to build an addition to the massive basement. When the task was completed, Ramonne celebrated moving into his new home by feasting on the blood of the contractor.

He liked the hustle bustle of the hospital; the life-or-death tension in the air invigorated him. He settled in his coffin and sighed. Soon he would have the answer to questions that had been burning inside him ever since he acquired the object that Nakimira-*san* had sought.

Miaow was thorough. She had stayed at her task throughout the day and into the evening. When Ramonne went to visit her, she had nearly completed the translation. As she continued, Ramonne sat and read her notes. It was as he thought. The information must never get into Lord Jim's hands—or, for that matter, anyone else's.

While he read, the girl finished her task. She sat motionless and awaited further instruction. Ramonne read the final pages, put them aside and thought. Then he dictated and the girl wrote a half-dozen more pages at his direction. When she finished, it was nearly midnight. Being a Monday, the Bamboo Bar was closed and Ramonne had the rest of the night. He took the girl to the bed and undressed her. He had partaken of her charms before and had found her a willing and capable companion. They spent the next few hours enraptured.

A few hours before the dawn, he woke the girl and told her to get dressed. He left the room and she followed obediently. He led her down the hall to a chained door. He opened the lock without problem and they climbed a decrepit staircase to the roof. The building was quite old and the roof was merely a forgotten formality. Buckets of cold black tar and petrified, rotted mops attested to the last time visitors had been up here. He led her by the hand to a bricked air duct.

Here, without ceremony or resistance, he took her life. He drained the blood from her veins, and when she was gone, he laid her gently down on the floor. He imagined that she'd be reduced to bleached bones before she'd ever be discovered. As an extra precaution, he fused the lock on the chain so that no key could open it.

He traversed the rooftops back to the hospital as the night sky turned azure and the purple veins of the sunrise started their progression on the eastern horizon.

———

The Bamboo Bar didn't open until ten, so Ramonne made arrangements to meet Jim Thompson earlier in the evening at the beer garden of the Cathay. Ramonne was already seated when Thompson arrived carrying several bolts of fabric.

"What do you think?"

Ramonne laughed. "You look like a Turkish rug merchant. All you need is a fez."

"It's silk." He fingered the material.

"I know it is. The street stalls are filled with this material."

"Not like this…feel it."

Ramonne took the cloth between his fingers. He had to admit it was smoother and finer than the silks he'd seen in Bangkok's numerous markets. It was a very superior weave. Several of the threads glistened as they caught the light.

Thompson turned over a corner from each of the other two bolts and insisted that Ramonne inspect them, as well. They were of the same, if not slightly better, quality as the first.

"The markets of Bangkok may be full of silk, my friend, but not of this quality. Nor the markets of Europe. Not the Harrod's emporium. Nor the luxurious *magasins* of the Champs Élysées.

Nor the big department stores of Manhattan. Their shelves are lacking." He refolded the bolts and placed them on the chair next to him.

"That, my fiend, is where these fine fabrics are destined. And I will take them there. This…" He patted the material. "This is my destiny. This is my future."

By the gleam in his eye, Ramonne knew that his friend was most serious. He lifted his wine glass in salute. *"Bon chance,* my friend."

"Thank you." Thompson snapped his fingers and a boy appeared. He ordered a gin fizz.

"Now, what have you got for me?"

Ramonne produced a packet of papers. He handed them to Lord Jim, who opened them with nervous hands.

"You found your translator?"

"Of course."

Thompson took out the handwritten pages and then looked in the envelope. "Where is the journal?"

Ramonne appeared perplexed. "It's not with the translation?"

"No…it's not."

"I'm sorry. The job was done in haste, and I'm afraid the journal was left behind. Don't worry, I'll retrieve it."

Jim Thompson had a look of concern. "You must. It's invaluable."

Ramonne shrugged. "Don't worry."

Thompson's momentary concern was replaced by the wonder of the document before him. He began to read. His drink arrived and he dashed off an order for a curry and rice without asking to see a menu.

Ramonne concentrated on his wine. Lord Jim was so consumed in his perusal that he failed to offer his usual sarcastic comment on Ramonne's lack of appetite.

Silent minutes passed. Ramonne studied his friend. He actually could hear the words as he read—broadcast to him through the veil of Lord Jim's thoughts. If he chose to, Ramonne could read the minds of all mortals. This had proved overwhelming when he was first transformed, but he soon managed to control it and was now able to turn it on and off at will. So he wasn't surprised when Thompson stopped reading and put the pages down.

"It's not…" He flipped through the remaining pages. "It's not what I thought."

Ramonne professed innocence. "Oh?"

"It's a journal, as I thought. But there's no mention of the…" He chose his word carefully. "The artifact he was seeking."

Ramonne smiled. The original word Lord Jim wanted to use was 'weapon.' Then he almost said 'device.' He finally settled on 'artifact.'

"There are some phrases in English," Thompson pointed out.

"Yes?"

"They seem to be his own attempt at learning the language. I'm surprised. I thought he was quite adept in English."

"Speaking, yes. Reading and writing are entirely different matters."

"I suppose you're right." Seemingly crestfallen, Thompson returned the leaves to their envelope. "Disappointing to say the least."

"I'm sorry."

Thompson's food arrived. The pungent aroma wafted across the table, and Ramonne had to discreetly cover his nostrils. The smell of cooked meat was still most offensive to him.

"As usual you are not eating, my friend."

Actually, I ate earlier. And I will have something at the club. Are you coming? It's Monsieur Witherspoon's last night."

Lord Jim seemed distracted. Ramonne knew that he was greatly distressed by the phoney translation he had provided. Although it was ninety percent truthful, the ten percent either omitted or changed had eliminated the very reason for

Nakimira's, and now Lord Jim's, desperate pursuit. Ramonne had decided that this information, coupled with the actual item of their attention, was too dangerous for mortal men.

He would be its guardian and protector. This meant that he had to deceive his friend, but as regrettable as that was, it was ultimately for the good.

Having lived for so long and seen mankind's folly explode in two unimaginable world wars, Ramonne—the vampire—felt that he had the authority to make this decision.

10

Bangkok, 1949

The Steinway pounded under the tutelage of Jay McShann. Ben Webster on saxophone filled in the gaps left for him by McShann, and Gus Johnson on drums drove the beat forward. Jimmy Witherspoon was perspiring heavily and continuously mopping his brow with a silk handkerchief while shouting the blues as only he could do.

The capacity plus crowd filled the room and overflowed onto the veranda. Ramonne, resplendent in his finest tailored tuxedo, took it all in from the bar.

> *"Big-legged woman,*
> *keep your dresses down."*

Spoon crooned, willfully making his lyrics more suggestive and risqué on this, his last night at the Bamboo Bar. The room was packed with the crème de la crème of Bangkok society.

The rich young women and their paramours sat stiffly at their tables with buckets full of Perrier and Mumm champagne. Generals and *gendarmes* in their military finest downed

100-year-old Scotch malts. And the expat community raucously made the night into an event. More than once Spoon admonished a member of the audience to "Shut the fuck up." He'd say it, get the quiet he demanded, and then graciously thank the offender and offer his compliments to his wife: "Is this your daughter?" Which elicited raucous laughter and applause.

It was a grand night. It seemingly lacked only one person to make it complete for Ramonne. And that oversight was corrected just as the last set began, when Lord Jim walked into the room—a gorgeous, sultry brunette on his arm.

Ramonne's radar was off; too many people, too much confusion. *Leave them to their own petty thoughts.* He preferred to listen to the band, and so he was caught by surprise when Lord Jim introduced his companion as Jane Farmer. Ramonne took her hand and kissed it while his mind processed the fact that this was the notorious Rubber Johnny Jane.

"*Bon soir*, Mademoiselle Farmer."

"*Enchante*, Monsieur Delacroix."

The accent was perfect. The woman was well-bred.

"Please." Ramonne led them to the two chairs he had been reserving throughout the night.

Jane Farmer was dressed in a beaded black Chanel that exposed her creamy white shoulders. Her hair was cropped just at the nape of her neck, and it bobbed as she walked.

All the right areas exposed. Ramonne watched as she settled in her chair, her gorgeous legs crossing. Just a wisp of perfume in the air. *Quite the package.* Lord Jim did not do her justice in his rant the other day.

The sound level in the bar was such that Ramonne had to bend down to Lord Jim for him to hear. "You didn't tell me that you were bringing such a special guest."

He turned to the lady. "I trust that you and Monsieur Thompson are not 'working' tonight?"

"Why, Monsieur Delacroix, whatever do you mean?"

Ramonne smiled. The woman, as were *all* women, was charmed by him. She blushed ever so slightly.

"Lord Jim mentioned that you were comrades in arms in the...resistance."

She leaned back and raised her eyebrows. "Yes, we were. During the war. But that was then. This is now."

"Of course. Foolish of me to mention it. Please forgive me."

With this he took Jane's hand and again kissed her long fingers. Thompson, having not heard a word of the exchange, was fascinated, as he always was, by his friend's way with women.

Ramonne turned back to Thompson. "Does she know about the journal?"

"No. She does not. Let's keep it that way, okay?"

"Agreed." Ramonne had no intention of providing Rubber Johnny Jane with any information. However, he was certain that she could provide him with much that he would find interesting. He'd have to arrange to be with her.

But for the moment, she would have to wait. Ramonne was preoccupied.

"I must see to my other guests." With one more smile to the lady and a nod to his friend, Ramonne turned back to the crowded room.

————

Bangkok, Present Day

Martin's day began at noon. Normally he would have been up before seven, taken his bicycle and ridden through Lumpini Park as the city's motorists locked horns in the daily morning commute. But today he was feeling a bit 'fragile' as his British friends always said. He'd downed two aspirins after breakfast and sought the solace of his studio.

He'd been granted the isolation he sought, as Areeya had

kept behind closed doors for most of the morning. The 'cold shoulder,' he supposed. Well deserved, he had to admit.

What the hell was I thinking? He loved that woman with all his heart. There was nothing he wouldn't do for her. No sacrifice he wouldn't make.

And yet he had bolted from her company and sought—sought what?

Solitude? If so, what was he doing on Sukhumvit—the most crowded pedestrian passage in this congested city. And what had happened after he'd left the Gardens of Babylon? He'd frozen in the middle of the Nana intersection, one of the most dangerous crossways in the city—perhaps the world. A sober, wide-awake pedestrian has little more than a fifty percent chance of making it across safely, let alone a sleep-walking zombie such as he had been. Taxis fly through the lights, making a left turn from Soi Nana to Sukhumvit with little regard for the green pedestrian light, never mind the living beings trying to get out of their way.

He remembered seeing only one thing—red. A red haze. And then only one thought...

Of him. Ramonne.

He'd left him long ago. He'd deliberately not traversed the scant fifteen kilometers from the orphanage in Siem Reap to the villa in Roluos. He'd not seen him, apart from two bizarre hallucinations in which he imagined he'd seen him in the light of day.

That had been over four years ago. He'd kept a silent promise to himself. He vowed that he owed it to his wife, his family, to remove that cursed tumor from his life forever. He'd kept his vow and had been rewarded for it. His boy Hon—for he was *his* boy, for certain—was healthy and happy. A joy. And now his wife was about to give birth to a daughter. A true, true blessing.

What was I thinking?

So what if she'd gone over the top in her decorating of the

Larue apartment. It made her happy, and that's what he wanted for her—happiness.

The mood swings, the irritability, he knew were hormonal and not personal. They would eventually subside. All he had to do was bear them out. Patience.

Never a virtue he possessed in any great measure, but one he recognized as valuable nonetheless.

He resolved to make it up to her. His loathsome behavior was inexcusable. Should she allow him back in to her good graces—well, he would be eternally grateful.

He rose from his desk and was about to go to her when the door opened. And she came to him.

Roluos, Present Day

They lay silent in each other's arms, amid the wreckage of their lovemaking. The sheets, new less than an hour before, were now torn, tattered and scattered, moist with their combined essences.

Kanchana stroked his thick mane of now mostly silver hair. He, in turn, reveled in the feel of her silken black tresses. They had spoken not a word for more than an hour. Awake and silent they lay there and stared into each other's eyes, seeing each other in the flesh for the first time in a very long time.

Finally Ramonne spoke. "It's been so long."

She smiled. She didn't know if he referred to her or to the act in general. It didn't matter. *Love is two people sharing the same dream.* She'd heard that in a song recently and liked it. Now she felt it.

She'd always loved this savage, magnificent man.

Loved and feared. Parallel emotions. His letter with a phone number in Cambodia had been like a bolt of lightning out of a clear blue sky. She had tried to forget him. Tried to put him out of her mind.

But it was impossible.

The man, some called him a beast, had been instrumental in ridding her of an incurable malady. She had fallen victim to a disease that had infected all the female members of her family for four generations, resulting in their cruel deaths. The cost had been high. She had been transformed by his repeatedly sinking his teeth into her and taking small amounts of her blood. She was becoming the same kind of beast as he. She reveled in blood as he taught her his killing ways. But her own reluctance and remorse had led him to seek a reversal of her fate, and miraculously his will had prevailed.

She owed her very existence to him.

Now, she wasn't surprised at all when, without a further word, he rolled her onto her stomach and entered her again. This was what she expected of her lover—the unexpected.

It was why she loved him.

———

Bangkok, Present Day

"I'm sorry. I've been a shit."

It was hardly what Martin expected to hear. But then the afternoon had been a complete surprise. Areeya had silently entered his office and, taking him by the hand, had led him to their bedroom. She had made love to him for the first time in three or four weeks, her swollen belly posing just the slightest bit of resistance to his amorous advances. The Kurt Elling CD *Night Moves* had been carefully selected as a present for her, and it had been playing softly in the background to their love-making—providing the perfect soundtrack to their climax.

She hadn't spoken until they were through. Her apology was unexpected, and, he felt, undeserved.

"No. Don't say that."

"It's true. I'm sorry."

"Please. I should understand. I know…well, I don't actually *know*, but I understand what you're going through. You're changing every day. Your body is doing amazing things. You—"

She put a finger to his lips. "Shut up. You're really not a romantic." She laughed.

Quit while you're ahead. He nestled his head into her outstretched arm.

Bangkok, 1949

Tables cleared, chairs straightened, glasses washed and hung up to dry. Closing and putting a nightclub to sleep is a ritual performed without ceremony every night, the world over. It is theater in its own right. The players—waiters, waitresses, busboys, bartenders—all participate with one goal: to restore order and prepare for the next night. Their props are the kitchenware, glasses, ashtrays, candles, tables and chairs. Their stage is the entire club. And every tomorrow is opening night.

Ramonne closed the safe, his own final act of the evening. Witherspoon and company had performed admirably and then gone off to the American ambassador's residence for what would no doubt be another grand event that would be spoken of in social circles for some time to come. The bartender locked the cash register, the busboy swept his way out the back door, and soon Ramonne found himself alone.

He waited.

It wasn't long.

Jane Farmer walked silently along the hallway and into the dimly lit, empty Bamboo Bar. She stared at him as if in a dream. Her eyes were glazed. Her hair, previously perfectly set and combed, had been blown in an evening breeze and she hadn't made the effort to rearrange it. She held her Cartier bag loosely at her side and clutched her white silk scarf to her throat.

She stood motionless. He knew that he could dispense with formalities. She'd fallen victim to a spell he cast on her earlier in the evening and, as bidden, returned at this hour of her own volition.

"Come with me." He offered his hand. She took it and he led her down the paved walkway to the pier. Here he passed a hand over her face. It was the lifting of a veil, and the real Jane Farmer returned with a jolt.

"What the fuck?"

"Charming."

She breathed deeply and then quickly reached into her purse, withdrawing a pistol. She aimed it straight at his heart. He raised his hands. "Please. I mean you no harm."

She looked quickly about while keeping the pistol leveled at his chest.

"I left here hours ago. How is it I'm back here now? And how did I get here?"

"I sent for you."

"What do you mean, you *sent* for me? I'm here alone. I don't remember anything except being dropped at my flat."

"You had a headache."

"Yes."

"Lord Jim graciously took you home."

"Yes."

"And there was a car waiting in front of your door. Rather than going to bed, you put on your coat and entered the automobile. It brought you here."

Ramonne spoke with his hands still raised, while Jane kept the pistol aimed at his heart.

"You drugged me."

"Not my style. No, I merely planted a suggestion in your subconscious. You acted upon it."

Her eyes never wavered from his. The pistol never moved.

"What do you want?"

"Tell me about the Oracle."

Her eyes widened at the mention of the word. "The Oracle…? Who told you of this?"

Then her eyes narrowed like a snake. She hissed and spat out the name: "*Thompson.*"

"No. I've known of its existence for quite a while."

Now she grew coy. She shrugged her shoulders. "If you know about it, why bother with me?"

"Knowing a thing exists is one thing. True knowledge is another."

The gun was still pointed at his chest. He slowly lowered his arms and put a hand over the barrel. "Please. You don't need this."

She lowered the pistol. It stayed in her hand, but she no longer pointed it at him.

"What do you want to know?" she asked.

"Let's start with your interest in it." He smiled. "I know you are an OSS agent, as is Monsieur Thompson. Therefore, I assume your country has dispatched you and your comrades in intelligence gathering to find this Oracle."

Warily she nodded, slightly. "We were informed that a Japanese attaché was coming to Thailand. He was known to have ties to the Kempeitai and was to be closely monitored. This task fell to your friend *Jim.*" Again she couldn't help but spit his name.

Ramonne smiled. "Your friend, as well, I understand."

She lifted her eyebrows. "There was a time. A very *brief* time." Again she shrugged.

"This Japanese, he knew of the Oracle?" Ramonne felt foolish asking the question, but he needed to maintain his façade of ignorance.

"We presumed he did. He'd been an agent during the occupation. He was rumored to have been Black Dragon, too."

"Black Dragon?"

"A fanatical group devoted to their beloved emperor and a quest for world domination. If Nakimira was truly a member of this shadow group, then he would have been well aware of the Oracle. 'Unit 831' was a code name for their archives and collection of wonders plundered from Asia. The Oracle was the prize in their treasure trove. It was the end game.

"When the Japs surrendered and retreated with their tails between their legs, they hid their treasures. They secreted gold in caves in the Philippines, priceless artworks were sunk in the holds of ships in Tokyo harbor. The bullion was well known to the Allies. Its discovery was inevitable. But other treasures, other secrets, have remained mysteries."

She was speaking freely. She didn't know that this was not of her own volition. She had been silently commanded to do so by Ramonne. Her tale poured forth unabated, uncensored.

She continued: "The precious metals, the lost masterpieces—they were nothing compared to the real reason for the Japs' scramble to hide their spoils of war. The real booty, so to speak, lay in their metaphysical quests."

She had drawn closer as she talked. He savored her perfume. He was becoming aroused by this American saboteur. This wasn't necessarily a good thing—for her. He backed away and concentrated on listening.

"Their greatest treasures were their most secret. These were the results of their unmitigated quest for a power source of indescribable magnitude."

The pistol, he noticed, was now ignored. It had *slid* behind the fold of her dress.

"Like the Nazis," she continued, "the Japs were tireless in their hunt for anything that would give them supernatural abilities. You have heard rumors of the Nazis' search for the Ark of the Covenant?"

Ramonne had. He knew that had the sacred object—if it existed—fallen into the hands of the Nazis, it could have changed the tide of the war. He nodded. "Yes."

"That is nothing compared to the power of the Oracle. If used according to ancient scriptural references, it would have meant invulnerability for the Japanese. The consequences? Well, no doubt you can imagine."

He could.

"This is why it is so important to find it now. It was hidden —we believe—in the Oriental Hotel by the Japs as they fled Bangkok like rats from a sinking ship. And Nakimira. He came back for it."

Ramonne leaned back. *Knowledge is power.* This woman had knowledge, and since he was in possession of the Oracle, she had power over him.

She was very dangerous to him. A threat of incalculable measure.

He knew what he should do.

He looked out at the Chao Phraya. The mighty river flowed silently by. Sand barges glided by on their way to and from Ayutthaya. A single solitary figure walked along the bank on the Thonburi side.

The dead of night. No witnesses.

A simple twist of the neck, a flick of the wrist—over the rail and into the river.

Problem solved. *Finis.*

But Ramonne, against his much better judgment, decided to stay his hand. This strong-willed woman intrigued him. He knew he could wipe her mind clear of this night's conversation. She would have no memory of him other than the charming impresario of the club she'd visited earlier.

He decided. He placed a hand on her forehead. It was as if electricity had entered her brain. She gasped and then her features went blank.

Ramonne nodded. A figure emerged from the shadows and led Lady Jane Farmer away.

Ramonne stared into the dark waters.

11

Bangkok, 1949

Jim Thompson studied the intricate patterns of the brightly colored bolts of fabric that sat on the seat next to him. He was riding in the rear of one of the three black Citroën Legeres that the Oriental used as limousines for its guests. He had been on a successful trip to Korat, the gateway to Isaan, the northeast. He was elated to find so many talented weavers in the Pak Tonchai area, just south of the city. Except for a dozen or so weavers in the old Ban Krua district of Bangkok that Thompson was familiar with, the craft had virtually disappeared from the city.

Every day that he devoted to the pursuit of this delightful fabric, he became more and more convinced that his future lay in extolling its virtues to the capitals of Europe and America, eventually laying the path for its exportation on a select and rarefied level. To this end, Thompson was already planning trips to London and New York.

Outside the Citroën's windows, a panorama of tropical foliage gave way to acres and acres of rice paddies. Water buffaloes rolled about in the ditches and ponds, while snowy white egrets rode atop their flanks and plucked at the insects that swarmed about them. For the unfortunate buffaloes not at leisure, there were plows to pull and carts to haul. Thompson's car was the only motorized vehicle, other than some beat-up motorbikes that he had seen on the dusty road two hours ago.

This was not the case, however, for Jadesada, the driver, had been concentrating on the rearview mirror for the majority of the return trip. Unknown to Thompson, a vehicle had been following them—keeping a discreet distance, but following nonetheless. Jadesada had thought the dark-green car had been behind them on the journey from Krung Thep, but had paid it no mind as the traffic had been fairly heavy on the journey north—a dozen or so vehicles, he estimated, as well as some trucks and over-laden public buses. But the fairly new Humber Snipe had caught his attention on this trip.

They had stopped for lunch in Saraburi. He and Khun Jim had spent at least an hour leisurely feasting on *somtam*, a spicy papaya salad, and grilled duck. Thompson's Thai was improving and he had told tale after tale that made Jadesada chuckle. He enjoyed the company of this *farang*. And Khun Jim obviously enjoyed life in the kingdom. He seemed as at ease in the Isaan countryside as he was in the luxurious comfort of the Oriental. So Jadesada was always the first to volunteer when Thompson needed a driver on one of his silk-buying forays.

His attention was drawn to the mirror again. He made a decision. Without signaling his intent, as the newly drafted road regulations now stipulated, he made a left turn onto what was little more than a cow path.

Having made this maneuver with very little deceleration, Thompson was consequently thrown about the back like on a fairground ride.

"Jadesada. What are you doing?"

"Sorry, Khun Jim. But I need to know something."

He continued down the rutted road; all the while his eyes were on the rear mirror. As he suspected, the Humber also turned onto the track. Two wheels lifted off the road as it teetered on the brink. In a great cloud of dust, it accelerated.

"Khun Jim. Please look behind. Do you know that car?"

"What are you talking about?"

"Please. Just look behind."

Thompson turned in his seat and looked out the Citroën's rear window. He saw the green car driving very close to their rear.

"No. I have no idea who that is. Why?"

"They have been following us. At least from Khon Kaen. Perhaps all the way from Krung Thep."

"What? Why?"

"I have no idea. But maybe if we stop, we will find out."

Thompson thought about this. He was in a vulnerable position. Unarmed. Exposed.

There would be nothing to be gained in a confrontation here in complete isolation.

"No. Turn around. Head back to the main road."

"Yes, Khun Jim."

Jadesada applied the brake and, when he felt it was safe, he threw the wheel into a 180-degree turn. Lord Jim bounced on the seat again.

They passed the Humber and Thompson tried to ascertain who was in it. There was one passenger—a man. He and the driver were both Asian, but that was all he could discern as they sped past. He turned in his seat and watched as the Humber did a U-turn and proceeded after them.

"Faster," Thompson instructed.

He was preaching to the choir, as Jadesada's foot was already floored. The Citroën was nowhere near as muscular as the Humber. The Snipe had nearly twice the horsepower, and was quickly catching up to them. They were a few hundred meters from the main road when the Humber pulled alongside.

"Jadesada, get down."

Thompson barely got the words out when the passenger fired a shot.

"Christ. They're shooting at us."

Three more explosions split the air. Thompson felt a slug whistle through the window and hit the car's paneling.

"Hang on, Khun Jim."

Jadesada was half-crouched when he cranked hard on the wheel. He managed to turn the Citroën onto the highway without flipping the vehicle. As he floored the accelerator, Thompson snuck a peek through the rear window. The dark-green car was stopped on the farm road.

Thompson checked himself for injuries. He seemed intact.

"Jadesada, are you all right?"

"Yes, Khun Jim."

They made it back to Bangkok without further incident.

Two bullets managed to hit the car. One in the paneling of the rear door, driver's side (it had indeed come through Thompson's open window) and one was in the trunk. It had punctured the spare tire.

Thompson thought about reporting the incident to the police, but decided against it. He wanted some more information before he lit that fire. Yoshiro Nakimira's death had not yet been declared a murder by the authorities. The official statement pending the outcome and eventual release of the autopsy was that the victim's "heart had stopped." A convenient way of dealing with the suspicious death of anyone in the kingdom.

He instructed Jadesada to take the car to a shop, have the bullets extracted and the damage repaired. Jadesada assured him that all would be done as he requested and that the matter would remain their secret.

A driver who can keep a secret is a worthy ally, Thompson thought.

———

Jadesada unwrapped his handkerchief and displayed the flattened slugs. Thompson picked one up. They had a familiar look to them. "Thirty-two caliber." He frowned.

He took a matchbox from his desk drawer, emptied the contents and placed the slugs within it. Then he unlocked another drawer and removed a .38-caliber revolver. It was well maintained, oiled and wrapped in a chamois. He used the chamois to wipe it clean, and flicked open the chamber. It was loaded. He closed the chamber and tucked the pistol into a small leather holster. The holster had a metal clip, and he attached this to his belt, on his left hip.

Jadesada's eyes widened at this but he remained mute.

"Bring the car around, Jadesada."

———

Thompson dropped the two slugs onto the desk. Jane Farmer looked up over her reading glasses.

"What's this?"

Thompson merely arched his eyebrows, his arms folded across his chest. The office was, as the sign outside indicated, a travel agency. The necessary tools of the trade were in evidence. Maps dominated the walls, and a huge globe stood behind the desk occupied by Jane. The other desks were decorated with personal touches—photos, papers, pens, a typewriter. But only Jane's was occupied at the moment. The office was a façade. *A damn good one* Thompson thought to himself.

Rubber Johnny Jane was making lists in a ledger when Thompson appeared unannounced. She put down her pen and picked up one of the slugs.

"Hollow point...Nasty."

"Indeed." Thompson uncrossed his arms and leaned on the desk.

"They were aimed at me."

Now it was Lady Jane's turn. She leaned back in her chair, her arms folded across her breasts. "Really?"

"Really."

"And, pray tell, who was doing the shooting?"

"I have no idea. That's why I'm here."

"You think I had something to do with it?"

"No, but I'm hoping you have an idea who it was."

She closed the ledger and moved it to the side of her desk.

"Why James, you flatter me. I'm just a humble travel agent."

She fluttered her eyelashes seductively. Thompson ignored her attempt at charm. "Nakimira's death…has it been formally filed?"

"Today, yes. The Japanese government had no comment."

"Until someone took a shot at me." He nodded toward the slugs. "You know the caliber of those bullets?"

She rolled one in her hand. "They do look familiar."

"Thirty-two. Hollow points." Thompson winced at the thought of the hollowed-out bullet designed to expand when entering the target, and shred tissue and bone. "Practically unique to the Walther PPK, favored by Nazi officers and the SS."

She put the slug back down. "What you're saying is very dangerous."

"Don't you think I know that?"

She went to the front of the office and locked the door. Outside, Jadesada heard the turning of the key and looked through the car window. Jane closed the thick Venetian blinds against the harsh morning sun.

"The Germans surrendered. The Japanese surrendered. Any sign of collaboration would be seen as a breach of treaty. Why would the Germans take such a chance?"

"You tell me."

Jane paced the room. She gnawed at her knuckles. She went to the blinds. She stood still a few moments. Finally she turned back to Thompson. "They don't have it."

"Who doesn't have *what*?"

She looked him squarely in the eyes. "I assumed that in your bungling of the Nakimira case, that the Japanese or their collaborators had gotten the Oracle."

"The Oracle? What the hell is that?"

She looked at him like he was from Mars. "You really don't know?"

"No. I *don't* know."

She shook her head. 'You must have very low clearance."

"Just tell me."

"It has many names. Akashwani is one. Asiriri is another. We simply refer to it as the Oracle. It's a conduit of power. The Nazis pursued it through North Africa and Egypt and lost it. It finally fell into the hands of the Japanese. They hid it when they saw the end coming. The very fact that they took pot shots at you proves that they don't have it."

"Then who does?"

"Who knows?"

He picked up the slugs again, rolling them in his palm.

"Jane, I had enough of these fired at me in Italy and France to get to know them. The load, the caliber. *Nazis*. Is that possible? Now? Here…in Bangkok?"

Jane lit a cigarette. She hissed out the smoke. "No. I think not."

"Then who?"

"Are you sure you want to know?"

"They shot at me. Of course I want to know."

"In for a pound…"

"Damn it."

She took a long drag on her cigarette. "Black Dragons. You have heard of them, haven't you?"

"No."

"Jesus, Jim. You told me Nakimira was Kempeitai. Well, we suspect he was more than that. Black Dragons are Japanese paramilitary. They're keeping the movement alive. They're fanatical and dangerous. German agents could never operate here. Too conspicuous. Too obvious. But the Black Dragons perform their operations behind the yellow mask. As Asians, they blend in. Pure and simple. They're in China, Korea, Indonesia and here in Siam. They're picking up the pieces left by an undignified surrender."

"Why are they targeting me?"

"Because they believe you have the Oracle."

"That's insane. I have no idea where it is. I don't even know *what* it is."

"I just told you."

"Yes. You did. I wish you hadn't. But I still don't know what it is or what it does."

She stubbed out her cigarette. "Jim. Face it. You're involved. You can't be a part-time OSS agent. You're either in or out."

"Okay. I'm out."

"Too late."

"Jesus Christ. I said I'd baby-sit Nakimira because I thought it was the right thing to do. I didn't know I was putting my life back on the line. I left that side of this in 1946."

"No…you didn't. You were discharged from the Army in '46. You never left the OSS. You merely went inactive."

"Jesus, Jane…I want to go into business. I want to have a life. This…*espionage* isn't part of it."

"Jim, much as I hate to admit it, you're good at this. You're an asset. We…this is hard to say…We need you."

He put the slugs in her hand. He closed her fingers around them and held her fist tightly closed.

"I'm through, Jane. I want out. Tell them."

He released her hand. "I quit."

He left. A little bell made a friendly chiming sound as he opened and closed the door.

12

Bangkok, Present Day

Love in the afternoon. Martin always thought that it was the sweetest form of *amore*. Afternoon delight.

He lay with Areeya curled in his arms. It had been almost five months. They hadn't done it since she'd found out she was pregnant. Superstitious, no doubt. Cautious.

And then the tension set in.

But when she opened his door wearing nothing but a towel —triggering an instantly rejected memory of his dalliance with Noi—he had welcomed her with a passion unknown to both of them in a long time.

It felt good. It felt right. It felt…perfect.

"Ma ma."

And of course the bliss was soon shattered by little Hon's appearance.

"Honey…What is it sweetie?"

"Small Talk have baby."

"That's impossible, honey. Small Talk is a boy."

"Small Talk have baby," Hon insisted.

Areeya sat up. Martin remained prone.

"Aiiiieeee!" She screamed. Martin shot upright. Hon was holding the scruffy cat in front of him. He was the only one who could really touch the feral feline. In Hon's outstretched arms, the contented Small Talk had a freshly killed mouse in its mouth.

By now Areeya had her head buried in the pillows.

This was the woman he'd seen take an M-16 and put a round through the head of a Khmer Rouge guerrilla who was threatening her family. A woman who had been kidnapped and held for ransom by a vampire. A woman who had seen her corrupt police chief father murdered in front of her eyes. Through all of this, Martin had marveled at her strength.

But now she was terrified by a mouse. A dead mouse at that. And he was also perturbed that somehow a disease-carrying rodent had gotten into the penthouse apartment. He'd have to have a word with the management about that.

"Hon. Honey…that's not a baby."

"Baby. Small Talk have baby," Hon insisted.

"No sweetie. He has a mouse. Put him down."

Reluctantly the boy listened to his father. He always did. He put the cat down and the cat dropped the carcass on the floor, turned and hissed at Martin, picked up the dead mouse and slinked away.

Martin poked his wife.

"Its okay, honey. He's gone."

She peeked out from under the pillows.

"Gone? Gone where?"

"He has a cat door. He'll go wherever it is he goes to."

"Don't. I don't want to know." She reached down for her boy, and Hon climbed into bed with them.

"Night time already?"

"No, honey. Not night time. Mommy and daddy were just taking a little nap."

The boy got between them. Martin activated a remote control and the louvers on the windows parted just a little, letting a small amount of light into the room. The remote-controlled blinds had been one of Areeya's remodeling touches that he actually liked.

He drew them both closer and kissed each of them on the top of their heads.

Life was good in Larue mansion.

It was good to be king.

Roluos, Present Day

Blood-red wine. Blood-red meat.

A blood-red sun setting outside over the vineyards.

Kanchana and Ramonne ate in silence. There were questions unanswered and un-asked spinning around in both their heads.

It was all too new. Too strange.

Too weird.

Better not to ask. Better to take things slowly. Better not to talk. Better just to eat and drink in silence.

Let time pass.

Bangkok, 1949

"In the end we all must walk alone."

For some reason Jim Thompson thought of the line from the Buddha as he walked along the pier in the dead of night.

It had been a week since his tête-à-tête with Lady Jane. He'd heard nothing. No news is good news, he reasoned. A late-night poker game with a few consular friends had left him feeling light-headed, and he'd chosen to walk the half-hour trek back to the Oriental. Clear his head from a bit too much gin.

The familiar smells of cooking wafted from the carts that

were set up to offer nourishment at this ungodly hour to the captains and deckhands who would soon ready their boats for a day spent ferrying passengers along the river. This was a moment of relaxation for them, and they smoked and ate noodle soup as it was scooped up and slopped into their bowls.

Fog was forming in the damp dark, and he turned up his collar as he left the riverfront and negotiated the back alleys that he always used as a shortcut to the grand hotel he called home. As he put his hands into his pockets, he felt the comfortable bulge of the .38-caliber revolver on his belt. He had kept his jacket on and his shirt untucked to disguise it, and he felt reassured by its presence. He reached the end of a little alley and was but a hundred meters from the hotel's rear entrance when the night's fading stars came cascading down.

The searing pain on the back of his skull was followed rapidly by a blow to his rib cage. He cried out as he lost his footing. He fell backward, careening into a stack of crates that fell with him to the greasy pavement. He struggled to maintain his consciousness, his right hand feebly trying to extricate his pistol. But he was hit again. This time across the forehead. He had a foggy vision of two figures—his assailants—before he tumbled into blackness.

As soon as Thompson was unconscious, a dark-green Humber Snipe pulled into the alley. The two assailants lifted the limp figure by the shoulders and ankles and hoisted him into the back seat. Thompson's head bounced off the door frame as he was tossed like a sack of laundry.

"Hai. Layo layo." The driver ordered the two thugs to hurry when a silent fury erupted. The man closest to the driver suddenly began gurgling and moving spasmodically. A fine red line appeared along his throat and crimson ran down his neck in rivulets. He fell backward and was quickly joined in the next life by his comrade. The other man's throat was completely severed and his headless corpse was upended and thrown into the passenger seat.

The driver, frozen in a white sheen of unimaginable terror, attempted to accelerate. But the car wouldn't move. His foot pressed on the accelerator, the engine raced, but the car went nowhere.

Thompson was pulled out of the vehicle and laid gently on the pavement. His place in the back seat was taken by the lifeless body of assailant number one. The door was slammed and then, to the driver's utter horror, the severed head of the second assailant was tossed through his window, landing on the passenger seat with a sickening squelch.

Wanting to see nothing, wanting to know nothing, wanting only to get the hell out of there, the driver, against his own will, turned to look at the assailant.

Ramonne held a long serrated blade, dripping with blood. His black hair blew in the breeze, his yellow eyes glowing. As the driver tried desperately to work the car through the gears, his foot pumping the accelerator, Ramonne stared at him and then licked the glistening blood from the blade. Just as the driver feared his heart would stop from fright, the car lurched forward and he sped away with his nefarious cargo.

———

Ramonne carried his unconscious friend easily. Lord Jim weighed close to 200 pounds, but was only a slight burden for the vampire. With his limp friend across his shoulders, Ramonne quickly crossed the hotel grounds and up the stairs to Thompson's chambers.

He laid him on his bed and examined his injuries. The ribs seemed to be not much more than bruised. The concern, he knew, would be with the blows to the head. He prepared a cold towel and held it on Thompson's temple to staunch the swelling. He could feel the American's blood pulsing through his temples. A good sign, he reasoned.

Ramonne stayed by his friend's side for over an hour, before he finally regained his senses. Thompson slowly opened his eyes.

"Ramonne...?"

"Good. Now, who is the president of the United States?"

"Harry Truman...Why?"

"You were unconscious. I read somewhere that you should ask the person who the president of the colonies is. Seems very prejudicial. Why not the president of France? But perhaps you don't know that."

"Vincent Auriol."

"Very good."

"What happened?" Thompson tried to sit up—the blood rushing to his head causing him to nearly black out again. He lay back down.

"Take it very slow, my friend. You have suffered a blow to the head. We must monitor you for a while."

"I was attacked."

"You were. Fortunately I was just returning to the hotel, and managed to scare your attackers off."

Ramonne brandished a stout walking stick he was carrying. He neglected to produce the serrated blade.

"Thank God." Thompson was able to sit up now. As he did, he felt the sharp pain in his ribs. "Arrgh!"

"Yes. You were struck there, as well. Do you want me to summon a doctor?"

"No. I'll see Khun Pisit in the morning." Wyun Pisit was the Oriental's resident physician. He mainly dispensed malaria prophylactics, diuretics for dysentery and injections to combat venereal diseases. Ramonne considered him the resident quack. A charlatan. He was concerned that perhaps Lord Jim needed better attention for his trauma. He decided to take matters into his own hands—literally.

"Lord Jim. Allow me to check for something."

He placed his left hand on the American's forehead, his right flat against the rear of his cranium. He applied gentle pressure.

As he did, he monitored Thompson's vital signs. He felt a strong pulse, steady blood flow. He attuned his senses to the skull itself. He scanned it. He detected no cracks or fissures. Next, hands still in place, he tuned in to Thompson's thoughts themselves. They were lucid. He was questioning the vampire's sanity, but the thoughts were clear and strong.

He released his grip.

"You are all right, my friend. You can rest assured. But do seek out the doctor in the morning and heed his advice. I am but a layman."

Thompson knew there was nothing simple at all about this Frenchman. He felt strangely resuscitated by the 'placing of hands,' and started to stand.

Ramonne stopped him. "*Non*, Lord Jim. Please. Stay seated. Do you want something? Some water perhaps?"

"A whisky would be more like it."

"Water…let me get it for you." Ramonne poured a glass from the pitcher on the dresser and handed it to the American, who scowled but drank the glass down in one long draw.

"More?"

"No. Thank you…So, you got in some good blows, did you?" Thompson smiled now, thinking of his attackers being dispatched by the questionable fighting skills of his unusual friend. He surmised that Ramonne caused enough of a ruckus that they felt exposed and chose to flee the scene.

"Let's say they were *dispatched*. They left a little the worse for wear, but wiser."

One headless, and both very dead. But he chose not to mention this.

"Bloody good show. I owe my life to you."

"I'm not sure they intended to kill you, monsieur. They had a driver, and that would indicate to me that they intended to take you with them—alive, I assume."

"A kidnapping?"

Thompson was on his feet now. Ramonne didn't protest. He knew it was useless.

"I was shot at, my friend. Just one week ago. In Isaan."

"*Mon dieu.* They missed, no doubt. Were you alone?"

"I was in the car. Jadesada spotted someone following us. He pulled onto a farm track and they pursued us. They fired four or five shots before we managed to get back to the main road."

"The car—was it green?"

"Yes."

"The same as in the alley tonight." Ramonne frowned. "Who are these men?"

Thompson hesitated. He wasn't sure how to answer this question. For one thing, he wasn't certain he knew the answer. But there was a bigger problem. If he answered the question—no matter how vaguely—he would involve his friend. Involve him in the intrigue that he thought he had walked away from. Involve him in the danger that Jane had no doubt tried to warn him of.

Involve him in something that could get them both killed.

He had tried to walk away. Tried to put whatever this Oracle involved, behind him. Tried to forget about it.

Forget about being shot at? Not very smart.

He knew better. He'd been *taught* better. His training in Europe and Catalina had been aimed at intercepting adversaries. Foiling their plans. Not turning your back.

He knew now that he had to face these people. And in doing this, Ramonne presented a potentially formidable ally. He had just proven his worth in street combat. Dispatching two assailants.

He decided.

"My friend...what I am going to tell you is a state secret. It involves liaisons between the Allies and Thailand that are outside the armistice. It evokes nationalism and, I think, the supernatural. By disclosing this to you, I am possibly exposing you to great physical danger. As you encountered tonight. And, I might add, you proved yourself sufficiently skilled to handle."

Ramonne nodded, accepting the compliment. *If he only knew how sufficiently skilled I really am.*

"The Jap—Nakimira—he wasn't here to retrieve any family heirloom. He was here to bring back to Japan the Imperial Army's greatest treasure. The Oracle. More valuable than all their gold, the Oracle is apparently an all-powerful mystical device. It was entrusted to the Black Dragons—a secret paramilitary group—to protect. It was brought to Bangkok, where, it was assumed, it would be 'off the radar.'

"Nakimira was the perfect foil. He hid it without knowing its worth, and he told no one where he kept it. So, it was he who was dispatched to retrieve it."

"And now, where is this…Oracle?"

"Nobody seems to know."

I do. Ramonne smiled to himself.

"That's why I am being targeted," Thompson continued. "Seems that this Black Dragon group thinks I may have it."

"And your organization—the OSS—they are in pursuit of these Black Dragons?"

"Not on the record, no. Officially the OSS doesn't exist."

Ramonne was amused by this. "Really?"

"Yes. And officially, these Black Dragons don't exist either."

Ramonne seemed even more amused by this. *Rather like vampires.*

"Truth be told, I could use another hand," Thompson added. "All I can offer you is my gratitude."

Ramonne smiled. "That is more than sufficient, Lord Jim. I would consider it an honor to join your band of invisible agents to battle this non-existent evil force."

And so, Ramonne Delacroix, 122-year-old French vampire, became an unofficial member of the American OSS.

13
———

Roluos, Present Day

The second night of their passion was no less intense. If anything, Ramonne enjoyed these new raptures more, as he now knew that his condition was in check. It had been his great fear that he would lose control as soon as he entered her. That the intensity of the act would awaken in him the beast. That he would devour her, drain her. In spite of his assurances to her, he hadn't been sure of himself. Not until the very moment of penetration.

Although this was their second night together, they were still mainly silent. Neither seemed to have found a voice. Words didn't seem necessary.

Words between a man and a woman had never been important to Ramonne. For a century and a half his romantic conquests had often ended in the bloody demise of his partner. No need for chit chat.

In general he was with whores. Women of the night. These he could ravish and dispatch without fear of reprisal. As long as they were well compensated, he could enjoy his perversions, generally leaving them intact. He had learned that much control.

His victims, by and large, were the wretched of society. Its invisible people. Not missed when they were gone, because they weren't noticed when they were alive. Kanchana—she was the first woman he had been with that he felt something other than lust for, in a long, long time.

The first since Giselle. Over 150 years ago.

Giselle had been his lover when he was mortal. It was beautiful, young Giselle that he had pledged to return to on that fateful day in 1858 when he and the explorer Henri Mouhot had set sail for the wilds of Indochine. Two years later, exultant from the thrill of unwittingly unveiling ancient Angkor, he had foolishly ventured alone into the temples at night, where he was set upon by the devil Zhoupeng, a 1,000-year-old Chinese vampire. This led to his own transformation into a creature of the night. The vampire had been too weak to kill Ramonne on his first attack; consequently, rather than ending up a corpse, Ramonne became a vampire himself.

In all the intervening years, he never forgot his beloved Giselle. He often crept into his crypt with a silver pocket watch adorned with her sepia-toned photograph.

He had foolishly allowed this yearning for a woman long-deceased to almost cause his demise when he encountered an amazing facsimile of her in a young American woman on her honeymoon in Pattaya. And lately, there was the uncanny resemblance to the girl who worked for Martin at the orphanage. He deemed this too dangerous to pursue, and deliberately avoided Siem Reap.

"What game shall we play tonight?"

These were Ramonne's first words in almost 24 hours.

"Game?"

"Our existence—your *life*—is a series of games. Here we are, two lovers, adrift in our own *amore*. We should indulge our fantasies."

"Sorry…but I thought we already were."

———

Bangkok, Present Day

The grainy black-and-white image on the tiny screen went through a series of jerking, wavy patterns, mainly gray and nebulous. Then suddenly, there it was—a tiny little being. In the center was a small, dark shape that pulsated at its core.

It was Martin and Areeya's daughter. The sonogram showed a developing fetus of 24 weeks old.

Martin squeezed Areeya's hand. She squeezed back. Tears were rolling down both of their faces. He looked to the doctor. He was a young Indian man whom Martin had determined to be the best obstetrician in Bangkok. His cheerful yet professional demeanor had suited Martin's demand to be included in the practice of medicine as it related to his wife and her coming maternity. This wasn't the case with most Thai physicians. They and their patients were used to a general lack of communication. Thai doctors gave their patients a diagnosis and dispensed advice and medication without discussion. Often they never even bothered to give a diagnosis, but merely wrote a prescription or ordered surgery or other procedures. This was followed unquestionably by the Thai patient. After all, 'The doctor said…' It removed the burden of responsibility safely from the patient's shoulders and onto the physician's.

However, Martin clung to his stubborn Western ways when it came to doctors and the practice of medicine. So, he was concerned now that Dr. Namazi was not wearing his customary smiley face.

"Doctor? Is everything all right?"

The doctor moved the transducer on Areeya's belly slightly. On the screen, the image got larger. He was zooming in.

"The heartbeat is still not as strong as I would like."

Martin stared at the pulsating bead of light in the center of the screen. The pulse rate was transmitted to a graph at the bottom of the screen. Lines rose and fell in repetition. Like a seismograph.

Martin squeezed Areeya's hand again. "What does that mean?"

Dr. Namazi removed the instrument and turned off the screen. The nurse wiped the gelatin off Areeya's belly, and she pulled the hospital gown back down. The doctor took off his glasses.

"We are in the developing stage. Organs are forming and maturing. She is slightly smaller and weaker than she should be."

He turned his computer screen so that they could both see it. He pointed to a line with the day's date on it.

"This is the test we did today. It shows the presence of fibronectin in the fetal membrane. This is normal up to 22 weeks. It should be gone by now."

"And what does that mean?"

"Your wife…" He looked at Areeya. "I'm sorry…you are in danger of having a pre-term labor. You could go into labor prematurely and lose the child."

Martin squeezed his wife's hand harder.

The doctor took out a small pad and pen, and looked again at Areeya. "I'm going to give you an injection today, and I want to follow up with daily injections for the next two weeks."

"An injection of *what*?" Martin wanted to know.

"Progesterone." It should stimulate fetal growth and help eliminate the fibronectin." He handed the prescription to the nurse. "Will you need to come in for the injections?"

"No. I can do it," Martin said.

Areeya cocked an eyebrow at this. "Martin? Are you sure?"

"I had a diabetic cat."

The doctor pointed to a spot just below Areeya's naval.

"Here. Every morning. After a light breakfast. The nurse will give you the medication and syringes."

Dr. Namazi and the nurse left the room. Areeya got up from the gurney and went behind a small dressing screen. They were both silent, lost in their own thoughts.

A weak heartbeat. It should be stronger. Not the words they wanted to hear.

Areeya stepped from behind the screen. She stood looking at him.

"You had a diabetic *cat*?"

Martin looked at her and they both laughed. She came into his arms and he held her tight. Tears and laughter mixed with the mutual release of tension.

———

Roluos, Present Day

The temperature was perfect. Although the days seldom dropped below thirty degrees Celsius, within two hours of the sun setting it was comfortable in the mid-twenties.

Ramonne and Kanchana walked in the early morning along the road that bordered the vineyard. A harvest moon was on the wane as the night began to wear out its welcome.

"Where are we going?" she asked.

"Be patient, my dear."

Soon they crested a small hill and the hamlet of Roluos was below them. It consisted of a sprawling market, a few dozen homes and shops, and a temple. On the outskirts of the mainly deserted village were scattered clusters of colored lights. Known to foreigners as *fairy lights*, each delineated a small bar or restaurant. There were a half-dozen between the walking couple and the nearest lights of the village.

Kanchana knew that these places were where the local men did their drinking. Cheap whisky would be sold. A group of men would buy a bottle and settle in while buckets of ice and bottles of soda were continually replenished. One bottle would lead to another and another and then, inevitably, to a fight.

Some of the bars featured cheap karaoke machines. And girls. A man with slightly deeper pockets could buy the same bottle of whisky for a slightly higher price, then instead of drinking with friends he could drink with one of the girl 'singers' and eventually pay to take her off to one of the shacks behind the bar for a tryst. Considerably more expensive than drinking with your mates—but less likely to end in a punch-up, a knife fight or, occasionally, a shoot-out.

These were, despite their fairy-light façades—rough places.

Ramonne liked them. He didn't frequent them. *God no.* Even a *provincial vin rouge ordinaire* would never be found behind their tattered, crate-board bars. But there was a time, when he first moved to the area, when he preyed on the clientele.

"Here." He stopped at the base of a giant banyan. Vines fell through its branches and secured their tentacles in the earth, forever imprisoning the great behemoth in their tangled web, destined to grow through the trials of time—as one.

He sprang effortlessly into the air, catching a thick lower branch about four meters off the ground. He pulled himself up until he straddled it. Then he leaned down and extended his hand. Kanchana jumped and grabbed it, and he pulled her up until she was seated next to him.

He stood, reached for a higher branch, held out his other hand and pulled them both this way through the maze of branches until they were a good ten meters off the ground. From here they looked down on the bars. They formed a semi-circle, their glow like a luminescent serpent.

"What now?" Kanchana said when she caught her breath.

"We wait."

"Wait for what?"

"Our victims."

Kanchana gripped the branch through a fear of falling. "Victims? What do you mean?"

"It's a game, Kanchana…just a game."

Soon a ragtag band of drunken louts emerged from the bar closest to their station.

"Now it begins," Ramonne whispered.

His steely gaze focused on the drunks as they began their stumbly, bumbly, weaving walk home. Instinctively she stood next to him.

"Watch how they *group*."

She understood what he meant. The half-dozen inebriates had already broken into twos and threes. In the front, the loudest and boldest still clutched a whisky bottle. He passed this alternately to two mates who stayed close at his heels. Next were two who were arguing. Whether it was serious or jovial couldn't be determined at this height.

Finally there was the straggler. A very drunken, sorrowful excuse for a human being, who lumbered along at a pace midway between a tortoise and a slug.

"Our victim," Ramonne intoned.

Kanchana watched as he dropped down onto the lower branches. He was as silent as a cat, as skilled at maneuvering in the dark as a bat. And deadlier than a cobra.

"Ramonne," she whispered.

He heard nothing. He was focused only on the target. On the prey.

The man reeled and lost his balance. He was now a good ten meters behind his pals. He soon fell out of the faint circle of light afforded by the bar's fairy-tale exterior. As he staggered into the shadows, he was directly below Ramonne.

Ramonne hissed. His eyes lit up. No longer blue, the yellow that had been there the first time she saw him those many years ago, had returned.

He parted his lips and sneered. He was poised. Ready to pounce.

"Ramonne," she said. This time it wasn't a whisper.

He heard her and turned to look up at her. There was a fury on his face. A demon had been interrupted in full hunting mode. His head snapped back to the man on the ground. By now he was stumbling, panting and struggling to put distance between himself and what he had just seen in the tree.

The moment passed.

The last of the silver moon sank below the horizon and, as it did, the color went out of Ramonne's eyes. He pushed himself to an upright position, brushed his hair back with his hand. And smiled.

"It's a game…only a game."

14
———

Bangkok, 1949

The game has begun, Ramonne thought to himself as he left Thompson's suite.

No doubt the repercussions of his attack on the two assailants would be forthcoming. He could hardly expect the severed head to go unnoticed. Someone would be looking for revenge. It was just a question of where and when.

He had suggested that Lord Jim leave town for a while. Either that or get a bodyguard. He knew that such men existed in Bangkok. They were a by-product of any war. Men who had grown used to the daily adrenaline rush of battle. Thompson said he'd look into it, and promised to be careful.

The evening was still young for Ramonne, and the earlier bloodletting had left him thirsty and hungry; in fact, he had just set off on the prowl when he'd spotted Thompson in trouble.

The vampire took to the rooftops. He could cover great distances, virtually unnoticed, traveling by rooftop. He would leap from the crimson tiles of the homes of the noble and wealthy, to the wooden shanties that crowded the river's edge. He headed south for the port at Klong Toey. There, he knew, he would certainly find a drunken seaman. He would drain the hapless sailor and never have to bother dragging the corpse to Hernando's Cemetery. The man would vanish without a trace, and if anyone noticed his disappearance, it would be assumed that he'd been shanghaied. Such forced conscription had virtually disappeared in the civilized world, but was still prevalent in the ports of the Orient.

Ramonne followed the river as it flowed south. He poised to leap across a chasm that separated two godowns, when below he noticed the green Humber. The driver was scrubbing out the interior of the car with a brush and a bucket of foamy water.

Ramonne smiled. The man had his work cut out. Bloodstains were nasty, he knew. He slipped over the edge and used a fire escape to silently drop down behind the car.

"*Nam som sai chu,*" he said, just above a whisper.

The driver pulled his head out of the car and stared at him.

"*Nam som sai chu,*" he repeated. "Vinegar…it will get the blood out."

A look of horrified recognition crossed the driver's face, and he screamed and flung the soapy brush at Ramonne's head. Ramonne ducked, and the driver jumped into the front seat of the car. Ramone pulled him out, kicking and screaming, and grabbed him by the throat. He applied enough pressure to stop his squawking.

"Shhh." He put a finger to his lips and the terrified man went silent.

—————

Two men in butcher's aprons were engaged in a grisly endeavor. They were removing the extremities of the two corpses that Ramonne had made of their comrades. One had a hacksaw and was laboriously working on the left hand of the headless body, while his partner was hacking away with a cleaver on the feet of the other; the hands of this corpse had already been severed.

It was messy work, and they had put tarpaulins down on the floor. The tarps were soaked in blood and gore. They paid little attention when the driver walked into the room. The one with the saw, Narong, spoke without looking. "The car is clean?"

The driver didn't reply.

"Are you deaf? Is the car clean?"

Still no reply. Now Narong stopped what he was doing and looked up. That's when he saw the figure behind the driver.

"Who's this?" He put down his saw and picked up a pistol. A Walther PPK. "Who the fuck are you?"

The driver was standing still and silent. He stared straight ahead. Showing no emotion. Seeing nothing.

Behind him Ramonne stood with both hands resting on the pommel of his walking stick. He stared intensely at the man with the gun.

"Hey!" Narong moved a step towards Ramonne. "I asked you—who the fuck *are* you?"

Ramonne spoke. "You're not the one I seek."

"What the fuck are you talking about? Put your hands on your head."

It was the other one, Rung, who spoke now. He also had a pistol, and he gripped it in one hand, the cleaver in the other. He moved slowly towards Ramonne.

Ramonne fixed his gaze on Rung. He shook his head slightly. "It's not you either."

"I don't give a fuck what you have to say—put your fucking hands on your head. Do it now!" Narong was walking behind Rung now, his pistol extended.

They were less than three meters from Ramonne. Still he had not moved. They stopped when they got to the driver.

"What the fuck is wrong with you?" Rung snapped his fingers in the driver's face. No reaction.

"What have you done to him?"

Ramonne ignored the question. They advanced on him. He was about to strike when he heard a voice behind him.

"Turn around, slowly."

Ramonne pivoted cautiously on his left foot, looking over his shoulder. A tall man in a dark suit was just inside the doorway. He too had a pistol. Another Walther PPK.

Ramonne decided that this one deserved his attention, and he swung around to face him.

"Now it's my turn to ask," the man said. "Who the fuck are you?"

Ramonne smiled. "You're the one."

The man scowled. "I'm the one *what*?"

"The one I want to talk to."

The man, like the others, was Asian. His hair was combed back from a formidable widow's peak. He was heavy set, but not fat. His suit was well-tailored. His broad shoulders and large hands made the Walther, a small handgun to begin with, look effeminate in his grip.

"You came in here…" He motioned at the bloody tableau. "To talk with me?"

"Yes."

The man laughed. "You should have just phoned. Then I wouldn't have to kill you."

Ramonne smiled. *A sense of humor.* He liked that.

The man kept his gun pointed at Ramonne. He studied the enigma. His ice-cold calmness with three pistols pointed at him. His disregard for the grizzly scene he had walked into.

"You did this…didn't you?"

Ramonne nodded.

The moment froze. No one moved. No one spoke. No one breathed. Time stood still.

Finally, "You two, put your guns down. Get back to work."

The two would-be butchers were reluctant to comply.

"Do it."

They did as told and went slowly back to their gruesome task—all the while looking over their shoulders at the trio by the door.

"We don't want to talk here," the man said.

Ramonne shrugged. "I don't mind."

"I do. Follow me."

The room, considering its warehouse location, was surprisingly warm and inviting. There were comfortable leather chairs, an inlaid wooden table, a side bar with decanters, and a Turkish rug on the floor. With the exception of the large metal desk and filing cabinets at one end, it had the appearance of a St. James' gentlemen's club.

The man led Ramonne to the desk. It was obviously his, and he sat in the swivel chair behind it. He motioned for Ramonne to sit. Ramonne noticed for the first time that the man was missing two fingers on his left hand.

"I prefer to stand."

They had left the driver behind. He was comatose and useless.

The man laid his pistol on the desk, within easy reach. "Now, perhaps you will tell me your name."

"It is not important. Yours, however, is."

"Let me get this straight..." The man entwined his fingers and leaned back in his chair. "You killed two of my men tonight—"

"They were attacking my friend."

The man held up a hand. "They were attempting to *persuade* your friend to come and talk with me." He pointed to the door. "Do you know what they are doing out there?"

Ramonne nodded. "Yes. Getting rid of their identifying features."

"Exactly. In a way, you helped out a little. We only have to cut off one head."

Ramonne shrugged.

"Now you've waltzed in here..." He shook his head. "I'm perplexed...I've tried English. I've tried Thai...Let me try French: What the fuck do you want?"

"Who are you?"

The man thought for a moment. Then: "Akira Hashimoto."

"Why do you want to bother my friend, Jim Thompson? Why did you shoot at him? Why did your men attack him and attempt to kidnap him?"

Hashimoto leaned across the desk. "First, I didn't do any of those things you just mentioned. I've been right here running my import-export business. But, yes, I did ask my associates to bring Mr. Thompson in for a little chat."

"I am here in his place."

Ramonne pulled a chair to the desk, sat down and put his hands on the table. "Let's talk."

Hashimoto lit a cigar. He offered one to Ramonne, who declined.

"Mr. Thompson is either in possession of, or knows the whereabouts of, an object of my desire."

"The Oracle," Ramonne flatly stated.

Shocked, Hashimoto held the match until it burned his finger. He dropped it.

"How the fuck do you know about the Oracle?"

"That's not important. What is important is that you understand that Jim Thompson knows nothing about it."

"But obviously, you do." Hashimoto picked up the pistol. "I don't know who the fuck you are, but I will get the Oracle. If you know anything, you had better start talking."

Ramonne was silent. For the moment. Then: "I've spoken my piece. Jim Thompson is to be undisturbed." He stood.

Hashimoto stared at Ramonne, aiming the pistol at his head.

He laughed. "You don't actually think you're walking out of here?"

"I do."

Hashimoto laughed again. "You were dead the minute you walked through that door."

He fired.

Ramonne moved with lightening speed. The bullet missed.

"You're wrong. *You* are the dead man here."

He sprang on to Hashimoto as he reflexively fired again. This bullet tore through Ramonne's shoulder, taking with it a great chunk of flesh and cartilage. Ramonne sank his teeth into the man's neck and drank voraciously.

He had been seeking sustenance. He just didn't know it would come with such a feeling of vengeance.

He drank deep.

15

Bangkok, Present Day

"Ouch."

"Sorry…shots hurt."

"Not when the doctor does it."

"Really? Sorry I'm not a professional."

Areeya pulled her top back down. "Your cat must have hated you."

She kissed him, Thai style, her lips brushing his cheek, her nose sniffing. When she left the room, Martin put the plastic hypodermic in its disposing pouch, sealed it and put it in a plastic box with six others. It had been a week since the sonogram. Areeya had been virtually a quadriplegic at Martin's insistence.

Martin would have shackled her to the bed if he thought he could have gotten away with it. Hell, he would have bought his own sonogram machine if he thought he could read the images. Doctors must spend seven years in college learning something.

He had Googled 'pregnancy, 24 weeks' and spent three hours reading the advice, opinions and medical facts. The prevailing wisdom seemed to be: 'Be thankful for the pregnancy. That alone is a gift from God. Relax. Let Nature take its course.' For a pragmatist like Martin, this wasn't much comfort. He felt impotent and helpless. All his millions, hell, even all daddy's billions, couldn't change what was going to happen right here in his apartment in the next few weeks. Either a new life would be allowed to develop, endure and survive...or it wouldn't.

A chime sounded. The door bell.

Martin ignored it. He assumed it was the doorman with his mail. In any case, Gai, the maid would get it.

"Khun Martin...there is a man here."

"Who is it?"

"I don't know. But he says it is important."

It must be important. Martin lived in the penthouse. No one came up in the elevator unless cleared by security. This had been the practice for years and was rarely violated.

Martin knew that there had been times when the security left the desk for toilet breaks and the like, and it would be possible to enter the elevator. But you still needed a key to get to his floor. He went to the door.

A tall Asian man he didn't recognize was already standing in his entryway. Gai had let him in.

Martin frowned. "Yes?"

"Mr. Larue?"

"That depends. Who are you?"

The man smiled and presented a business card.

Martin read it. "Toshiro Muraki...Japanese?"

"Yes...from Tokyo. As it says on the card."

Martin put the card in his shirt pocket. "What do you want?"

"Can we please sit, Mr. Larue? My questions are many."

"No, Mr. Muraki. I am not allowing you any further into my apartment until I know the nature of your business." Martin had his hand on the phone that was a direct line to security downstairs.

"Ramonne Delacroix."

That was enough for Martin to release his grip on the phone and admit Mr. Muraki to his parlor.

The shaded room with its large French doors leading onto a balcony overlooking Lumpini Park was one of Martin's favorites. It was completely screened, and in the early evenings he threw open the doors and enjoyed the relatively cool air and slight breezes that blew over the Big Mango. But in the heat of the afternoon, as now, the louvers were drawn so that only slits of light entered and the air-conditioner cooled it to a very comfortable 23 degrees Centigrade.

Martin led Mr. Muraki to a rattan couch fitted with cushions encased in Provencal fabrics that he had acquired on one of his many trips to the south of France. They had survived Banana's whirlwind. Without a word, the maid placed two glasses of iced water on the table that separated them, and stood waiting.

"Thank you, Gai. That's all for now." Martin was not about to extend his hospitality any further for this intruder. She bowed slightly and left.

"Now, Mr. Muraki, perhaps you'll tell me why you are here."

"I'm looking for Ramonne Delacroix. I was told that you know him."

"Knew him, yes…he's dead."

The man smiled. "Really?"

"Really."

Muraki sipped from his water, placing it down precisely on the bamboo coaster. Beads of condensation ran down the glass.

"How did he die?"

Martin shrugged. "He drowned. In a fight with a police lieutenant seven years ago."

"Interesting. I heard he was blown up in the terrorist bombing on Silom Road in 2005."

Martin shrugged again. "I heard there was a man who threw

himself onto the bomb. Very heroic. But he couldn't have been Delacroix."

Muraki smiled again. "I also heard he was recently involved in an incident in Cambodia with a band of ex-Khmer Rouge who were smuggling artifacts. In each of these incidents, Mr. Larue...you were there."

Martin leaned back in his chair. Silent.

"The last one that I just mentioned occurred in front of an orphanage that you personally endow."

Martin knew this day would come eventually. Someone would put it all together and come looking for him. Looking for Ramonne.

No amount of self denial, no amount of rejection, no act of physical removal—he'd moved his family to Bangkok mainly to be away from *him*—could eliminate the fact that their lives had been entwined for years. Ramonne had been incinerated and reborn, destroyed and reborn, eviscerated, entombed and trans-mogrified—and yet, he remained. Martin assumed he would, forever.

That's the way it is with vampires.

"You seem to know a lot about Ramonne Delacroix," Martin stated.

The stranger nodded. "We have been interested in him for a long, long time." He leaned on the table, his hands splayed flat before him. "We know *what* he is, Mr. Larue. We just don't know *where* he is."

Did they really? Martin had had this conversation before, in this very room, eight years ago. When he had been a non-believer. Jonathan Peyton had come from America to bring down the vampire who had killed his wife and destroyed his life. Now, here was another believer seeking the vampire.

What should he do? What should he admit?

————

Roluos, Present Day

Nights turn into days. Days into weeks. Soon Kanchana and Ramonne were an old, comfortable couple.

Ramonne had played their 'game' twice again. Once more in the tree near the village, and then another time near the town of Nikom to the south.

Tonight he had the professor drive them to the outskirts of Angkor. Here, rhesus monkeys lined the road morning and evening, paws outstretched, begging for handouts from the tourists.

But it was well past midnight and the monkeys were settled in the trees. Those that weren't sleeping were chattering to each other.

The tourist station that monitors the visitors during the day becomes a guard station at night when the park is closed. Ramonne, however, could cross any border, get through any portal. The guards never saw them.

Kanchana was excited. She had never seen the temples of Angkor, and the prospect of seeing them at night, with no tourists, was alluring. Ramonne seemed pleased that she was excited, but his own enthusiasm was markedly dampened. She knew the story of his battle with the demon Zhoupeng and was well aware of his origin as a vampire in the temples so many years ago. So she understood his trepidation at returning to the scene of the crime, as it were.

They were soon traveling along a large, open body of water. It glistened in the moonlight. After a quarter-mile it curved to the right and suddenly the great temple of Angkor was revealed in all its sacred glory.

Its stone towers were set back a great distance from the lake and the road. A stone causeway led across a giant terrace to the temple itself.

The professor parked the van and Ramonne led Kanchana

up the wide stone avenue and onto the temple grounds. "It's fantastic, my love. Thank you for this gift."

He held her close.

"This, my love, is *axis mundi*. The center of the universe. We are following the path of divinity, as did the ancient Khmer kings."

They walked through the portals and ascended to the tower stairs.

"It is written that in the reign of King Prasadharma, there was a golden tower just beyond the temple. Each night the king climbed the tower and slept in the summit. Each night he made love to a different woman. One of his 200 wives. He turned into a *naga*, a nine-headed serpent, to give him the strength to perform the act night after night."

She smiled at him. "You would need no such transformation, my love. Your stamina is amazing."

He slipped his arm around her waist and led her slowly back along the balustrade, across the bridge and back to the road. In front of them, a long road led to a massive stone gate. It was topped by a large head. The same massive head faced all four points of the compass. On each side of the causeway, railings were fashioned with dozens of figures performing some monumental task. The heads were missing from the majority of the bodies.

Kanchana pointed to the gate. "What's that?"

A cloud crossed the moon, and with it a shadow fell across the landscape. "That is known as the South Gate. It leads to the temple of the Bayon and the walled city of Angkor Thom. The figures on each side represent the ancient Hindu myth of the 'churning of the ocean.' On one side the figures pull the tail of a giant serpent, while on the other the figures pull the snake's head in the opposite direction. The snake's body is wrapped around a mountain, represented by the temple of the Bayon, beyond the gate. As they pulled, the ocean began to churn and the mountain was split into the earth below and the cosmos above."

He took her hand and they headed for the van. "We will not be going there tonight."

She did not resist. The gate…the temple. These must hold terrible secrets for him. His hand grew cold in hers.

Dr. Kaestle was looking at the gate and seemed lost in his own memories.

"Professor," Ramonne quietly called. This brought Dr. Kaestle back from his contemplation, and he hastened to open the doors to the van. Ramonne held the door open for Kanchana but his gaze was directed off in the distance. Beyond the gate. It was as if something beckoned him.

A slight breeze began to rustle his hair. He inhaled deeply. The breeze grew stronger.

"Ramonne," she whispered.

His nostrils were flared now, and his head arched back. The breeze became a wind. It swirled around the van.

She tugged on his arm. "Ramonne…let's go."

Slowly he turned to her. His eyes had changed color again, as they had the first night of their lovemaking and on the nights they played the 'game.' She tugged again on his arm. He was solid. Immobile.

She became frightened. "Professor!" she shouted. Then she noticed that the good doctor was also outside the van. He too was facing into the wind, his eyes fixed on some faraway spot, through the tangled vines and stout boughs of the banyan trees, beyond the massive gate.

She had heard enough stories of Ramonne's times in Angkor to know that, although they couldn't see it, their attention was riveted on the Bayon. It must be the source of the ill wind that was now blowing with increasing fury.

Desperate, Kanchana released Ramonne's hand and slid across the seat. She opened the door and stepped out. She brushed past the professor and yanked open the driver's door. She slammed her hand down on the pommel in the middle of the steering wheel. Immediately the blast of the horn cut through the howling wind.

She held her hand there for what seemed like forever, but was in fact just a few moments. The jarring, blaring noise broke the spell, and Ramonne turned away from the forest and looked to her. She kept her hand on the horn.

The wind continued to blow his silver mane. It blew around his face like Medusa's coils. He turned back to face the wind once more and then walked slowly to the driver's side of the vehicle. He reached in and lifted her hand off the horn. The shrill noise ceased and the wind slowly abated.

The night returned to an eerie silence.

She looked up at him. His eyes were losing their amber tint and returning to what she now regarded as normal. He smiled and pressed her head to his chest.

"I'm sorry, my love."

"What was that?"

Ramonne looked back once more to the Bayon and then shrugged, seemingly dismissing it.

"That…? Just a call from an old friend. It was nothing."

He took her hand and she climbed out of the driver's seat. Professor Kaestle was back to his version of normal, and he opened the rear doors for them.

They left Angkor and drove back down the tree-lined road. Ramonne cracked his window a bit and listened to the chattering of the monkeys. Kanchana wondered if he understood them.

There were many things about this man that would remain mysteries.

Bangkok, Present Day

If he knows this much, how can he not know of Ramonne's where-abouts in Cambodia?

The answer was that no one knew of Ramonne's existence in Roluos. No doubt Villa des Oiseaux was purchased or leased in the professor's name. Whatever nefarious business needed to be done would transpire under the cover of darkness, and whatever witnesses there were would, no doubt, be disposed of.

Continued denial. This was Martin's only recourse.

"Mr. Muraki. You are sorely mistaken. As I said, I was once acquainted with the man you mentioned—a few years ago. But he is deceased. For him to be linked to these other two incidents is quite impossible."

Muraki ignored him and took out a manila envelope. "Is this the man you knew as Ramonne Delacroix?" Muraki slid a yellowed newspaper photograph, encased in a plastic folder, across the table. The photograph was taken at a formal occasion. It featured two men and two women. The two men, dressed in tuxedos, raised glasses in a toast. The man on the right was tall, blond and seemingly quite at ease. He smiled broadly for the camera. The man on the left, however, seemed unhappy with the act of being photographed. He stared directly at the camera, his brow furrowed and his mouth a straight line.

"The man on the left is Ramonne Delacroix. Yes?"

Martin nodded. He had never seen a photograph of the vampire before, but it clearly was him.

Muraki lifted the photograph from its plastic sleeve and unfolded it. It was a good color Xerox of the society page of the *Bangkok Times*. The caption read, 'Expat entrepreneur Jim Thompson hosts a reception to launch the Oriental Hotel's newest addition—the Bamboo Bar.' Others in the photo were identified. No mention was made of Ramonne.

The newspaper was dated 1947.

"Now, tell me, Mr. Larue…how is this possible?"

Martin stared at the photograph, dumbfounded. He spoke without thinking. "It's a fake."

"I assure you, it is not. Your friend was employed by the Oriental Hotel in 1947. He was the compère of the music bar. He disappeared in 1949. And resurfaced fifty years later, seemingly no worse for wear. Unfortunately we have no photographs of him at this time, but he was witnessed in a battle at the Temple of Dawn that resulted in the death of Lieutenant-Colonel Boonsong. However, he is not listed in the police report."

He slid the article back in its plastic sleeve and put it back in the envelope.

Martin had grown very uneasy. He realized he had been sinking into his seat, and he straightened his posture. He wanted this tiresome man and his irritating questions out of his apartment. Out of his life.

"What is it you want, Mr. Muraki?"

"I want to know where Ramonne Delacroix is today."

He paused to let this sink in.

"I am greatly concerned with something of immense value that belongs to my organization. Something that we are convinced is in his possession."

"Your *organization*?"

"I am not at liberty to discuss that."

"Something that belongs to you?"

"I am not at liberty to discuss that either...but I can tell you this: What I seek is an object of such power that it is no doubt responsible for your friend's extended lifespan and seeming immortality."

Now Martin's head was truly spinning. *Ramonne is a vampire. That is the key to his immortality.* How could this man know so much and yet not know that? And what the hell was this 'source of power' that he was talking about?

"I'm afraid you've lost me. You actually believe that Delacroix is immortal due to his possession of some secret power source? Do you realize how absurd that sounds?"

Muraki tapped the envelope containing the photograph. "How do you explain this?"

"It must be his father...or grandfather."

"It is not."

"How do you know?"

"We have our sources. Our search for our missing property has been going on for a very long time."

"You have your *sources*? Mr. Muraki...this is childish. Beyond belief. I must insist that you leave now."

Muraki swept the envelope off the table and into his pocket. He stood and walked slowly into Martin's space.

"Mr. Larue, my associates are dangerous people. Your failure to cooperate may put you in jeopardy."

At this Martin stood. He walked to the front door, Muraki trailing behind. "I've wasted enough time on this nonsense." He held the door open.

Muraki stood in the entry. "I suggest you keep our conversation confidential."

"Good day, Mr. Muraki." Martin closed the door on the Japanese man's back.

"Who was that?"

Areeya was toweling her hair, wearing a white cotton robe.

"Nobody."

16

Bangkok, 1949

The Silver Palm Cabaret. Ramonne loved the word. *Cabaret*. It sounded naughty, and that was what Ramonne liked about it.

The Bamboo Bar was closed for the next few nights while they scrambled to book a fitting follow-up to Jimmy Witherspoon. An offer was out to legendary guitarist Django Reinhardt, who was at the moment in Hong Kong, and Ramonne sincerely hoped it would pan out. Otherwise he would have to endure the tiresome local trio that consisted of the only proponents of stand-up bass and jazz drumming in the kingdom, accompanying a piano player who made his living giving lessons to the daughters of the Bangkok social glitterati. Ramonne had heard of more than one complaint that the pianist's hands were prone to wander up his students' skirts. But his ability to teach the keyboard was so unique that his transgressions were tolerated—for the moment.

C'est la vie. Ramonne had let the man know more than once what he thought about him, and yet—as they say—he and his trio were the only game in town.

Enough business. Ramonne was out, in his element. The

Silver Palm reminded him of the cabarets of Paris, and he would treat himself to a night of entertainment of which he had not the slightest involvement. He was seated in his customary box, a bottle of Bordeaux before him. On stage a juggler rode a unicycle and clumsily tried to flip pie plates onto a tower atop his hat. He missed more often than not, gaining a visual reprimand in the form of a heavy scowl from the emcee standing in the wings. But no matter how many plates crashed to the stage or juggling balls were missed, he always received a stirring round of applause when he unseated himself from the cycle and took a bow.

The nattily attired emcee—a pure white tuxedo, white vest and cummerbund, white gloves, top hat and cane, topped off with two sweeping strokes of glitter alongside his iridescent eyes—returned to the spotlight and introduced the singer, the enchanting Lady Marivel. Ramonne was entranced by her coquettish charm. He immediately dispatched one of the waiting staff with his card and instructions to invite her to his table. He knew he could seduce her without effort, as all women were prey to his vampiric wiles, but he found it intriguing to play the role of jazz impresario to the hilt on occasion. She was Filipina, as it seemed all the chanteuses were of late. Her blonde wig made her even more irresistible to Ramonne, and he led the applause for her as she finished her brief set.

Next was the chorus line. All Thai girls, all wearing wigs, petticoats and bustiers. They high-stepped and kicked in their own imitation of the famous French cancan, and Ramonne encouraged their flailing attempts at choreography with his exuberance. He was in mid-whistle when he noticed that a beautiful, raven-haired girl was shyly waiting outside his box for him to notice her.

"Lady Marivel?"

"Just Marivel, sir," she said in perfect English.

"Please, join me." He motioned to the chair next to him, and she sat demurely, keeping a respectable distance between them.

"Would you care for a drink? Wine?" He pointed to his half-full bottle. "Or champagne, perhaps?"

"Champagne would be nice." *Of course.* Even a nice girl like Mademoiselle Marivel knew enough to order champagne when offered a drink. The house would send its most expensive bottle, and she would receive her cut later. But Ramonne cared not for this triviality, and ordered the bottle to be brought.

An hour later, he and the girl were rapturously inebriated. Two empty Beaujolais bottles and a Dom Perignon were upended in the silver bucket. Ramonne now had his arm around the girl and they were singing along to the show's finale.

That was when Ramonne spotted him.

Brigadier-General Natiwat was seated in a box directly across from them. He was in dress uniform, row upon row of medals pinned to his chest. He was accompanied by two men in civilian attire. Ramonne knew these men. He had met them once before. At that time they were wearing butcher's aprons and engaged in the task of dismembering the bodies of the men he had slain in defense of Jim Thompson. All three were now staring intently at Ramonne.

Ramonne attempted to ignore the trio. But his mind was racing. *General Natiwat? In conspiracy with the Black Dragons?* What was it that Thompson had said about them—they were Japanese saboteurs. In this case, the nefarious general could well have been a collaborator during the war. Many Thais had worked openly and willingly for the Japanese.

Ramonne turned his attention back to the charms of the delightful Miss Marivel. She had, literally, let her hair down, at about the time of the third glass of champagne. Her raven locks framed her face and set off her smoky eyes. Ramonne was enchanted.

"If I may be so bold, Mademoiselle Marivel, would you do me the honor of accompanying me this evening?"

She blushed. "Sir, I am not sure what you mean?"

He vamped. "I am in need of a singer at the Bamboo Bar. Perhaps you could audition for me in my parlor?" Ramonne had an arrangement at the Oriental whereby the keys to any unoccupied room were his for the asking.

Again, her cheeks colored and she cast her eyes away from his. "I cannot accompany a gentleman without a chaperone. It would not be right, sir."

To hell with this. Time to forgo the formalities of seduction. He turned her head to him, with his hand gently propping up her chin. He looked deep into her eyes and simply *willed* her to come with him.

"I need to get my things," she said.

"Of course." Ramonne smiled and stood while she left the box.

He turned his attention back to the general, but he and his accomplices were gone.

"Looking for someone, Khun Ennomar?" The general was now standing at the entry to Ramonne's box. He was alone.

"Yes. I was looking for you."

"Look no further. May I join you?"

"No. I have company."

"I saw your *company*." The general sneered. "The Lady Marivel has been courted by most of Krung Thep's gentlemen of leisure. They have all failed to bed her."

He looked at the empty seat. "I see you too have failed, as well. She is gone."

The general started to enter the box. Ramonne put a hand to his chest, stopping him.

The general looked indignant. "There is something important we must discuss."

"The lady has gone for her purse. I am busy, General, and I wish you to leave. "

The general attempted to back away from Ramonne's hand. Ramonne kept it in place.

The general spoke in a loud whisper. "You have overstepped your bounds, my friend. My patience has run out. Kindly remove your hand." He placed his hand atop Ramonne's and attempted to remove it. Ramonne's arm was like a steel tendon.

"Killing the little Jap, that was the first mistake. Much as you would like to claim otherwise, I did try and cover that up for you. But when you walked into that godown in Klong Toey, you sealed your fate. I can no longer protect you, Khun Ennomar, if that is your name. The Black Dragons are not a legion to be trifled with. If I were you, I'd leave Krung Thep." He glared. "If I were you, I'd slit my wrists, but perhaps you are the kind that fancies a long, lingering death."

Ramonne turned his hand and clutched the material of the general's uniform, pulling him towards him until his hot breath was on the man's face.

"Listen to me and heed my words. I have paid you well. I can only assume that they are paying you more—for I know that what you do, you do not out of allegiance to anyone but yourself. These Black Dragons that you speak of are buffoons. Blunderers. Amateurs. The last I saw of the men you were with tonight, they were covered in the gore of two of their comrades that I had slaughtered. They were attempting to conceal their identities. I then dispatched their leader, and I can easily deal with them. I would advise you, General, to stay out of my way."

The general was speechless. Ramonne's retort had taken him unawares.

Ramonne released his grip.

Shaken, the general attempted to straighten his uniform. "You…you have no idea who you are dealing with."

The general bent to pick up his hat from a chair. Without ever having seen him move, Ramonne was now in the row of chairs before him, the general's hat in his hand. His eyes had fire in them that the general could only attribute to the reflection of the chandelier above. But the theater was closing and the chandelier had been dimmed.

"No, General Natiwat. You have no idea who *you* are dealing with." He held out the hat.

"Sir, is there a problem?" The maître d' was standing near the general, his words addressed to the policeman.

Reassured of his stature, the general ran a hand through his heavily pomaded hair, and placed his hat upon his head.

"No, Manat. Everything is quite in order."

He nodded stiffly to Ramonne, turned on his heels and left, the maître d' in tow.

The place was practically empty now, and it was with relief that Ramonne noticed Lady Marivel waiting patiently, clutching her handbag. He picked up his walking stick and moved to her. He offered his arm.

"Mademoiselle. We'd best be off for your audition."

She took his arm and they departed.

———

Roluos, Present Day

The brush was dipped into the palette, taking a bit of burnt sienna and mixing it with cadmium orange to make warm amber. The brush returned to the canvas and was deftly used to make a shadow under the chin and below the arm of the woman in the painting.

The painting was done in a flat, slightly impressionistic style. The background, a vibrant vineyard, had already been rendered, and the woman in the foreground was now being completed.

Ramonne painted from life; his model, Kanchana, was posing in his studio in front of an open window—the vineyard resplendent beyond. She was naked from the waist up, a shawl wrapped across her shoulders and gathered in her folded arms that were crossed just below her breasts. Her attitude and expression were reminiscent of the Mona Lisa.

Ramonne worked unhurriedly, obviously enjoying the process of creating. Behind him, the walls of the studio were filled with charcoal sketches. Landscapes, anatomical studies, the neighbor's dog, and of course Kanchana. Her hair up, hair down, dressed, undressed. At her boudoir, in the bath, and strolling the vineyards. A half-dozen full-color canvases lay stacked against the base of the wall.

Ramonne had returned to the legacy he had left behind in that dimly-lit temple so long ago. He had been an artist in Marseilles; his beloved Giselle was his model. It was his artistic talent that had attracted the explorer Henri Mouhot. He had wandered on a whim into the café that Giselle maintained, and had taken note of the paintings and sketches on display. She had run home, and breathlessly begged the morose artist to leave his cups and come meet the charming Monsieur Mouhot. Ramonne, despondent that he could not support Giselle as he would have liked, had at first refused, but she literally dragged him to meet his destiny.

"Ramonne. Can we stop for a while?" Kanchana's back was beginning to ache from holding the position for close to half an hour.

"Just a moment, my love. I'm almost finished." He studied her without moving his brush, his eyes darting between the model and the canvas. He then made two small dabs with the darkened amber and put the palette and brush down.

"*Finis*," he announced. Kanchana sighed with relief and drew the shawl across her breasts. She cracked her neck and rose from the stool. She crossed the room and stood next to him as he studied his work.

"It's beautiful," she exclaimed.

"It's all right. I think I failed to capture your inner beauty, my love. Although I did manage to capture your areolas."

"My what?"

"Your nipples."

She looked at him with a smirk. "So that's what it's all about. And I thought you were an artist."

He laughed. "An artist is only as good as his subject." He pulled her to him." And you, my dear, are sublime." He kissed her as she put her arms around him and pressed him to her.

She put on a blouse and they went outside, walking hand in hand through the vines. The setting sun backlit the stately rows of grapes. They shone with an emerald hue that Ramonne would have been hard-pressed to mix on his palette. They were alive with light.

Her head was on his shoulder and he stopped beneath a gnarled old shade tree. He had placed a slatted bench under the tree when he first rediscovered the joys of the sunset stroll, and they sat beneath the stately old tree.

Not a word was spoken for a long moment.

Finally, "I've never been happier, my love."

She looked into his crystal-blue eyes.

He took her hand and kissed it. "You've brought true joy to my life."

"And you to mine, my love."

The sun began its evening change from gold to scarlet as it descended below the distant hills. The breeze picked up and the red poppies, purple hyacinths and grape vines waved softly, each shimmering with the luminescence provided by the setting orb. The world glowed and the two lovers were silent as they admired what Nature had wrought.

"Darling, I must return to Bangkok soon."

He turned to her with a quizzical look. "Why?"

"I have a business, my love. It needs me."

Kanchana had inherited a silk business, one that had benefitted immensely from Jim Thompson's campaign that had made Thailand's unique silk desired internationally. She had showrooms in Bangkok and Chiang Mai.

"You don't need a business."

She smiled. She knew that this argument would be forthcoming.

"I do need it, my love. It's what I do. What my family has always done."

Now, for the first time since she had known him, she sensed he was unsure what to say. She took his hand, squeezing it to her breast. "What we have here is not going anywhere. I'll be back as soon as I can."

He looked to the hills. A hawk rode the evening thermals and silently searched for prey. He rose and fell with the swells of the breeze. Ramonne envied him his freedom. He knew that the purloined thoughts he was suppressing were primeval instincts that had served him so well for so long. These *emotions* —that was the word—would eventually be his downfall, as they were to all humans. At this very moment, he knew that were he to pursue this path, it would lead to his ruin. Was that what he truly desired?

He thought back—about a century ago—and remembered a scene in Ayutthaya. A soothsayer was begging for his life while his compatriots celebrated the lunar festival of Loy Krathong— lighting candles and floating them out on the river in tiny banana-leaf boats, along with their hopes and wishes for the future. They were in the shadow of the Queen's summer residence, and the fortune-teller had demanded compensation from Ramonne for a tossing of bones. "Why should I pay for such a miscast prophecy?" The bones had predicted that Ramonne would live a long life only to fall victim to deception by a woman. It seemed ludicrous to Ramonne, the immortal young vampire, that he could ever succumb to such folly. He had let the old seer live but had taken out his angst on a group of drunken revelers who unfortunately crossed his path that same eve.

"Ramonne. Please. You're not listening to me."

He was snapped back to the present. The sun went behind

the hills and the first stars of the night appeared. He stared at his lovely woman.

"Oh, but I am."

She was afraid to look into his eyes, but at last she did. They were, as she feared, yellow.

In that moment she lost her will. She felt it slip away like a silken bed sheet sliding silently off her soul.

He leaned in to her and she unconsciously unbuttoned the top button to her blouse.

She felt a slight tingling sensation. She sighed.

17

Bangkok, Present Day

Martin could tell before the doctor spoke—it would not be good news. He just prayed it was not the *worst* news.

"The heartbeat still isn't as strong as I'd like."

As strong as 'you'd' like? Who cares what 'you'd' like. It's my daughter. Is she going to live? Will she be born? Will she graduate high school? Go to Vassar?

Martin realized *his* heart was racing. He took a deep breath. The doctor turned off the sonogram and the image faded.

Martin looked at Areeya. She was just staring at the blank screen, her eyes moist, the tears not yet falling.

Not again. Not again. He held his wife's hand while the nurse wiped her stomach.

What the hell is wrong? Areeya was young, strong, healthy. He would have been the questionable one, Lord knows, but once his soldiers of sperm had surmounted the sixty million-to-one odds, and one of them had stormed the proverbial gate, his part was done.

Why? Why was this happening to them? The hand he was holding was cold.

"Martin?"

"It's nothing. He's just being cautious."

———

In his small office, the doctor handed Martin two pages of small grainy images from the sonogram. Martin groaned. *For our collection.*

"I'm going to continue the injections for another two weeks. In addition, I'm prescribing some oral medication."

"What?"

"Cortico. It will, hopefully, speed up the fetal development."

"Steroids? Is that absolutely necessary? I've read that that's the last thing you want to introduce into a pregnant woman's bloodstream."

"You've obviously spent time studying this on the Internet. You should know there are two schools of thought on this—pro and con. I am of the former. Your wife's history of miscarriages leads me to suspect that she has an auto-immune deficiency. In any case, if we don't do something drastic at this stage, I am afraid we will lose the baby."

'We' again.

"Of course the choice is entirely up to you and your wife."

Martin looked at Areeya. Her face was blank, emotionless. Stunned. This was a decision that he would have to make.

"All right. Give her the medication."

The doctor wrote a prescription and handed it to his nurse.

"I'll see you in two weeks." He smiled the smug little doctor-patient condescending smile that Martin hated.

Martin helped Areeya stand up. She barely had any legs at all, and he practically carried her through the door.

In the car they rode in silence. Martin had hired a driver when they returned to Bangkok, vowing to never again have to personally negotiate the notorious and frustrating gridlocked city streets.

They sat in the rear of their new Lexus SUV, staring at the city whose appearance changed daily and yet never seemed to change.

He looked at her profile silhouetted against the window. She had changed little since he'd first met her, nearly eight years ago. She was called Yaya then. Society's child. The spoiled brat of a police lieutenant-colonel. Known for her wild escapades that taxed not only her father's patience, but his pocket. He regularly bribed the media to cover up her indiscretions. She had been caught up in his involvement with the vampire quite innocently. Ramonne had taken her hostage to gain access to, and ultimately harm, her father. She and Martin had met under the worst of circumstances, and went their separate ways when their ordeal was over. It was a year later when Martin returned from purging his demons in a hillside Buddhist temple that they met again. She had been through her own involuntary exorcism, having been committed to a mental institution for the tales that she dared to speak about what had happened at the Temple of Dawn on Bangkok's riverside. Two wounded spirits had formed a bond that led to a love affair more intense than any Martin had ever known.

They needed this baby. It would make them whole. They both loved little Hon with all their heart, but a child of their own had been their dream since they first united. They had talked about it until they were blue in the face. They'd driven their friends crazy with their obsession with her pregnancy. They employed ovulation prediction kits, had sex at the optimum time for fertilization, and used the missionary position exclusively. All to no avail. Areeya erected altars in their house, lit candles and incense in the morning, prayed in bed at night, and dragged him to temples he never knew existed.

Martin took the practical approach and enrolled in an in vitro fertilization program. His sperm was frozen and her eggs were extracted. Embryos were created and inserted. A long, elaborate and expensive process.

And then they had their first success. Alas, it ended in miscarriage. As did the next, four months later. Now they were 26 weeks into this journey, and the noose was being dangled again.

"Martin…shut up."

He looked at her, stunned. "I haven't said a thing."

"No, but you're thinking too much."

She reached across the seat and took his hand. "We're doing all we can. At this point it's no longer up to us."

She was right. He knew it.

He just wasn't sure who it was up to.

———

Roluos, Present Day

He carried her lifeless body through the vineyards silhouetted against the immense rising harvest moon. She was as light to him as a feather.

The professor saw him through the kitchen window. He thought at first that the woman must be ill, and he put down his dish cloth, preparing to rush outside.

But no, she wasn't ill, and the master wasn't walking to the house. He was walking away from it.

He turned off the tap and dried his hands.

He knew this moment would come. He knew the master very well. All the attempts at normalcy were doomed to fail. All the pretensions Ramonne had assumed in his vain attempt to regain humanity were doomed to fail.

He didn't know what particular alignment of stars had allowed this temporary reprieve from the curse, but he always knew it would be just that—temporary.

He had been keenly aware of the mood swings, the shifts that were more than mere acquiescence to the stress of the moments. He knew that the master was strong enough to banish each of these foibles if he desired. But he had watched as the master accepted and allowed these intrusions.

However, more than that, he had been privy to the master's relationship with the woman. He knew that the master had attempted to enter into a true relationship with her. He had allowed her access to more than just his bedroom. He had allowed her access to his heart.

But that wasn't the problem. The master had no heart.

Professor Kaestle was a scientist. An entomologist. One of the first things he had done when he gained the master's confidence was to do a physical examination of the vampire.

He had been astounded. Blood work showed that the term 'living dead' was completely false. Ramonne was in a state of hyper-existence. His blood cells multiplied and regenerated constantly under the microscope. He had virtually no body fat. But the most astounding thing was…

He had no heartbeat. No pulse.

He had no heart.

There was an organ that circulated blood to his extremities, but it was not a heart. It was something else. Something that his former heart had evolved into. And this organ required constant replenishment of the fluid that sustained him. For even as it was regenerating to repair any tissue or organ damage, it was also constantly thinning out and dissolving.

It was a cycle. It was not life as we knew it, but something else.

As amazing as this had been then, it was more amazing now. The professor asked the master to let him examine him again, after his battle with Zhoupeng had left him with an apparent tolerance to the rays of the sun. The results were only slightly different than they had been a year before.

All physical exams start with the stethoscope. The heartbeat. The pulse.

Ramonne had none.

No matter what had occurred on the battlefield. No matter

what the master had learned from the study of the ancient Sanskrit scrolls of Angkor, no matter how much he was able to rationalize the change he was experiencing, no matter how much he justified it, no matter how much he sanctified it…

It was never going to last.

Ramonne had been given a temporary reprieve.

He wanted to change. That was obvious. He wanted to love this woman. That was obvious. But the professor knew that this too had been only temporary.

He had seen the signs here, as well. The false love. The veil of lies. And now, what he knew would eventually happen had transpired.

The master had gone over the edge. He had crossed a fragile divide. He had been treading like a tight-rope walker with his pole.

The master was gone.

The master was back.

18
___

Bangkok, 1949

"James…how's your wife?"

Jim Thompson thought this was rather an odd question from a woman who was currently sharing his bed. But he had learned to expect the unexpected from Lady Jane Farmer.

"We're divorced, Jane."

"No shit."

"She has no interest in living here."

"She doesn't like malaria, cholera or syphilis?"

"Not particularly."

"Go figure. Hand me an ashtray, love."

Lady Jane sat up, pulling the sheet with her. She shook out a cigarette from the pack on the nightstand. Thompson lit it for her with his Zippo. She drew in the smoke and surveyed the room."

"So this is the grand manor of Lord Jim Thompson."

It was a comfortable suite. It had been one of the first rooms renovated when Thompson and his partners acquired the hotel after the war. The Japanese officers, by all reports, had treated the hotel with a certain amount of respect. But it served as an

American military hospital after the surrender, and in the mistaken notion that the Japanese had built the hotel for themselves, the GIs had done their best to trash the place. The first four months of renovation were mainly spent removing rubbish and tearing down burnt drapes and shutters.

When they got the old gal stripped down to her wooden girdles, she showed Thompson and his partners the promise that he had always known she had.

They thoroughly renovated the colonial building that his suite was situated in. The rooms were arranged along open verandas that the guests referred to as 'bowling alleys.' The plumbing was antiquated and needed a complete overhaul. Some rooms still had giant *klong* jars of water in the rooms to be used for bathing. Thompson's room was the first to acquire a real bathtub.

"It's home for now. But soon, I want to build my own house."

Jane tapped her ash and looked at the rugged, tousle-haired man in the bed next to her.

"A house? You know what comes with that, don't you?"

"No...tell me."

"Trouble, James. Our kind are meant to be footloose and fancy free. That was a compliment, by the way, about your 'grand manor.' I like hotel rooms."

"So do I. But I have aspirations, Jane. You know what those are, don't you?"

"Humor me." She stubbed out the cigarette.

"Silk. Beautiful, hand-woven Thai silk. I want to excite the world about this marvelous fabric."

"Isn't that a little effeminate, James?"

Thompson pulled down the sheet. "I'll show you who's effeminate."

She screamed in mock objection, then pushed his head down. "Ahhh."

They made love for the second time since she had arrived

unannounced, just as he was about to retire. The Oriental being the kind of establishment it was, single ladies were not allowed entrance to gentlemen's quarters, but with Jim Thompson being who he was, she had been allowed upstairs without accompaniment.

She had been drinking, that was obvious. But it wasn't just sensual lust that had sent Lady Jane Farmer to his door. She had an expression on her face of confusion. He'd admitted her to his room and fixed her a bourbon and water, the drink he knew she preferred.

"What is it, Jane?"

"That man...the French one in the Bamboo."

"Ramonne?"

"Yes. That's him...who is he?"

Thompson fixed himself a gin and tonic.

"I don't know. As you said, he's French. Been here a while. Why?'

"He gives me the creeps."

He smiled. "The *creeps*? What do you mean?"

"I was there tonight. With Johnny Wester and Alex Mac-Donald. He greeted them by name. Neither of them had ever met him."

Thompson mulled this. "He does that, yes. I assume it's his business. He keeps tabs on who's who."

"No...it was more than that. He knew me, too."

"Yes. He does. We were there together. Two weeks ago."

"No, James. He *knew* me. Knew things about me. Things I don't tell."

"What do you mean?"

"I can't quite explain it. It's a feeling. He looked at me, and I swear, I blushed like a schoolgirl."

Thompson laughed. "You...? Never."

She punched him in the arm. Hard. He winced.

"I'm serious, James. He took me aside and asked me how the *quest* was going."

"The 'quest'?"

"That's the word he used. I feigned ignorance but, I swear, he started talking about the Oracle.

He tried to look shocked. "That's absurd."

"That's what I thought…but then he winked at me."

"He winked?"

"He winked."

Thompson vowed to have a few stern words with Ramonne. There seemed to be a few things about 'our secret' that he hadn't quite understood.

"I was so flustered, I faked a headache, begged out on Alex and Johnny, and left."

Thompson finished his drink and put it down on the dresser. Jane had made her own refill and was now sipping while seated on his massive antique Chinese wedding bed. It was elaborately carved and had a full canopy.

"So…that's why you came here."

She smiled over the top of her drink. Her bangs fell over her hazel eyes. "Well…not the only reason."

"What? What did I do?"

"You scared her, that's what you did. What I told you was in confidence."

"But she was the one who told you about the Oracle. I don't see why I couldn't talk about it with her."

Thompson was beside himself. It was all he could do to keep from hitting the little 'Frog.' Of course, he thought better about that. 'Frog' Ramonne might be, due to birth, but he wasn't little and Thompson had no idea how a physical challenge to him would turn out.

They were at the Sani Château, an after-hours club suggested by Ramonne when Thompson said they needed to talk. Why Ramonne couldn't meet in the afternoon like normal people, he had no idea. Thompson supposed it had to do with the hours Ramonne kept in running the bar. He was definitely a nighthawk.

The Sani Château was virtually deserted. Ramonne had typically ordered a bottle of their only wine, and Thompson had a gin rocks. Ramonne had started to tell Thompson about the brilliant chanteuse he had discovered, Lady Marmalade or something like that. Thompson had no patience and got right to his point.

"Look, the whole point of the OSS is that it's a secret organization. By the way, how did you know Johnny Wester and Alex MacDonald?"

"I didn't," Ramonne lied. "Lady Jane introduced them."

Thompson studied the Frenchman. No tic, no sideward glance. Nothing to indicate he was lying. Maybe Jane was wrong about that. He let it slide.

"Anyway, we can't go around blabbing about this so-called Oracle. As you well know, it's being sought by some very dangerous characters."

Ramonne shrugged. *Not so dangerous.* He'd already killed three of them without exertion. "That is open to debate."

"I beg your pardon? They shot at me. They attempted to kidnap me. If you hadn't been there—"

"Ahh, but I was. By the way, do you know General Natiwat of the Bangkok police?'

"No, why?"

Ramonne decided he'd keep the general his secret. "No reason. Just curiosity."

Thompson shook his head. "I like you, Delacroix. I really do —but you're a very odd fellow."

Ramonne had no reaction to this.

"Look, I appreciate your interest in this…*case*, but we—the OSS, that is—are handling it. By their allegiance to the Japanese, these Black Dragons are international criminals. The OSS, MI6, the Thai police and the US Army are all searching for them."

"I wouldn't be so sure about the Thai police."

"What? Why would you say that?"

"No reason." Ramonne leaned across the low table they were sharing. "Do you want to know where their headquarters is?" he whispered.

Shocked, Thompson shouted his reply. "What? How do you know—"

"Shhh," Ramonne cut him off with his finger to his lips. "Hush hush."

Thompson lowered his voice. "How in hell do you know where the Black Dragons are?"

"I stumbled across them. It's not far."

Thompson sat back in his chair. "Jesus, man...when were you going to tell me this?"

"Tonight. I thought I'd surprise you."

Thompson shook his head again. "Ramonne, this is not a game."

"I know that, Lord Jim. I would have told Miss Farmer, but she left the bar unexpectedly."

"Thank God you didn't. Look, you tell me where this place is, and then you forget about it. All right...? You forget about this whole thing that you think you're involved in."

"Oh, I'm involved. That I assure you."

"You're involved because you helped me. You bounced your stick off a few bad apples—and I thank you for that. But that doesn't mean you're involved. Giving me the directions to these Black Dragons will be helpful. We'll organize a proper military operation. We'll storm the gates, as it were, arrest these hooligans, and hopefully we'll learn where this Oracle is, and that'll be that."

Ramonne smiled.

"They don't have it, Lord Jim. You told me that yourself."

"They may have found it by now."

"They haven't."

"How can you be so sure?"

Because I have it.

"They told me."

"They *told* you?"

"Yes."

"What the hell are you talking about?"

"I asked them why they wanted to bother you? Then I talked to Hashimoto—"

"He gave you his name?"

"Yes. He said that he wanted to ask you about the Oracle."

"The Oracle?"

"Precisely. That's what I said."

"You spoke about the Oracle with them?"

"Yes, why not?"

Thompson ordered another drink.

"No reason…but I'm quite surprised you walked away from them."

"Hashimoto was, too."

"What do you mean?"

"Never mind. I told him not to bother you anymore. That you knew nothing about the Oracle."

"Really? You said that?"

"Of course."

"And then?"

"Then he got quite indignant. Used rude language, threatened me. Etcetera, etcetera."

"Jesus, what did you do?"

Ramonne leaned in again and whispered.

"I killed him."

———

Roluos, Present Day.

The light of the setting sun danced off a solitary, slender thread spun by a spider between the pepper mill and the salt shaker atop the wrought-iron table.

He studied it, tilting his head right and left to determine its course. Tiny sparrows flitted on the evening breeze, bouncing between the stone ramparts of the villa's outbuildings and the jacaranda trees. A dark, finger-shaped cloud cut the setting sun mid-way, and its edges glowed like a halo. The light that had for the last hour illuminated the vines from the rear, allowing them their iridescent glow, was turned off, as if by the flick of a switch. A bell tolled in a distant church tower. A legacy of the French occupation so long ago.

Ramonne sighed.

The last sunset.

He was robed in thick black cloth, a hood atop his head. Dark, almost opaque sunglasses shielded his eyes.

He had only dared to venture a few paces from the shelter of the villa, and only just as the sun had begun to set. He'd extended his left hand into the waning light and immediately felt the searing heat. He withdrew it into the folds of the robe. He knew that if he had left it for a few seconds longer it would have gone ablaze.

When the darkness of night replaced the light of day, he removed the dark glasses. His eyes were yellow orbs that shone like a cat's.

He sighed again.

His fate was inevitable. The die had been cast irrevocably over a century and a half before. He'd been given only a slight reprieve, granted, he was aware, as a token for his resuscitation of the boy. And then recanted, he was certain, for his betrayal and murder of his beloved Kanchana.

He sighed again and pulled the hood from his head. He unfastened the robe and let it slide to the ground. He arched his head back and let loose with a piercing cry. The howl echoed for miles around and brought a shudder to the soul of each who heard it.

He abruptly stopped. Then strode swiftly, boldly into the night.

The hunter.

In search of his prey.

19

———

Bangkok, Present Day

"Mr. Larue. How good to see you. I trust you are well?"

Kurt Wachtveitl stood to greet Martin. He was tall and trim, with gray hair and a warm smile that lit up his handsome, tanned face. Although he was officially retired, he was dressed immaculately in a charcoal gray Italian suit. He was seated at his personal table in Le Normandie, the gourmet restaurant whose renovation was one of his first projects in 1967 upon the start of his long-running tenure as general manager of the Oriental Hotel.

"I'm well, Kurt, thank you. May I say, you look very fit." Martin was suitably attired in a lightweight suit that he recalled wearing only once before. He took the outstretched hand and received a strong, firm handshake.

"I have time now to indulge myself," Kurt replied. "I've always loved tennis, and now I play almost daily." He motioned and a white-jacketed waiter uncorked the bottle of young Mosel Riesling that had been cooling in a silver bucket to his right. The waiter poured a small amount into Martin's glass for him to taste. Martin sipped it.

"Wonderful."

Their glasses were poured and Kurt raised his.

"*Chok dii*." They clinked their glasses and drank.

Kurt put his glass down and leaned back in his chair. "So tell me, old friend, what can I do for you?"

"I have some questions about the hotel's past. I can't think of anyone else who knows more about this place than you."

"I started here in '67. Before you were born. Correct?"

Martin nodded.

"I arrived in '65. But immediately it was home. It was as if I'd lived a previous life here. You can't imagine what it was like." He looked out the window to the river below. "A lifetime devoted to the serious business of giving pleasure to others."

He turned back to Martin. "Makes me sound like an old harlot, doesn't it?"

Martin smiled. "My questions go back to long before even you came here." He took an envelope from his jacket. It bore a *Bangkok Times* logo and the single word 'Archives' was stamped in red below the newspaper's name. He extracted a copy of the same ancient photograph that Muraki had shown him. Kurt smiled as he studied it.

"Do you know these people?" Martin asked.

"Germaine Krull." He tapped a finger on the handsome woman to the right of Jim Thompson. "I knew her quite well. She had my job long ago. A fascinating creature. Sophisticated, debonair, and yet she took the naughtiest photographs." He looked up at Martin. "I collected some of her prints. I should show them to you."

He moved his finger slowly across the photograph. "Jim Thompson I only met once. Shortly after I took over and right before he disappeared in 1967. He was interested in doing a renovation of the Tower Wing. We had lunch." Again, he looked up at Martin. "He had a cockatoo that sat on his shoulder and went everywhere with him. A huge white bird that would raise a shock of orange on top of its head and whistle at you." He smiled at the memory. "As you are no doubt aware, he and Miss Krull were responsible for saving and restoring the hotel after the war."

Martin nodded and then pointed to Ramonne. "What about this man?"

"I never met him, but I know who he is. I've forgotten the name, but he was French. He was with the Bamboo Bar at the start. As I understand it, he booked the music and was a sort of host. Legend has it that he suffered a tragic early demise."

"What happened?"

"I don't know the details, but apparently somebody tried to kill Jim Thompson—something to do with his OSS involvement."

"In the Second World War?"

"Yes. This was 1948, I believe. Or '49. Anyway, a Japanese gang had been stalking former OSS agents. They killed some, I believe, and they were after Thompson."

"A Japanese *gang*? Yakuza?" Martin could hardly conceal his eagerness to hear more.

"Affiliated, no doubt, with the Yakuza. Anything nefarious in Japan would seem to be. But these were called..." He thought for a moment. "I believe it was the Black Dragons."

The waiter refilled their glasses and Kurt paused to enjoy the wine. As he did, another waiter set a bowl of light-green soup in front of each of them.

"I have ordered for us, by the way. Steamed turbot. They make it with ginger and soy sauce. Divine. But if you like, you can see the menu."

Martin smiled. "Not necessary at all. I trust and value your judgment. Thank you." Martin picked up his spoon and tasted the soup. "This is fantastic."

"Spinach velvet soup. One of my favorites." He sipped his wine without tasting the soup. "Now, where was I?"

"The Black Dragons," Martin offered.

"Ah, yes. They were apparently on some sort of vendetta,

terrorizing Bangkok when they cornered Jim Thompson. This fellow..." He tapped Ramonne's picture. "He saved Jim, but was killed in the process."

"Do you know what happened?"

"No, I'm afraid all I know is what I've told you. And that was only gleaned after many nights in the Bamboo with Khun Ling, a bartender who was a bellboy back then."

"Is Khun Ling still the bartender?"

"No. He retired ten years ago, and passed away last year. I went to his funeral."

Kurt looked out the window again. "When he retired it was due to his ill health. He didn't want to go. He told me he couldn't have imagined any other life than the one he lived." He turned back to Martin. "I feel that way, too, Martin. I can't imagine any other life than the one I lived here.

"Today human beings have become machines. That's why young people are leaving the industry. Perhaps one day we will teach robots to smile and say, *have a good day*."

As Martin listened to the grand master of the Oriental reflect upon the past and expound on the present, he couldn't help but be reminded of the similar tales and philosophy that he'd given a rapt ear too less than eight years ago in this very hotel. On only their second encounter Ramonne had given Martin a tour of the Oriental, and he now knew why the vampire was so intimately versed in the legend and lore of the place.

He needed to know how the vampire met his supposed demise in 1949.

The first of his many demises.

———

Bangkok, 1949

"There it is."

The warehouse loomed ominously in the moonlight. It had

been time-consuming finding the building on ground level. More than once Ramonne had almost told the driver to stop, so he could leap to the rooftops and ascertain their true position. He and Thompson were in a saloon car with Lady Jane and a very large, ginger-haired OSS officer known only as 'Babe' at the wheel.

Thompson had insisted on calling Lady Jane and telling her about Ramonne's discovery. She, in turn, insisted they check the warehouse immediately. Thompson suggested they contact the Army but Jane said they'd go it alone. "If there's any danger, we'll call for them. But let's see for ourselves, before we get anyone else involved." And so, against Thompson's better judgment, the four of them proceeded to search for the warehouse. Babe had the forethought to bring four .45-caliber pistols. This meant that now there was an extra gun in Babe's jacket pocket, as Ramonne refused the offer to bear arms.

Babe pulled the car into a loading dock and shut it off. They sat in the shadows for a few minutes in silence, just watching. Except for a few stray *soi* dogs that scampered by, nothing moved. Ramonne started to get out of the car. Babe reached over and stopped him.

"You stay put," he whispered, and pulled the pistol's slide back and chambered a round. It made a distinctive metallic *click*. Ramonne raised an eyebrow at the sound. The big man slipped silently out of the car. Two more *clicks* sounded in the back seat and then the rear doors opened and Thompson and Jane stepped out. Ramonne started to open his door again, but Jane held it shut. She put a finger to her lips and shook her head.

"Stay here, Monsieur Delacroix. This is a job for professionals." She patted his arm. "Wouldn't want you to get all dirty, would we?"

Ramonne sighed, crossed his arms, leaned back and watched as the three musketeers approached the warehouse.

Mortals. Such fools.

The first door they came to, the street entry, was locked. Chained and padlocked.

"They're gone," Jane whispered.

"Not necessarily." Babe held his pistol in front of them and motioned for them to follow him.

They rounded the corner and were faced with a cinderblock wall running at least a hundred meters, seemingly without a single entry point. But a fire-escape ladder was situated about twenty meters away from where they stood. Babe motioned them forward.

He jumped up and pulled on the ladder. It didn't move.

"Damn." He dropped back to the ground. "It's locked at the top."

"Boost me up." Jane was stashing her pistol in the back of her pants. She was wearing the military outfit that Thompson had seen her wear at the wharf when they became re-acquainted.

"Jane, don't be foolish," he hissed.

"He's not going to lift the likes of you up there. Come on, Babe, give me a boost."

Babe linked his fingers together, and Jane put a toe of her riding boots into his palms and grasped his shoulder. He lifted her to the ladder with relative ease. He hefted her to where she could grab the third rung and pull her legs up. She started climbing and was soon on the landing.

"Unlatch it and drop it to us," Babe said in a loud whisper.

Jane checked the ladder and found it was padlocked in place.

"No good." She pulled her pistol from her waistband and started across the landing.

"Jane. Don't be foolish," Thompson admonished louder, but she was already at the metal door. She tried the handle. It turned and the door came toward her as she pulled.

"It's open."

"Jane. Stop. Wait—"

Rubber Johnny Jane went through the door, her pistol extended in front of her.

Thompson was visibly agitated, and leaned back against the building, his hands on his knees, looking up at the ladder. He shook his head.

"Relax," Babe attempted to reassure him. "It's empty."

Then a shot rang out from inside the warehouse.

"Jane!" Thompson shouted.

Another shot echoed from within the walls, followed by muffled shouts. Thompson stood erect and racked his pistol.

"Come on." He went charging down the narrow alley that ran along the side of the massive warehouse. Babe quickly followed. As they ran, there were more shots and yells from inside.

"Jesus Christ." Thompson slid on some wet leaves and slammed into a chain-link fence.

"Locked, of course." Babe rattled the padlock. The three-meter high fence was topped by barbed wire.

"Here." Babe started climbing the fence and then grabbed for a low-hanging branch of a tree that was wedged into the corner. Its roots and vines were intertwined with the rusty fence. He managed to pull himself up onto a bough of the tree. He extended his hand for Thompson and pulled him up alongside him. Babe reached for a branch on the far side and swung to the ground. Thompson followed.

They found themselves on the river, straddling a rickety pier. To their right the warehouse doors were flung wide open and a long wooden chute ran down to the water.

"It's an ice factory," Thompson noted.

"It *was*," Babe countered. The chute and what they could see of the darkened interior showed no sign of life or activity. It appeared deserted, abandoned.

"I know this place." Babe flattened himself against the building, his pistol extended before him. He inched his way toward the opening. Thompson was right behind him.

"Be caref—" Thompson was cut off as a bullet pinged off the wall, inches from his head. He turned in the direction of the shot. Two men were in a small boat. One was casting off a line while the other was taking shots at them.

"Babe. Get down." Thompson dived behind some rusted barrels, quickly followed by Babe.

Shots hit the barrels, which were fortunately full of rainwater. The water stopped the bullets. Babe crept to the edge of the barrels and returned fire. He got off three shots before diving back for cover. "They've got Jane," he shouted.

"What?"

Thompson stuck his head up and was able to make out a figure lying in the boat just below the gunwales. The engine started with a roar and the boat headed away from the pier.

Thompson shouted, "Jane!" and fired at the departing craft.

Babe pulled Thompson's arm down. "No. You could hit her."

They both ducked down as two more rounds smashed into the barrels. They stayed down and listened to the boat leave the dock. When there was no more gunfire, they stood up.

The boat was heading downriver. The two men stood watching with their guns still pointed in front of them. The wake from the departing craft lapped up on the old ice chute as the boat slipped away on the Chao Phraya.

First Babe and then Thompson lowered their pistols.

"That went well."

The voice came from above them. They both instinctively raised their pistols. They looked up to see Ramonne standing on the roof of the warehouse.

———

"During the war the Japs used this as storage for their booty." Babe spoke softly as he followed Thompson into the cavernous warehouse. It was humid, musty and empty. Thompson had a flashlight, but it barely lit any of the interior. Fortunately there were dirty panels of glass above the massive riverside entrance, and there was still sufficient moonlight reflecting off the river to be able to make out some details.

"I was right out there." Babe pointed to the river. "With a group of Thai resistance, disguised as fishermen. We watched as crate after crate was loaded under armed guard onto a 'hospital' ship."

Thompson and Babe still had their pistols in hand as they cautiously moved through the factory.

"Some hospital ship. We found four more of them… freighters painted white and covered with red crosses. They went unmolested to Tokyo loaded with looted gold and antiquities."

Babe lit a cigarette, offering one to Thompson, who declined.

"The most important thing about war isn't how much you conquer. It's how much you steal. Gold, paintings, cultural treasures. Six thousand tons of bullion looted from Nanking alone."

Two huge refrigeration compressors stood idle alongside one of the walls. Miles of pipe and rusted ducts ran everywhere. Numbers were stenciled in rows on each wall, stretching to the center of the building. Scissor-type tongs were hung from suspended poles and there were large, thick-slatted workbenches lined in rows near the center.

"With the surrender we finally saw the inside of this place. The Japs were long gone by then. There were huge cauldrons and furnaces right here." He pointed at the open area before the workbenches. "We found molds for 75-kilo bars. They were cutting up golden pagodas and Buddhas and melting them down. What they couldn't get out of the port was probably dumped in the river."

Beyond them, a wooden wall divided the room. It had a metal staircase running up to a second floor. The second floor had windows that had been papered over with oil cloth. A light went on and the papers glowed with an amber hue. A door opened and Ramonne appeared. He leaned on the rail and looked down on the two men.

"That is where they dismembered the two that I dispatched in their botched kidnapping of Lord Jim."

Thompson and Babe looked at the workbenches.

"They were doing *what*?" Babe stared up in disbelief at the Frenchman.

"They were cutting up the bodies. I imagine they threw them in the sea."

Thompson shone his torch on the bench in front of him. The light played over what appeared to be dried bloodstains on the thick wooden slab.

"Blood," Ramonne remarked.

"Maybe." Babe studied the stains.

"It's blood. Take my word for it."

Ramonne motioned to the open door behind him.

"Gentlemen. Join me."

He went back through the door, and Thompson and Babe climbed the stairs. They found Ramonne in a large, vacant office. It had been stripped of its 'gentlemen's club' furnishings and all that remained was the metal desk and two filing cabinets. A half-full bottle of Dewar's Scotch sat alone on a shelf on the back wall.

"This is where I had my little chat with Hashimoto-*san*."

"Who?" Babe scowled as he sniffed the whisky bottle.

"Akira Hashimoto. The apparent leader of this little group of Black Dragons."

Babe bristled. "Black Dragons? What makes you think these men were associated with them?"

"Lord Jim told me they were. And Hashimoto admitted that they were seeking the Oracle."

Now Babe was astonished. He stared at Ramonne in open-jawed shock. "*The Oracle*. What do you know about the Oracle?"

Thompson stepped between the two men. "He knows nothing. Only that there supposedly is such a thing and that the Black Dragons are after it. Apparently they think I have it or know of its whereabouts."

"Do you?"

"Do I *what*?"

"Have it, man. Do you have the Oracle?"

"Of course not. Do you think I'd know if I'd found it? I know where it *was*. That's all."

Thompson turned his attention to the desk. He opened the drawers. *Empty.* He slid them all the way out and reached his hand in to the rear to make sure there was nothing in them.

Babe was beginning to perspire. He moved to a window and forced it open. It hardly made a difference. A faint draft came through. He used the Dewar's bottle to wedge it open.

"Your little *chat* with this Hashimoto...what did he tell you?" Babe stood by the window.

"Very little. I told him that they should leave Jim alone." Ramonne remained near the door.

Babe grinned. "You told a Black Dragon to leave Jim alone?"

"Yes."

"And what was his reaction?"

"He shot at me."

"He shot at you?"

"Yes."

"And?"

"*And*?"

"What happened?"

"He missed...and I killed him."

Babe had to sit down. He landed on the desk, as it was the only surface available. Thompson was going through the filing cabinets, but stopped and looked at Ramonne.

Babe turned to Thompson. "Were you aware of this? I don't recall it in your report. In fact I don't recall the mention of any dead Japanese."

Thompson shook his head. "He told me tonight. Right before I called Miss Farmer."

Babe had a handkerchief, and wiped the back of his neck. He looked at Ramonne. "Did this Hasha..." Babe couldn't remember the name.

"Hashimoto. Akira Hashimoto."

"Hashimoto. Did he happen to tell you anything else before you...before you killed him?"

"No."

Thompson opened the last filing-cabinet drawer.

Babe looked away from Ramonne. "Find anything?" he asked hopefully.

Thompson shook his head. "Nothing."

Before closing the drawer, he returned to the top of the cabinet and pulled the first drawer all the way out. He extracted it and dropped it on the floor. He did this with all the drawers until the cabinet was empty. On the bottom, inside the frame of the cabinet, was a lone scrap of light-green paper. He lifted it out gently.

"What is it?"

"A receipt." The paper was torn and only the amount—26 baht—was legible. He shone his flashlight through the back of the paper and a watermark appeared.

"What is it?"

"I don't know. But there aren't that many printers who do watermarks. It should be traceable."

"Good. Rubber Johnny Jane's a royal pain in the ass, but she deserves to be rescued." Babe pushed himself off the metal desk and stood. It took some effort. "We'll get the Army to send a forensics unit in." He looked around the room. "Cheeky bastards to set up here. I suppose they thought it was the last place we'd look for them." He moved to the window.

"They were right." He took the Dewar's bottle from the window and it slid closed. Bottle in hand, he moved to the door. "The boat was riding quite low in the water. It was heavily loaded. I suspect we got here just as they were abandoning this place. I don't know how much you saw from the roof, but did you recognize the men in the boat?"

"They were the two doing the dismembering." Ramonne decided there was no need to mention seeing them in the company of General Natiwat.

"Good. We'll count on you to help us find them."

"It will be my pleasure." Ramonne smiled and held the door for him.

"I suspect we'll be hearing from them," Thompson offered. "We've got something they want, and they *think* we have something of theirs."

Thompson picked his pistol up off the desk and followed Babe and Ramonne out the door.

"How *did* you get onto the roof?" he heard Babe ask Ramonne.

20

Roluos, Present Day

"Professor!"

Dr Kaestle *heard* the call long before his ears did. He hurried from the house, dropping and breaking a nineteenth-century crystal decanter.

Outside, the night was still, as quiet as a churchyard. Funny metaphor, he thought. There was a faint breeze but the rustling in the vineyard was barely audible.

"Come. There is no time to lose."

The master was suddenly walking in front of him, heading back for the house. *Where did he come from?* Dr. Kaestle hurried to catch up with him.

"Master? What is it? What's wrong?"

"We need to leave. Now."

"Leave? I don't understand."

Ramonne was already inside the villa. He took the keys to the van off their hook and tossed them to the professor. "Start the car. Move it around to the back. I'll meet you there."

Dr. Kaestle caught the keys. He stood in the doorway, staring at the master's departing figure.

"Go!" Ramonne commanded, and the professor jumped, dropping the keys. He picked them up and then hurried out to the car.

———

In the few minutes that it took the professor to start the van and maneuver it around to the rear of the villa, Ramonne had, alone, dragged his own coffin up the steep cellar stairs and onto the driveway. Dr. Kaestle got out and opened the rear door to the van. Ramonne reappeared with a small valise that he tossed into the van.

"Our papers. We'll need them at the border."

"The border? Why are we go—"

"Help me." Ramonne began hoisting the massive casket into the rear of the van. "Guide it in," he barked, and the professor took one end while Ramonne lifted the other and started to push. Its small pedestals caught on the van's bed for a moment but then gave way to Ramonne's brute force. Once it was in the van, Ramonne slammed the doors.

Dr. Kaestle stood looking blankly at the villa. Both the front and rear doors were wide open and a number of lights were ablaze within. He didn't know what to do.

Ramonne was already in the passenger seat. "Professor!"

Dr. Kaestle snapped at the shout.

As they pulled through the gate of the villa, the professor saw at least a dozen headlights coming towards the house from the west.

They headed east.

Two hours later, they were almost at Poipet. Dr. Kaestle felt it was appropriate that the name of the miserable border town rhymed with 'toilet.' He had been there less than two months before, when he arrived to escort the lady Kanchana to the villa. That was the first time he had driven on the newly completed highway between Siem Reap and Poipet. It was a slick, unblemished miracle. When he and the master had arrived four years prior, the road had been a nightmare. Then it was mainly dirt, with holes that could swallow a saloon car. The slightest rain and it turned into a swamp. Trucks would get bogged down and cause traffic jams that backed up for kilometers, blocking the road for hours. Hardly anyone dared make the journey at night.

But tonight Dr. Kaestle had been able to average almost 100 kilometers per hour. He had to. The master wouldn't allow him to let up for any reason. He was terrified during the entire journey.

As for the reason for their rapid departure, the master had said little. Only that he had made a mistake. He alluded to being 'out of practice,' which the professor thought was an odd thing to say for a vampire, but he stayed silent and concentrated on driving as fast as the vehicle would go.

Mercifully they finally had to slow down as they entered the dusty town. Garish neon Christmas trees lined a road that led to a three-story casino. The casino, one of many, contrasted sharply with the squalor that was the border town itself. As the road into town reverted to packed clay, swarms of young beggar children gathered about the van. The only vehicles present were parked outside the border gate—mostly long-distance trucks, their drivers asleep in the cabs. The huge gate was decorated with Khmer-style pagodas. As the professor expected, it was closed for the night.

"Master. It is as I said. The border shuts at eight o'clock."

Ramonne was seated in the passenger seat, his eyes fixated, as they had been throughout the entire journey, on the rear-view mirror. Two small boys were trying to get his attention A little girl began to soap his window. He scowled at them and they scampered away.

"Proceed."

"But, it's closed."

Ramonne looked at the professor. His glare left no question as to what he wanted done.

Dr. Kaestle pulled the van up to the gate.

No one paid them any notice, except for another group of street urchins, who crowded around the van.

"Use your horn."

"Master, I don't think we should—"

Ramonne reached across the wheel and leaned on the horn. Its blast sent the urchins running, but seemed to have no other discernible effect.

"Master, please…We should wait."

"We can't wait." He blew the horn again.

A light went on in a guard shack. Ramonne released the horn, and in a few moments the door opened. A guard tucked in his shirt, zipped his fly and put on his hat. He didn't look happy. The professor slouched down in the driver's seat and tried to become invisible.

"We are closed. Can't you read?" The guard jerked a thumb to a faded sign that gave the opening hours in Khmer, Thai and English. The hours in English were listed as "07:00 a.m. to 19:00 a.m." Apparently there was no p.m. in Poipet.

Ramonne spoke: "We need to pass now."

The professor slunk even further into his seat. As if to make sure there was no doubt as to who had spoken, he nervously pointed his finger at Ramonne and tried to smile.

The guard took out a crumpled pack of Golden Goat cigarettes. He struck a wooden match on the side of the tin shack, lit up and inhaled deeply. As he smoked, he slowly walked around the van to the passenger side. Ramonne lowered the window. The guard studied Ramonne. Ramonne, in turn, studied the guard.

After a moment, the guard blew a small stream of pungent smoke out of the side of his mouth. He jerked a thumb back toward the line of trucks, trailers and buses. "You see those?"

Ramonne looked over his shoulder.

"They are waiting for the border to open." The guard put his hands on the window and leaned his weight on the van. "What makes you any different from them?"

Ramonne smiled and reached into the valise that sat between him and the professor. He opened it and extracted a thick wad of banknotes. As it caught the light, it was apparent that this was a stack of US 100-dollar bills. It was wrapped with a thick elastic band. Ramonne counted out ten of the bills and slipped them from the binding. He handed them to the now wide-eyed border guard.

One thousand US dollars. Over four million Cambodian riel. He would literally need a wheelbarrow to carry it in local currency.

The guard promptly stuffed the wad of bills in his shirt pocket. "Your papers—quickly." He held his outstretched hand while looking nervously around.

Ramonne handed him their passports. The guard disappeared into the shack. Shortly, the distinct sound of a rubber stamp being zealously put to work could be heard. The guard re-emerged with the passports and a large ring of keys. He walked to the passenger window and handed the passports to Ramonne.

"The Thai border is also closed. However, I made a phone call. My counterpart is expecting you."

Ramonne took the passports and smiled. "I'm sure he is."

The guard turned to leave.

"One moment, Heng."

The guard stopped. "How do you know my name?" As he turned to Ramonne, he felt a force wash over him. He froze in his tracks.

"Haven't you forgotten something?"

Heng opened his shirt pocket and extracted the American money. Without hesitation, he handed it back to the vampire.

"Thank you, Heng. That will be all."

Heng snapped his boot heels together and saluted. Ramonne

raised his hands in a slight *wai* and the professor moved the van across the border.

The same exercise was repeated at the Thai border post, and within twenty minutes the van was speeding away from the town of Aranyaprathet on the Thai side, on the road to Bangkok. Ramonne took his eyes from the rear-view mirror and relaxed.

About forty kilometers outside of Bangkok, the sky began to lighten. The professor stopped the van and Ramonne climbed into the silk comfort of his coffin and went to sleep.

———

Bangkok, Present Day

"Martin…? I hope I didn't wake you."

Martin fumbled for the clock. *Six thirty!*

"No," he lied. "Who is this?"

"It's Kurt. I'd call later but I'm leaving for Germany this morning and I thought that you might want to talk with Babe."

Martin sat up in the bed and stretched. He covered his mouth to suppress a yawn. "Who is Babe?"

"A very old man…But he knew Jim Thompson. He was with him in the OSS."

Martin opened a drawer and took out a small notepad and a pen.

"How do I find him?"

"Call Khun Suzie at the hotel. She still has my Rolodex."

"What's the name?"

"Babe…just Babe. That's all I know."

"Thank you. Thank you very much…Have a safe trip."

Martin put down the phone and went back to sleep.

———

The Foreign Correspondents' Club was located on the top floor of the Maneeya Center on Ploenchit Road. The area, known as Ratchaprasong, is classier than the street market of Sukhumvit, just to the east. It is what Orchard Road is to Singapore, Knightsbridge to London: Glitzy shopping malls, five-star hotels and the clientele that patronize them. Elevated walkways connect the shops, hotels and skytrain for three long blocks. The Maneeya Center was a showcase when it opened in 1988. Seventeen floors made it a skyscraper. Now it was a dwarf in its surroundings and had a 'doomed' atmosphere

Martin stepped off the elevator and into the vacant marble lobby. A bust of Jorges Orgibet, one of the club's founders, greeted arriving visitors. A paneled wall outside the club was covered with faded color photographs of members, guests and events, the Dalai Lama and the ousted premier Thaksin Shinawatra taking up the most space. Martin pushed open the glass doors and entered the club's bar. It being early afternoon, it was deserted. If he had waited a few hours, the place would be packed, as it was most evenings, with journalists stationed in the area or on assignment, writers who had settled in the city, and expats who enjoyed the conversational opportunities provided by this motley group of intellectual alcoholics. The long narrow room was equally divided between bar and dining area. The end of the room was a stage with a curtain and podium for the guest speakers and events the club held throughout the year.

Martin said hello to Tony, the bartender, who was in his usual attire—white shirt, black vest and bow tie.

"Your friend is on the patio, Khun Martin."

Martin nodded and went to the glass door to the narrow patio-cum-balcony that ran alongside the club's dining room and bar. Outside, an Asian woman of indeterminate age was standing at the rail. "Khun Martin?"

"Yes." They exchanged *wais*.

"Khun Babe is here." She gestured to the left, and Martin

followed her to a table where an elderly man sat contentedly puffing a cigar.

The man was facing away from Martin, who saw only the back of his head of pure-white hair, close-cropped and flat as a ruler on top. The head drooped forward slightly. It didn't move as Martin walked around the table and extended his hand in greeting.

"I'm Martin Larue."

The man made no move to take Martin's hand. He continued puffing on the huge cigar while studying Martin with what seemed to be his one good eye. The other was clouded over and seemed devoid of a pupil.

"Of course you are."

The face was creased and worn. The man wore a safari-type shirt that hung on his bony, leathery frame as if it were meant for a man twice his size. Great giblets of skin gathered in folds and fell from his neck.

Martin withdrew his hand and looked to the woman. She indicated that he should sit down. He did. She continued to stand.

There was a bottle of white wine in a bucket next to a large potted banana tree that shaded the table. The woman motioned to the wine. "Would you like a glass?"

"Yes, thank you."

As she took the green bottle from the bucket, Martin noticed another one chilling behind it.

The old man raised his glass in toast. "John Huston's one great regret before he passed away was that he wished he'd drunk more wine and less whisky...So do I." The old man smiled as he said this. Martin liked the smile. It reminded him of Mick Jagger. All wrinkles, lips and teeth.

"Mister—" Martin realized he didn't know the old man's name.

"Babe." He sucked on the cigar as he said it.

"Babe...An unusual name. I take it it's a nickname?"

"Of course. My father was a Yankee fan." The old man took a sip of his wine and studied Martin. "I know what you're thinking. Don't ask. I'm not telling you my name. I've lived in this town for over sixty years as just plain Babe. Nobody asks anymore. They just don't."

Martin sipped his wine. *Not as good as Kurt's Riesling, but not cheap either.*

"I don't need to know your name, sir, but I do want to ask you a few questions."

"Let me guess. You're writing a book about Jim Thompson's disappearance." The cigar went back in and the old man gloated.

"No. I'm not writing a book, and my questions aren't about his disappearance."

The old man raised a bushy eyebrow. "Good. I finished talking about the Cameron Highlands twenty years ago."

"I want to know what happened in 1948."

"*Forty-eight?*" He laughed. The laughter turned to coughing. The woman handed him a glass of water. He waved it off and took another sip of the wine. In a moment the hacking ceased. He wiped his mouth with his napkin.

"That was a very long time ago."

"I realize that. But I believe you and Mr. Thompson were acquaintances then."

"Acquaintances?" He smiled his Jagger smile again. "That's one way of putting it." He put the wine down as a waitress set a plate before him. A cheeseburger with French fries. He put his cigar aside without snuffing it out. The woman opened a bottle of ketchup and handed it to him.

"Sorry. They know me here. I don't mean to be rude, but they bring this to me whether I order it or not…Would you like to see the menu?" He smothered the burger with the ketchup and made a small pile of it next to the fries.

"I know the menu here. You've chosen well. I'll join you."

The old man motioned and the woman started for the bar.

"He has his blood rare," she said. "I assume you want yours cooked?"

"Medium rare, please." Martin figured the old man had ordered wisely, for all cooks in Thailand tended to overcook any Western meat dish.

The old man cut his burger in half and took a healthy bite.

"Ahh. Perfection."

Martin sipped his wine and tipped his chair back while the old man ate. It took about three minutes and he was finished with the burger. He hadn't touched the fries. He wiped his face clean, took his wine and his cigar and also leaned back.

"Once a week, Mr. Larue, I must have the epitome of American cuisine—the lowly hamburger. Not a *teriyaki* hamburger, no fried egg on top, no chili peppers, black beans or bacon. Just a nice hunk of ground beef thrown on a grill and topped with a thin slice of cheese."

Martin waited until the old man seemed content before he raised the question again. "You and Jim Thompson...1948? What happened?"

The old man sucked at his cigar. He studied Martin for a few moments. Finally he took the cigar out of his mouth and tapped it in the ashtray.

"You've heard of the OSS?"

"Yes. Of course. The Office of Strategic Services."

"Nice name, ain't it? Makes one seem right respectable." He took a single French fry and dipped it in ketchup. "Fact is, we were taught to lie, steal, kill, maim, spy, deceive, terrify and destroy. It was the Ten Commandments in reverse." He dangled the fry over his mouth and then slowly chewed it.

"We came from everywhere. Wall Street, Harvard, Yale. Liberal and conservative. Some were veterans who'd fought in Spain and the European theater. Mostly we were a bunch of adventurous, upper-class types. We shared one thing in common—our boyish enthusiasm for excitement." Another fry was dragged through the ketchup and consumed.

"I first came here in late 1944. I came in from Ceylon on a British submarine. It was a hellacious voyage. The weather was absolutely miserable, forcing us to stay submerged off the Thai coast for over a week. It was hot and it stank. Finally we got a break in the weather and two of us slipped into harbor in a rubber dinghy.

"There were a few others already in place. Scattered about the country. We infiltrated deep behind Japanese lines and our government allowed us free reign to carry out our operations, but we were totally dependent on our brothers in the Free Thai movement. We were a year away, at least, from the possibility of an Allied invasion. Our mission's top priority was to prepare the Thai army to fight the Japanese. To that end we were to win the hearts and minds of the Thai people and eventually take over the leadership of their resistance movement."

The old man started coughing and the woman handed him the glass of water. He gulped it down and reached for the cigar, which had gone out. She lit it for him and he puffed until he had a mouthful of smoke, which he slowly hissed out.

"That's better." He took a slug of wine and continued. "As more and more men and supplies parachuted into the jungle, I joined a group that had a few secret locations around Bangkok, and began covert activities aimed at providing intelligence to the coming Allied invasion.

"I won't bore you with the details, but when the war ended, we'd laid the groundwork for an ongoing intelligence presence in Southeast Asia."

"The CIA," Martin offered.

The old man neither confirmed nor denied this as he methodically ate a few more fries.

"What about Jim Thompson?"

"Thompson literally arrived on the day the war ended. He and a group of combat-trained OSS officers were air-bound for the Cambodian border. They were to parachute in and provide assistance to what was looking more and more like a liberation than an invasion. He told me they got word of the Japs' surrender on the plane. They took off their 'chutes and landed their C-47 in full view of the enemy.

"After the war, a few of us, Thompson included, stayed on. We seemed to have an affinity for the place. And there was work to be done in the transition. Officially we were now working for the Strategic Services Unit, an office opened by Thompson and Alex MacDonald. Unofficially we were still OSS. Thailand's politics, then as now, was a mess. Power was traded through a succession of coups and intrigues. We were relegated to facilitating American liaisons between the almost daily shifts in government.

"By '47 Thompson was running the Oriental and MacDonald had started the first English-language newspaper in Bangkok. There were only a handful of us left. Myself, Rubber Johnny Jane—"

"Rubber Johnny Jane?"

The old man shrugged. "I can't remember why we called her that. She was quite a gal. Gams that wouldn't quit. There was her, Johnny Wester, me and a few more whose names I can't recall. By now we were working for the Black Eagle Trust."

"The Black Eagle Trust?"

"After the war, MacArthur did return to the Philippines. He went looking for the booty, the loot. President Truman set up the Trust so that the stolen gold, art and relics that the Golden Lily had sequestered would be commandeered by MacArthur and—"

"The Golden Lily?"

"Yes, the Golden Lily." He looked up at Martin with his single eye and frowned. "Young man, if you're going to interrupt me every other sentence, I'll be dead before I have a chance to tell you the story I believe you wanted to hear. Obviously you never cared for history. You seem completely ignorant."

Martin said nothing. There was nothing he could say.

"You have a notepad, don't you?"

Martin nodded.

"Then I suggest you use it. Later, when I've been left in peace, you can go to your infernal computer and look up all these little historical bits that seem to confuse you."

Martin sheepishly pulled out his little Moleskin journal and his Sensa pen.

"The Golden Lily were Kempeitai agents."

The old man waited for Martin to write down the two names.

"As the inevitable conclusion to the war loomed, they struggled to either hide their massive treasure trove or ship it to Tokyo. They managed to get two boatloads of plunder out of a warehouse in Klong Toey before the Allied forces moved in. The Black Eagle Trust was a secret slush fund set up by Truman's secretary of war to retrieve this enormous stash of precious metals and gems and use this wealth to fund clandestine operations after the war."

"The CIA," Martin offered again.

Again the old man refused to comment. He shoved his plate aside and reached for his cigar.

"How this relates to me and Jim Thompson, this is what I think you're looking for, isn't it?"

Martin nodded.

"The Japs didn't get everything they wanted out of Bangkok. So they came back for it. They sent in the Black Dragons." He paused while Martin wrote. "There was one...*relic* in particular that they really wanted, and they had reason to believe Jim Thompson was in possession of it. They made several attempts to kill him before we managed to locate them. Thompson, Lady Jane, me and this rather odd friend of Thompson's."

"This man?" Martin produced the photo of Ramonne and Jim Thompson.

The old man reached into his pocket and took out a pair of half-framed reading glasses. He slid these down on his nose and took the photo. He moved it back and forth, apparently trying to get his one good eye to focus. Finally he stopped and smiled.

"Yes. That's him."

He took off his glasses and put the picture down.

"Thompson was chased once in his car, and shots were fired. A second time he was jumped in an alley behind the hotel, and it was just by chance that this chap..." He tapped the photo. "Ramonne?"

Martin nodded.

"He came along and ran them off. At least that was what Thompson thought. He'd been knocked unconscious. Later on, this Frenchman, Ramonne, told Thompson that he dispatched the two assailants and their apparent leader."

"*Dispatched?*"

"Killed. He said he killed three very dangerous men."

Martin's lunch arrived, and the old man took the opportunity to enjoy his cigar and take a few long draws, savoring the smoke in his mouth. Between puffs, he rolled the cigar in his fingers, finally setting it back in the ashtray, careful not to knock off the long cylindrical ash.

"He led us, the Frenchman did, to their hideout. It turned out it was the same riverside godown they'd used during the war."

"The Golden Lilies?"

"*Lily,*" the old man shot back. "Singular. It was a code name...And no—not the Golden Lily. The Black Dragons. The Golden Lily movement ended with the war."

Martin made notes and went back to his burger. Babe sighed and drained his glass. He addressed the woman. "Open the other bottle please."

"At first, I didn't know it was the same warehouse, as we approached it from the rear. From the street, rather than the river. There seemed to be no way in until Lady Jane climbed up the fire escape. She went inside against our advice. Shots were fired and Thompson and I made it to the river in time to see her and two Japs in a small boat heading down the river. Jane was trussed up like a fish. We exchanged a few shots while they hauled ass.

"We had no idea where they were taking her, but we figured we'd hear from them." He took a drink of the new wine and wiped his mouth.

"Sure enough, within 24 hours Thompson got a note at the hotel."

21

———

Bangkok, 1949

Bring us the Oracle. We'll give you the woman. Mahakan Fort. Midnight. Come alone.

The note had been brought to the reception by the doorman. He got it from a cab-driver who pulled in under the hotel's *porte-cochère* and waved an envelope, without getting out of the cab. The envelope was addressed to J. Thompson. It, like the note itself, was typed.

Thompson arrived at the hotel in the early evening. He had spent the day with an Army forensics team at the ice factory looking for fingerprints and other trace evidence. Lots of fingerprints were found, but little else. Oddly, many of the prints were missing the fifth digit, or little finger. One set of prints consisted of only the thumb and the first two fingers.

The watermarked receipt turned out to be a dead end. It was a cash receipt for whisky made at a shop in Yaowarat over two months ago. Other than establishing the Black Dragons presence at that time, it provided no more clues to their whereabouts.

Thompson was scheduled to meet Babe for a drink, and was late. He was walking briskly across the lobby when his name was called. The receptionist handed him the note, and he opened it at the counter.

———

"Short and sweet." Babe handled the note by the edges and slipped it back into the manila envelope.

They were seated by the river. A welcome breeze stirred the night air. The lacquered wooden table reflected the light of a candle housed in a Chinese lantern.

"What should we do?" Thompson asked.

"We'll give it to the forensics people."

"But what should we *do*? We have a little over four hours."

"We don't have it."

"No. We don't."

"They'll kill her."

"Yes. I'm sure they will."

Thompson drummed his fingers nervously while Babe lifted his glass of Scotch and soda off its coaster and moved it around in little circles of moisture on the slick table. Neither spoke.

"What don't you have and *who's* going to kill *who*?"

The voice shocked them both. They had neither seen nor heard anyone approach.

It was Ramonne. He stood at the end of the table wearing a dark suit and an inquisitive smile.

"Show him the note," Thompson instructed.

Babe opened the envelope and extracted the message. He held it close to the lantern, and Ramonne leaned over the table.

"Ah. They have made contact." He stood back up. "What shall we do?"

"*We*?" Babe frowned as he put the note away.

"Yes. We have just four hours. What shall we do?" Ramonne pulled over a chair and sat down.

Thompson looked to Babe and shrugged his shoulders. "We don't have the Oracle."

"But they think you do." Ramonne smiled.

"We don't even know what it is—do we?" He turned to Babe.

"No. The only description we ever had was basically biblical. An ancient Egyptian scroll referred to the Oracle as a 'vessel of eternal light.'"

"That's helpful."

Ramonne raised his hand.

"Yes?" Babe frowned again.

"Why don't we simply get a theatrical property and pass it off as the Oracle?"

"A *theatrical property*?" Babe continued to scowl.

"He means a prop," Thompson interjected.

"Yes. A decoy to lure them into thinking you have it. Distract them, surprise them and rescue Miss Farmer."

"Just like that? Nice and easy. Like a walk in the park," Babe scoffed.

"Well…a rather *dangerous* walk in a very treacherous park." Ramonne continued to smile.

———

Midnight.

Mahakan Fort's ancient and corroded cannons stood silent sentinel against a foe that had long since passed into history.

Jim Thompson had been across from the old fort for the past thirty minutes. He and Babe crept through a thick grove of rain trees that bordered Rajadamnern Avenue on the northern edge of the canal, staying in the shadows. When they were close enough to make out the details, they squatted behind a low wall that fronted the canal.

They were alone. Babe had virtually 'commanded' Ramonne to stay away. To Thompson's surprise, Ramonne had agreed, stating that he needed to tend to the bar. However, he took on the task of fabricating the decoy that Thompson was carrying.

Thompson figured the 'vessel,' the Oracle, had to be a portable entity, so the Frenchman had taken two empty cigar boxes from the club, filled them with sand from a cigarette ash can in the hotel lobby, and wrapped them as one in brown paper. Thompson hoped the ruse would buy enough time to bring whomever was waiting for him in the fort into the open long enough for their 'back-up' to take them out.

The US Army had limited manpower in Bangkok at this time. The occupation of Japan was entering its second phase, and an increasing number of troops were being deployed to Korea. They had been fortunate to find a forensic team available to search the godown at Klong Toey. But there were no military forces available to them on such short notice. So Babe made a call to the superintendent of police and was in turn quickly contacted by a provincial general who assured him that he would send a squad of his own men to assist.

"Where are they?" Babe whispered.

Thompson tapped his shoulder and pointed to his right.

Three men in dark uniforms appeared and crouched behind the wall. One of them had a rifle with a telescopic sight. Thompson looked to his left, and in the deep shadows, two more men could be seen. One was also armed with a rifle.

Thompson looked at his watch: 11:45 exactly. The general seemed to be a man of his word.

He went back to studying the fort through his binoculars. Constructed in the late eighteenth century on a moat that surrounded the Grand Palace and the city at the time, the fort was long ago swallowed up by the twentieth-century urban sprawl. The moat became part of the network of *klongs*, or canals, that gave Bangkok its 'Venice of the East' epithet. The fort remained aloof and untouched. Its white turreted walls formed a perfect octagon. Six cannons, long ago disarmed, thrust through the gun cavities. A steep staircase led up from a path along the canal to the cannons. A second set of stairs led up to an octagonal tower. It appeared to have just one small entrance and was topped by a tiled canopy in the shape of an inverted lotus leaf. A surviving section of the old city wall abutted the fort and ran out to Rajadamnern Avenue.

The trees that lined both sides of the canal were just as thick in front of the fort. These, Thompson feared, would limit the opportunities for the snipers to get clear shots.

Occasionally a *sampan* glided past on the *klong*—a lone fisherman or merchant on his way home, slowly working the single scull in the stern. Arrow-shaped wakes reflected silver in the moonlight as these small craft floated silently down the canal. Each side of the *klong* was lined with *sampans* covered with a curved, woven-mat roof. Lantern-light illuminated the interiors of some, indicating that the small boat was also a family home.

The fort was backlit by lamps on its far side. Thompson hadn't seen any sign of life. No movement of any kind. The only thing that gave him reason to believe he wasn't on a wild goose chase was the incongruous presence of the small motorboat docked adjacent to the fort. Even though it was covered with fishing nets, there was no doubt that it was the craft that had spirited Lady Jane away from the ice factory.

Thompson figured that whoever they were meeting had been there for a while, perhaps coming there directly from the old godown with the smell of gunpowder fresh in their nostrils.

He checked his watch. "Time to go," he whispered, and handed his binoculars to Babe.

Thompson stood and brushed leaves off his pants, and adjusted his holster. His nine-millimeter Browning rode high on his left hip, butt facing forward for a quick right-handed retrieval. He let his jacket fall back in place, and picked up the parcel. He stepped from the shadows and approached the narrow footbridge. Tree branches bent under the bounteous weight of their fertile boughs and waved in the breeze, casting ominous moving shadows onto the opposite bank and along the white wall of the old fort. Thompson paused and crouched at the foot of the little bridge. A figure had appeared on the top step below the tower. The man stayed in the darkness of the roof.

Thompson started across the bridge, taking his time. The bridge was about fifty meters east of the fort. It had a meter-high wall on both sides with lanterns encased in stone. Only one of these was lit, but it served to illuminate Thompson as he crossed. He placed his right hand on the smooth stone wall that ran along the canal on the southern side. It too had lanterns embedded in it, but none of them were working. The only light source, other than the moon, was a street lamp twenty meters behind Thompson, so he was almost a silhouette as he approached the fort.

It took about a minute to reach the entrance to the fort. The stone stairs loomed ahead of him. He looked up. The man was still in the shadows of the tower's roof. He waved a hand, indicating that Thompson should proceed up the stairs.

Thompson moved forward and slowly climbed the first set of stairs. They were steep, so he stayed to the right and used the wall for balance. He reached the landing and looked around. There were doors in the wall behind each cannon.

He froze.

To his immediate left there was a man with a rifle lying prone on the rampart's floor, sighting alongside the cannon. Thompson drew his pistol, but the man never stirred. It was this immobility that had made him invisible from the other side of the canal.

"Don't move," a voice came from the darkness.

Thompson looked up the stairs. He recognized the man who spoke. He was one of Jane's kidnappers. Thompson didn't know it, but the man's name was Narong. He had a gun leveled at Thompson, who slowly lowered his pistol. As he did, the door behind the man began to open. A glow emanated from within.

"Mr. Thompson." A man he had never seen before was now in the doorway. He too brandished a pistol pointed at Thompson. "My name is Takashi." He was large for an Asian, dressed in a ceremonial robe, with a thin mustache and slicked-back hair.

As the light fell on the stairs and spilled across the landing, Thompson could see that the cannon to his right was also accompanied by a man with a rifle aimed outward. The police would be sitting ducks. This disturbing thought was immediately replaced by the appearance of a figure next to Takashi.

"I believe you know Miss Farmer." Takashi gave his pistol a slight wave and she stepped forward. Her hands were bound in front of her, and the second man from the boat, Rung, had a pistol in her ribs.

"Jane. Are you all right?" Thompson raised his pistol and started up the stairs.

"Do not move, Mr. Thompson. Or she will not be all right. She will be dead."

———

Babe watched Thompson go up the stairs through his binoculars. He registered the man on the landing and assumed he was one of the men on the boat with Jane.

He held his breath as the second and third man appeared with her.

A thin, young policeman crawled up alongside him. He was the one with the rifle with the telescopic sight.

"Sergeant Tantipong, sir." He saluted. "There are shooters stationed in each of the front cannon ports."

Babe returned the salute. "Are you certain?"

"Yes sir." He pointed at the scope. The lens had a red glare. "Night vision, sir."

Shit. Now what do we do? He had hoped to pick off the three men with the pistols and be done with it. He didn't want a fire fight.

"Hold your fire. Let's see what happens."

"Yes sir." Tantipong snapped another salute and crawled back to his position. He spread himself prone and aimed his rifle. Babe squatted, very uncomfortably, on one knee...and waited.

———

Thompson kept his pistol aimed at Takashi, his eyes on Jane.

"Are you all right?" he repeated.

"Yes...roughed up. Nothing new. And nothing punctured or broken."

"Mr. Thompson, there are three pistols pointed at you. I assume you've also seen the men guarding the perimeter?"

"I noticed them, yes."

"You are alive because of what you are holding in your left hand. It is much too valuable to risk any damage to it."

Thompson held the package pressed to his chest. "I suggest, then, that we make the exchange we came here for."

Takashi lowered his pistol and made a backward wave with his left hand.

"Give it to me."

Thompson stared at the hand. It had only two fingers. Now he thought he understood the odd fingerprints in the warehouse. He moved the package away from his body and held it out in front of him.

"Release her."

Takashi motioned, and Rung slit the ropes tying Jane's wrists. She rubbed them and then started to walk. Rung stuck his pistol in her ribs. She stopped.

"Let her go," Thompson demanded. He raised his arm and slowly turned his hand with the package. "My arm is getting tired, Mr. Takashi."

Takashi motioned again and Rung moved the pistol away from Jane and pointed it at Thompson.

She crossed to Thompson's side. "Thank you."

"Get behind me." He motioned and she did.

"The package please, Mr. Thompson."

"Not until she's safe."

"Mr. Thompson. The package. *Now.*"

Thompson held the package higher. Over his head.

"She walks down the stairs. Gets to the bottom. Then it's yours."

Takashi and the two men stood silent, their guns aimed at Thompson. No one spoke. No one moved.

Finally Takashi broke the silence. "Go," he said.

"Jim?"

"Go...now."

Lady Jane looked a little dazed as she slowly descended the stairs. She reached the bottom and stopped. Thompson turned his head, just briefly. "The footbridge, Jane. Hurry."

"Mr. Thompson. My patience is worn very thin...The package. Now."

Thompson smiled. He swung his arm back and tossed the package high in the air.

"Catch."

Takashi, in shock, dropped his pistol and dashed forward—both arms extended before him.

As the package spun in flight, Narong and Rung both fired their pistols. Thompson, however, had already dropped to a crouch, and both shots missed. He fired and hit Narong in the shoulder.

The package landed in Takashi's outstretched arms. He fumbled with it and almost dropped it, before recovering his balance. He clutched the package to his chest and smiled.

Immediately a fusillade of bullets splattered the area. Rung was cut down by at least four shots. His pistol fell to the ground and Thompson snatched it up.

Takashi scrambled for cover behind the rampart wall, while Thompson dived headfirst down the stairs. As he rolled end over end, he saw continuous gun blasts from the other side of the canal. These were being returned by the men in the cannon ports. He hit the walk at the bottom and fell flat—his two pistols pointed back up the stairs.

It was pandemonium. Gunfire rained from both sides.

Takashi had recovered his pistol and seemed desperate to reach the door to the tower chamber. He had Narong with him and one other man armed with a rifle, who had obviously abandoned his post to defend Takashi and the Oracle.

Thompson fired off a quick volley and rolled to his left. He flattened himself against the wall of the fort. The men at the gun ports above him couldn't see him from their positions. He tried to catch his breath and gather his wits.

"Jim."

He looked to his right. Lady Jane was crouched, her back to the wall. Her hands had been over her head, but she removed them and stared blankly at Thompson.

"Jane." He looked at her briefly before taking her in his arms and drawing her to him. She was frightened. He'd never seen her this way. She felt vulnerable.

He held her close and hugged her. "It's all right. Babe's right over there. He's got a squad of police."

"Babe's down. I saw him get hit."

"What?"

"Give me a gun," she said.

Thompson gave her the captured pistol. Immediately when she took it, he saw a change in her. She brushed the hair out of her eyes and focused.

Something had happened to her. Something bad. She would probably never talk about it, but whether she bore physical scars or not, she'd been wounded. Seriously wounded.

"Babe!" he shouted out.

No response. He shouted again.

"Jim." Jane pointed to her right.

Two men in black were advancing. The police. Sergeant Tantipong was in the lead. They hugged the wall and ran in a crouch. He snapped off a quick salute and squeezed by Thompson. "Sir."

"What about my partner?"

"He's been hit."

"How bad?"

"Head wound. We wrapped it, and my last man is staying with him."

"Your *last* man?"

"Yes, sir. I've lost two men. We can't fire from there without exposing ourselves. And we can't hit them. That's why we're here. We'll take them from the stairs."

"Okay." Thompson turned to Jane. "Go. Get on the other side. Help Babe. We'll cover you."

She shook her head. "The best help I can be is with you."

"No. We need that gun at our back." He pointed across the canal. "You need to relieve their man."

Impulsively, he pulled her to him. He kissed her. Sergeant Tantipong's eyes went wide.

She slipped from his embrace and ran, crouching low. They all watched her go. When she reached the bridge the man opposite them fired a volley of shots, giving her the cover she needed to cross safely.

"Let's go," Thompson ordered, and Tantipong started for the stairs. Thompson was next, with the other policeman at the rear. Sporadic gunfire was now coming from across the canal. Thompson said a silent prayer for both Jane and Babe.

Just before they turned the corner and started the stairs, Thompson whispered, "I'll go up the far side. There may still be someone in the other gun ports." Tantipong nodded.

Thompson crawled on his belly to the far side of the stairs. They started up, making their way quickly, but no one seemed to be watching. Thompson figured Takashi had made it back into the tower.

The lone cop was doing a valiant job of providing cover fire for them, and they made it to the top without hindrance. Thompson raised his pistol and nodded at Sergeant Tantipong.

They made their moves.

Thompson found no one on his side of the stairs. He quickly headed back, then heard the sharp crack of Tantipong's rifle. Once, twice, three times.

Then: "*Stop!*" The voice bellowed through the fort. It was followed by immediate silence. Thompson saw a man approaching up the stairs. He wore a police officer's uniform. He had a holster on his right hip and a pistol in his hand. He wasn't dressed for combat as were the others. He had stars on his epaulets and the brim of his hat.

"General?" Thompson asked, lowering his pistol.

The man reached the landing. He clicked his heels together and snapped off a rigid salute to Jim. "Brigadier-General Natiwat."

Thompson returned the salute.

The general turned to his left. Sergeant Tantipong and his partner had their weapons trained on a lone gunman. He was wounded. Two others lay dead at the feet of the cannon that had protected them.

Tantipong lowered his rifle and saluted.

General Natiwat shot him once between the eyes.

"General. What are hell are you—"

Before Thompson could finish his sentence, the general shot the remaining policeman and the wounded Black Dragon marksman. He swung the pistol around and aimed it at Thompson.

The general started to speak but was cut off by a piercing scream. The door to the tower flew open. Gas lanterns scattered throughout the room backlit the figure of Takashi as he came through the door. He was followed by Narong, carrying a pistol and clutching his wounded arm.

"Sand!" Takashi had the two torn cigar boxes, one in each hand, and the grains poured from them. "You brought me *sand.*"

He threw the boxes onto the stone floor.

"Kill him," he commanded the general.

As the general cocked his pistol to do as ordered, Thompson raised his gun and aimed it directly at the general.

"Put the gun down."

"No. I'm not putting my gun down." For the second time in less than an hour, Jim Thompson found himself staring down a pistol in a Mexican standoff.

"Lord Buddha, I should have killed you earlier." Takashi pulled out his pistol and aimed it at Thompson.

Suddenly a figure appeared on the tower's roof above them.

'I have something for you.'

It was Ramonne. His arms were raised, and he had a package in his left hand. The breeze blew his long hair and his eyes glowed.

What the fuck? Thompson held his pistol on the general. But his attention, as was the others', was riveted on Ramonne.

"It's him," Narong sputtered.

"Who?" Takashi barked.

"He's the one who came to the warehouse. He killed Hashimoto."

"*You* killed my brother?" Takashi's brow furrowed and he swung his pistol up to Ramonne. Unfazed, Ramonne lowered his hands and stepped to the edge. He dropped six meters to the landing. He fell slowly and landed without effort.

The guns did not fire. Nobody moved.

"Ramonne. What the hell...?"

The vampire put a reassuring hand on Thompson's shoulder and walked slowly between the pointed pistols, to Takashi.

"Your brother?" Ramonne studied Takashi. "Ah. Yes. I see

the resemblance." Takashi was virtually identical in appearance to his brother. He seemed a little larger. Stronger.

Ramonne extended the package. It was similar in shape to the one carried earlier by Thompson. "I believe you've been looking for this."

Takashi and his men became animated again and Takashi waved his pistol. "Stop right there."

Ramonne paused.

"Another trick?" Takashi sneered.

"No trick." Ramonne slowly removed the wrapping paper. As he did, the object within began to glow.

"Lord Buddha," Takashi uttered.

The paper fell to the ground and Ramonne held in his hands a golden box. It was semi-opaque and radiated from within. It was inscribed on all sides with ancient symbols.

"It's the Oracle." The iridescent blaze grew stronger, and soon all were bathed in the golden light.

Takashi reached for the vessel of light. "Give it to me."

Ramonne smiled. "I think not."

He pulled the shining object of desire to him. "I merely brought it to tease you…Taunt you."

He held it close to his chest, its light now restrained and reduced to amber. "*Your kind* must never possess…" He moved it slightly in Takashi's direction and then withdrew it. "This."

Takashi's eyes grew wide. His face flushed and he fired his pistol at Ramonne.

The bullet struck just above where the heart would be. It passed through the vampire, spinning into the night.

"Ramonne," Thompson yelled. His gun was now leveled at Takashi. His finger squeezed the trigger.

Ramonne put up a hand. And smiled. "Worry not, my friend…This is *their* demise, not ours."

He crossed without effort to the Japanese, extending his right arm and seized Takashi by the front of his robe. Narong raised his pistol and fired directly into Ramonne's side. There was no reaction, and Ramonne twisted the robe, strangling Takashi and ignoring Narong. A shot rang out and Narong fell to the pavement. Ramonne turned briefly to Thompson, his eyes now blazing a ghastly yellow.

Takashi gasped and groaned.

"Stop!" The general screamed. His gun was at Thompson's head.

"Let him go."

Ramonne smiled. He said one word.

"*No.*"

And continued to wring the life from Takashi.

The general's finger on the trigger did not move. The general didn't move. He *couldn't* move. He could do nothing but watch the vampire suffocate the Japanese.

Thompson, however, was free. He moved away from the general's aim, leveled his own gun at him, and watched the macabre play unfold.

Takashi finally expired and Ramonne let him drop, like a rag doll, lifeless, to the floor. The vampire was left holding the robe, revealing a multitude of tattoos covering Takashi's lifeless torso. Ramonne turned slowly to the general. Thompson had never seen his friend like this. He radiated *evil* that was a physical reality. As the saying went: You could cut it with a knife.

As Ramonne fixed his demonic gaze on the general, the general came back to life.

"No!"

Ramonne leaped on him. He bared his teeth and tore into the general's throat.

"Ramonne! Stop!" Thompson was horrified as his friend turned into a devil before his eyes. His gun now hung useless at his side. He helplessly watched as a second life succumbed to Ramonne. This one, however, provided sustenance and vitality for the vampire. When the insufferable minutes finally passed and the general's corpse slipped from his grasp, Ramonne was renewed. Invigorated.

He stood amidst the horror he had wrought. Takashi's corpse was slumped next to the general's. The bodies of Narong, Sergeant Tantipong, his aide, the three marksmen, were all scattered lifelessly about, as in some war tableau. Thompson and the *thing* he once knew as Ramonne Delacroix, stood alone amidst the carnage.

22

Bangkok, Present Day

"I suffered a penetrating eye injury. A 'fragmentation.' Today they'd call it shrapnel. In any case, I was fucked up. I was blinded, though my right eye eventually cleared up. I regained some vision in the left but lost it totally over the next couple years."

The sun was sinking and the lights of the teeming metropolis were turning on, as Babe finished the second bottle of wine.

"We were getting creamed. Two of the local cops were down. The Japs were picking us off like ducks in a pond.

"I saw Thompson get Jane down the stairs. Saw him shoot his way out and roll…"

Babe looked as the lights came on in the adjacent building.

"That's the last thing I saw."

Martin got up to stretch his legs, and give the old man a chance to go on.

"Tantipong left one guy with me. Why, I don't know. I was fucked. Useless. Couldn't see a thing. And the pain was excruciating. He shoulda' shot me."

Martin turned to him and smiled. "I'm glad he didn't."

"Next thing I know, Jane's with me. She's pressing me down behind the wall and the cop laying down rounds. It sounded like the sky was falling.

Other than that, I only know what Thompson told me."

———

Martin stayed in the club's bar after the old man left. It was familiar. Comfortable. And he needed to digest what he'd heard.

"Mr. Larue?" Tony inquired.

"Wine *daeng, khrap*." He ordered a glass of red wine.

The evening crowd was starting to enter and take their places. Printing presses rolled at night and reporters drank. The way it had been for eons.

That Ramonne was alive in 1949 was no surprise to Martin. He had just never thought about it before. That he was involved in intrigue connecting American OSS agents with treasure stolen by the Japanese wasn't surprising either. He knew that Ramonne was easily bored and relished role-playing whenever the chance presented itself. The impresario of the Bamboo Bar: that fit perfectly. He loved jazz. And the hours? They couldn't have been better. He also enjoyed hobnobbing with society's mavens.

The reference to the Oracle—a vessel of light that carried the secret to immortality—well, this was indeed something that would intrigue Ramonne. The quest to understand it could fill countless hours in the centuries he was destined to explore.

Last, but not least, the friendship—albeit short-lived—with Jim Thompson. This was perhaps the most intriguing of all to Martin. He remembered the vampire bemoaning his lonely existence so often, citing Martin as his one and only true friend in all his troubled years.

And yet, it seemed, there had been a predecessor.

Jim Thompson.

Babe's own account of the battle was a bit delusional, but what Thompson had told him was that Ramonne appeared and saved his life again. Unfortunately he was shot in the ensuing battle and killed. When Martin researched it further, Thompson's numerous biographers stated that in spite of being overwhelmed, he had survived with the assistance of the Thai police. The lack of mention of Ramonne wasn't surprising to Martin.

———

"Half a kilo. Same as a delicious box of chocolates."

Martin had just about had enough of doctor humor. They were back in Dr. Namazi's office and he—the doctor—had a big smile, or a satisfied smirk; Martin couldn't tell the difference. He looked away from the sonogram screen and made his little joke.

"Doctor...is she—"

"You and your baby are fine, Mrs. Larue. Her heartbeat is normal."

Thank God.

Martin had been using the unbearable 'waiting time' to seek out information on Ramonne and his relationship to Jim Thompson. Taking his mind off the waiting game.

But today was day 180. Twenty-six weeks into the pregnancy. Until today the sonograms had continued to show a baby with an unhealthy heartbeat. A slightly smaller-than-normal fetus. Not as strong as the doctor would like. Not as large as the doctor would like.

But today—today was different. Today they crossed a milestone. The baby's heartbeat was strong. She was healthy.

She's going to make it.

———

The one advantage Martin could truly say the Ethan Allen bedroom had over his former Boxetti minimalist set was that the duvets, pillows and cushions gave Areeya innumerable surfaces to bury her face in when she was overwhelmed with tears—as she was right now. The difference this time from the countless other times was these tears. They were tears of joy.

"I can't believe it." Her eyes were like a raccoon's, the result of smeared mascara. "We did it."

Martin smiled and pulled her and her handful of pillows to him. He kissed the top of her head. "*You* did it."

She looked up at him. "We're going to have a baby."

Finally they allowed themselves to say it. They allowed themselves to believe it. Everything was all right on Planet Larue. Martin relaxed for the first time in six months. He forgot about everything else.

He forgot about the Japanese stranger who had mysteriously appeared and threatened him. He forgot about the strange journey of discovery that meeting had led him down. He forgot about the feeling that had plagued him for months, that the sinister force that had dominated and offended him for so long was not left behind, like so much else of his life, in Siem Reap.

He forgot that something told him—was telling him—that Ramonne was about to re-emerge. That he was about to take that plunge into the dark again.

He forgot all of this for now. He was really going to be a father.

It was finally working. All the doctor's voodoo medicines, sonograms, injections, dietary restrictions, all the forced somnambulism—all of it—it had worked. Areeya was carrying a healthy child.

They weren't out of the woods yet, but they were on their way.

Their joy was boundless. They piled atop the Tuscany sleigh bed—Martin, Areeya, Hon and Small Talk. Martin and Areeya kissed, and Small Talk hissed. Little Hon just beamed, not knowing exactly what was going on, but savoring the pure goodness of it all.

———

Ramonne strolled the small street. Just off the madness of Sukhumvit Road, Soi 8 was a refuge. Less than 100 meters down the narrow street and the noise fell away and the neon dimmed. Traffic was limited to the few taxis that came and went, ferrying people to and from the condominiums and hotels that occupied the western end of the *soi* before it dead-ended.

In an area of Bangkok that now contained more buildings over twenty stories than any other, there were still a remarkable number of family houses with gardens in back and trees in front. There were small pubs and restaurants with outdoor seating and fairy lights in the trees. It was one of these small restaurants that Ramonne now called home. On the north side of the street, a French restaurant had occupied a remarkable piece of property for over twenty years. A large banyan tree covered the entire front, sheltering an old, two-story wooden house that served as the restaurant. Unfortunately the restaurant was one of the first victims of the kingdom's economic woes, and shuttered its windows and turned off its ovens. An agent who knew of Ramonne's fondness for the place—he had spent many evenings exploring the owner's wine cellar— contacted the professor just prior to their hasty departure from Cambodia, and Ramonne had immediately dispatched the funds to secure the property.

His coffin comfortably ensconced in the huge cellar fitted with a new steel door, Ramonne left the furnishing up to the professor. He had a storage vault filled with his collections, and the necessary items would be gradually transferred to the house —once it was suitably fortified.

It felt good to be back in Krung Thep. His rural retreat to

Roluos had been good for him. But there was no denying that he was a city dweller. He loved the electricity in the air. The crowds in Bangkok gave him energy, not the least reason being that they held his victims. What he didn't like about the modern metropolis was the *modern* part of it. He had no use for the computer, the television, cellular phones—he could count on one hand the number of times in his life that he'd ever used one.

Ramonne would walk tonight. He'd walk for hours, savoring the city. Its smells, its pulse, its life. When he desired, he'd tune into the thoughts of its denizens. But only rarely. In general, the thoughts of mortals were tedious, onerous, monotonous. Caught up their tiny, insipid little lives, it was too depressing for him to hear much of it.

Eventually, when the hands of the clock fell into the morning hours, he'd choose a victim. An isolated soul. Someone lost. Someone, preferably a female, who would not be missed. Perhaps, just perhaps, he'd seduce her first.

The prospect excited him. As it had in Roluos. He'd been foolish then. He would not make that mistake again.

In Cambodia he'd felt the bloodlust return with a passion. He'd been practically a saint for months—years actually. With the exception of his...he wasn't sure what to call it—affair? dalliance?—whatever it was with Kanchana, he'd not mixed sex with bloodletting in a long time. For decades, that had been his modus operandi—seduction, sex and the kill. But he had felt something for Kanchana, even if he no longer remembered what it was.

What he'd felt on that fateful last night in Cambodia had been bloodlust—pure and simple.

But what had, for decades, been such a simple act for him, had gone terribly wrong. He'd become rusty. Clumsy. Careless. He'd gone into the village. That was foolish. He should have gone in to Siem Reap. Tourist town. Filled with wanton lasses, massage parlors, karaoke dens—whores. But instead he'd seen a girl and followed her. She was dressed in a traditional costume. He assumed she was a dancer. She was young, probably no more than 22—if that. The moment he spotted her, he knew he had to have her. And that, he knew, sealed her fate. She was dead.

He followed her. Studying her. She had a purposeful stride. Her gait was strong. He liked that. She knew where she was going. What she was doing. The town's lights grew closer and he quickened his pace. He could not allow her to be seen. Not now. Not ever again.

Not alive.

He stepped to her side. She glanced his way. Caught his eye. And stopped.

That was it. All it took. She was his.

He told her to follow him. He led her back the way they'd come. At the edge of the village was a plantation of rubber trees. He'd always admired their stately aspect. They stood tall and straight in perfect parallel rows for acres.

They entered the grove and she followed obediently. Like a dog.

Like a lamb to the slaughter.

When they were safely away from the road, he motioned to her and she lay down on the soft, pungent earth. He undressed her quickly. Her skin was as smooth as riverbed stones. He caressed her, smelled her hair, her scent. He needed her.

He mounted her. He was inhuman—true—but he had been human once, and the carnal release of the seed still gave him great pleasure.

She writhed beneath him. He knew that his decades of experience made him an unnatural lover, and women always reacted the same way—lost in some ether zone that overtook their mind and body and suffused it with lust. She scratched his back, her nails digging deep into his flesh—rending it, tearing it. But as quickly as the flesh was shredded—the wounds healed.

He allowed himself to come, filling her void. She withered

beneath him, folding like a day lily at sunset. He withdrew and studied her. She was at peace. She could easily sleep the night away among the trees. He could slip away and in the morning she could wake and gather her belongings and resume her life.

But this would not be.

He parted her legs. She stirred. She smiled at him.

He sank his teeth into her vulva and drank. She succumbed.

And died.

When he was finished, he dressed and departed. He was refreshed. Rejuvenated. Restored. The girl was no longer.

He walked out of the plantation and onto the pavement. He paid no heed to the car lights that approached from the town.

He walked.

They stopped.

He walked.

Men got out of the cars. They had powerful flashlights. They headed into the plantation.

He walked.

The lights played among the rubber trees.

He walked.

The lights of one of the cars lit up like a carnival. Red and blue strobes exploded.

He fled.

She was not a dancer. She was the daughter of the village headman.

She was on her way to the formal affair at which she would be betrothed. She was late.

And then she was dead.

———

By 3:00 a.m. he was on Silom Road. His old stomping ground. He sauntered under the skytrain's massive canopy, watching as the last vendors rolled their carts back down Convent Road and the Phipat *sois* to tuck them away and trot them out again tomorrow evening. Most of the neon over Patpong Road's soiled red carpet was extinguished, and the centerpiece—the long market of imitation goods—was disassembled. The stalls too would arise again tomorrow evening.

He strolled down the *soi*, savoring the fact that although there had been attempts at reforming it, cleaning it up, nothing here had really changed. He continued until he saw the familiar sign, 'Tip Top,' and knew that—at last—he was home.

Martin rose early on Sunday. Before the sunrise. It was a ritual he had. Alone time.

He ground his coffee and picked up the paper from outside the door.

That was the mistake.

Once the door was open, it was thrust into his face with such force that it knocked him back across the foyer and into the vase that held his umbrellas and walking sticks. Two very large men followed the door into the room. One of them swiped Martin across the base of his skull with a sap, and he fell into a dark void.

When he awoke, he sensed he was alone. His head throbbed as he struggled to his feet. "Areeya," he called—without much force. He steadied himself by inching his way up the wall to an erect position. He called again. His voice sounded hollow in his own home.

They were gone.

The cry. It pierced the night, and yet it was heard by only one pair of ears.

Ramonne was on the roof of a flophouse called the Madrid when he heard it. The short-time hotel provided rooms, condoms, breakfast, booze and pizza. The customer brought the pussy. *Is there anything wrong with this?* Ramonne thought not.

He had taken his latest victim across the Madrid's threshold. He had enjoyed carnal lust, and then the true climax that he sought. Afterwards, he'd taken the body to the roof, where it would rot unnoticed and be consumed by the rats and crows.

The cry so unnerved him that he flew across Patpong in three swift bounds.

Although he was a mile or two away from the sound, the crossing of the city took him but a few minutes, and then he was on Martin's balcony.

Martin was seated on the couch, his head in his hand. His cell phone was on the table.

"Martin," he called softly.

Martin looked up, his eyes red, his face stained with tears. He registered no surprise at seeing the vampire on his balcony, thirty floors above the ground.

"They're gone. Areeya and Hon. They took them."

"We'll get them back. I promise you." Ramonne now stood in the living room. Dawn was rapidly approaching.

"You've called the police?"

"Yes. Just now."

Ramonne returned to the balcony. "Learn what you can. I will return at first dark. We will get them. They will be safe." And then he was gone.

———

"Mr. Larue. You say that this Japanese man threatened you. How?"

The apartment was full of cops.

Lieutenant-Colonel Somchai was looking at the business card the man had given Martin: 'Toshiro Muraki, Tokyo, Japan.' On the back was presumably the same thing in Japanese.

"He told me his associates were dangerous people and that

my failure to cooperate would put me in jeopardy. I believe those were his very words."

The colonel was writing in a small leather notebook, while a forensics team was dusting and photographing various parts of the apartment. There were male and female police officers, all in tight, dark-brown uniforms. They had arrived at dawn and had been in the apartment for close to three hours. Martin was tired, agitated…and frightened.

"And you say, Mr. Larue, that you've never met this Toshiro Muraki before?"

"No. I saw him just the once. When he came here."

"And threatened you."

"Yes."

"Why did he threaten you?"

"I told you, he was looking for someone and felt that I could help him locate this person. When I told him I couldn't, he became indignant, and I asked him to leave."

"Who else would want to harm you or your family?"

"No one."

"How is your relationship with your wife?"

My relationship with my wife? "My relationship with my wife is very good, Colonel. She's pregnant."

The colonel made note of this fact. "Would there be any reason why she might want to leave you?"

"She didn't leave me. She and our little boy were kidnapped." Martin was holding an ice pack to the back of his neck. "Do you think I did this to myself?"

"You will need to have that X-rayed. Other than the bruise you have, there is very little evidence of anything happening here."

Martin stood. "Nothing happened? The bedroom looks like a battle zone."

The colonel shrugged. "It has the appearance of possible domestic violence." A female officer handed a blue sheet of paper to him. He studied it for a moment. "There are no fingerprints other than yours, your maid, or the samples you provided of your wife and son."

"Then they wore gloves."

The colonel folded the blue sheet and put it in his breast pocket. "I need you to come down to my office, Mr. Larue. We will stop at the Police Hospital on the way and have you examined."

———

As the day wore on, Martin slowly regained his strength. He realized he had been in a daze. A concussion. Since seeing the empty bedroom, since being struck by the unknown assailants

Ramonne had appeared to him as in a dream, conjured up he knew not how. But there he was on his balcony. And he realized as he walked zombie-like through the emergency room at the Police General Hospital and the Pathumwan Police Station, studying their small collection of Japanese mug shots—all unrecognizable—that his best hope, his best chance of recovering his wife and son lay with Ramonne.

He and Ramonne were connected. They had been since their first forays together eight years ago, when Martin first succumbed to the vampire's power. Since that dark journey had ended at the Temple of Dawn, Martin knew that he and the vampire would be connected throughout Martin's life. Ramonne's reappearance was always preceded by a forewarning. A chill. A lapse. He knew the feeling he had been experiencing recently was this forewarning, just as he knew that the appearance of the vampire was a direct result of his cry upon discovering his family's abduction. Wherever the vampire had been, he had heard the cry, just as Martin had heard *his* forlorn cries, as well. This bond, whatever it was, was strong. He had tried to untangle himself from it, but to no avail.

Now, he found, he was glad that Ramonne had come. He

knew that the police would prove ineffectual in returning his family. His only hope lay with his friend—a vampire.

———

The phone rang.

Martin stared at it. Lieutenant-Colonel Somchai stared at it.

They had returned to Martin's apartment. The colonel told Martin that he would most likely receive a call from his wife's kidnappers, and that the police would attempt to monitor and track it. Martin had seen the movies, and knew that he had to keep the caller on the line for at least a full minute. He watched in silence as they attached a device to his phone.

The afternoon wore on. Martin showered and changed and drank tea and grew impatient. No one spoke or did much of anything. Like all Thais, the police had mastered the skill of doing nothing and enjoying it.

Then the phone rang.

Martin waited while a cop put on headphones and adjusted his laptop. On his signal, Martin answered the phone.

"Yes?"

"Mr. Larue?"

"Yes."

"It's Nat. Your dry cleaning is ready. You asked me to call."

Martin couldn't believe it. Across from him he saw two sets of eyes roll, and he paused a moment before replying.

"Thank you." He hung up the phone.

———

The phone rang three more times throughout the remainder of the day. One was Martin's solicitor, returning Martin's call. Martin had called him from the hospital. He no longer felt the need for any legal advice, and so he thanked him and said he'd call later. The other two calls were from friends. One was looking to go on a bicycle ride—Martin was in the habit of riding long distances out of town for exercise—and the other was a reminder of a luncheon date.

At 6:00 p.m. the police folded up their equipment and departed.

"I'm sorry, Martin, but there just isn't any evidence to support a continued investigation," Colonel Somchai intoned.

Martin pointed at the bandage on the back of his head.

"Yes…you bumped your head. But that doesn't really qualify for a police investigation, I'm afraid. If your wife and son fail to show up in the next…" He looked at his watch. "Let's say, 48 hours, please call me."

He extended a business card. Martin took it. Then the colonel clicked his heels, saluted and left.

Martin sat and waited. The sky turned mango, crimson, a velvety purple, and then indigo until the blackness of night took over.

He sat in the darkness for a while. Then he turned on a light.

He never saw him arrive. Suddenly—he was just there.

"It's the Japanese, isn't it?" The vampire was seated across from him, his elbows resting on his knees, fingertips supporting his chin.

"How did you know?"

"The Japs. They've been the bane of my existence since the end of the Second World War. And now they've included you in their quest."

"What is it they want?"

"Something they shall not have." The vampire rose and walked onto the balcony. "I'll tell you more, but for now it's imperative that we—"

The phone rang.

Martin looked at it. He thought he should turn the speaker

on, but quickly dismissed that idea. *He reads my thoughts...of course he can hear my phone conversation.*

He answered the phone. "Yes?"

"Your wife and the boy are safe...for now."

"What do you want?"

"You know what we want."

There was a pregnant pause.

"Bring him to us. We know he's with you."

Martin looked around. *How?*

It was obvious. When Martin had moved into the penthouse, he had been king of the world. He lived at the top of the highest building for twenty or thirty blocks. But in the last few years five buildings had risen up within easy sight of his apartment that completely dwarfed his building. Any one of them offered an easy vantage point if the kidnappers utilized the right optical assistance.

"Bring him to us."

Martin looked to Ramonne. He merely shrugged.

"My wife and son...how do I know they are unharmed?"

"You don't. You must trust me, Mr. Larue."

"I don't."

"Ah. But you must. There is no alternative."

Martin looked again at Ramonne, who now appeared to be bored. He was flipping through a magazine. Martin realized there would be no negotiating. All he could do was hear the demands.

"Mr. Larue. You are a very wealthy man. I must admit that this was not known to me at first, but it became apparent on my visit to see you in person. Therefore, in addition to your bringing Mr. Delacroix with you, I'm going to insist that you also bring a small token of your generosity."

Martin sighed. "Again...what do you want?"

"The Picasso sketch. The small one in the entry hall. It should easily fit into a shoulder bag."

The Picasso...Shit.

The sketch was no larger than six by eight inches. It depicted, in a few graceful lines, a woman preparing her bath. It was worth upwards of three quarters of a million dollars.

Martin walked deliberately to the entry hall and took the framed piece from the wall and stuffed it into a leather shoulder bag.

"Done. Now when do I get back my wife and son?"

23

———

Bangkok, 1949

Jim Thompson was flying. Without a plane.

The man-thing he'd known as Ramonne Delacroix had taken him by the hand and, via a series of powerful leaps, transported him up to the rooftops overlooking the Chao Phraya River. Thompson's heart was in his mouth as the fiend propelled them without effort ten or twenty meters through the air at a time.

Finally they halted. Ramonne and Thompson landed atop a large hangar-like structure that housed the King's fleet of royal ceremonial barges. The Grand Palace was behind them, and the graceful Temple of Dawn was directly across the river. Thompson, when he finally convinced his heart to stop racing and was assured that his feet were on a solid platform, marveled at the magnificent view. The river snaked north and south and was congested with the usual nighttime traffic— mainly rice and sand barges steadily making their way up or downriver.

Thompson allowed himself a mere moment's respite before the horror of the evening took hold again. He pressed himself to the railing of the structure and stared at Ramonne.

"My God, man, what *are* you?"

Ramonne ran a hand through his mane of silver-streaked hair and faced the river. "I'm a man, Lord Jim...a man betrayed." He turned to Thompson. "Betrayed a long, *long* time ago, by a beast. Betrayed by my own folly. Betrayed by time so that he who should have perished nearly a century ago, stands before you now."

"I saw you kill a man by drinking his *blood*. You were *shot*. It didn't affect you. And you carried me here by leaping across rooftops. You're not a *man*, damn you."

"That is correct. I *am* damned. I'm cursed."

He moved towards Thompson, who shrank back from him. "Stop."

Ramonne halted and raised his hands to placate Thompson. "I promise you, I will not harm you."

He let a moment pass. He knew that this was overwhelming for the mortal Lord Jim, and that his friend would need time to absorb what he would tell him. It would take time to regain his trust—if that would, indeed, be possible.

"I came here in 1858. This port was filled with great three- and four-masted ships plying their trade. Loading and unloading cargo." He smiled at the memory.

"How is that possible? You would have to be over 100 years old—"

"One hundred and twenty-two actually. I look good, don't you think?" He grinned, but Thompson just stared. "A little vampire humor, forgive me."

"A *vampire*?"

"Yes, Lord Jim. A vampire. The living dead. A forsaken one."

"How is this possible?"

"As I was explaining, I was a victim. A victim of my own folly. I was on an exploration in 1862 that traveled deep into the jungles of Cambodia. We were the first white men to come across the ruins of the Angkor temples. In my rush to satiate myself, I foolishly ventured into the temples alone at night. I was attacked by a very old, very frail vampire. He did not have the strength to kill me, and I wandered the day delirious before becoming his victim again at night. This time he finished his task and condemned me to join him in eternal damnation. I have needed fresh blood for my very survival ever since."

Jim Thompson was holding the railing in a death grip. "My God, man. I've known you for over a year. We drank together, dined together—"

"You dined, I drank."

"You've been my…my…"

"Your *friend*." Ramonne put his hands on the railing. "I *am* your friend, Lord Jim. I will always be your friend."

Thompson was torn apart. He could barely continue to stand. He was witnessing the end of all that he believed in. Until this very moment, life had had rules. Limits. Boundaries. Things made sense.

No more.

He had somehow crossed over into a netherworld without rules or control. Where nothing made sense.

He suddenly felt exhausted. His legs began to give out and he slowly sank to the deck. Ramonne caught him and gently helped him to a seated position.

Thompson looked up at Ramonne through heavy eyes. "You *look* the same."

Ramonne smiled. "I *am* the same. I'm the person you know. You just know more about me now."

"You really did kill those men that attacked me that night, didn't you?"

"Yes. I did."

"And tonight…you knew what would happen, didn't you?"

"I suspected it, yes."

Thompson looked at the box that Ramonne had carried throughout the night.

"What is that?"

"It's the Oracle."

"You've had it all along?"

"Yes."

Thompson marveled anew at how things had changed. Here was the Oracle. Men had fought for it, died for it, sought it for centuries, and here it was. Within his grasp. Ramonne had wrapped the paper around it, but the glow was evident within.

"What are you going to do with it?"

"Keep it safe."

Thompson looked at the river. It seemed the same as always, but it was in a constant state of flux. Ever changing.

He sighed. They watched the river together. Moments passed. Finally Thompson spoke. "Now what?"

Ramonne thought for a moment.

"I think I should disappear."

"Disappear?"

"Yes…I shall die."

"But you said you couldn't—"

"I won't actually die. Just disappear. But I'll die in others' eyes."

"How will you do that?"

Ramonne thought some more.

"You will do it for me."

———

Bangkok, Present Day

"Just like old times." Ramonne smiled.

Martin looked at him like he was crazy. "Old times? We have no good *old times*."

"Don't we?"

"No. We don't. I was insane then. You had me under some kind of spell."

"Oh, come on now. You made a deal with me. I spared your life and shared mine with you in exchange for a pittance of your fortune."

"A *pittance*? I gave you more than two million dollars."

"And I showed you things no mortal has ever experienced. The past. History. You experienced it. You lived it."

"And you took me with you on your murderous quests. You deceived me."

"I deceived you…? I *saved* you."

At this they both fell silent.

They were in the van. Professor Kaestle was at the wheel. It was Friday night and they were on Sukhumvit Road headed east, just below the Asoke intersection, stuck in a line of cars almost two kilometers long. They waited at what was perhaps the world's longest traffic light. They were frozen in time for at least six minutes. When it would finally change, nothing would happen for another full minute while the flurry of cars and motorbikes that had run the red light on Asoke raced to make it through. Then traffic would surge forward in a blare of horns and belching exhaust. Two minutes later and the traffic had crept forward a matter of a few meters. Then another interminable wait until the world's longest traffic light changed again.

Martin sat in the front with his leather shoulder bag holding the Picasso sketch. The endless traffic was doing nothing to calm his nerves.

"Why the hell is he going this way?" Martin scowled at the professor.

"He has a phobia about left turns."

Martin now frowned at Ramonne. "Like J. Edgar Hoover?"

"I suppose.'

Martin thought about this for a moment.

"That makes a little sense in America, where they drive on the right. It makes no sense at all in this country."

Ramonne rolled his eyes and shrugged his shoulders. "What can I do? He's the driver."

Ramonne, sitting in the rear, looked up longingly at the rooftops. "We don't have to wait here, you know. There are other, faster ways we could travel."

"Yes. We could take the skytrain."

"That's not what I meant."

"I know that." Martin chuckled. "We have time. And we'll need the van to bring my family home."

They fell into silence again. The professor hadn't said anything. He knew these two shared a past, and he thought it best not to interfere.

Martin turned in his seat and faced the vampire again.

"Tell me about Jim Thompson."

Ramonne sighed. He looked away from the street, and Martin saw the sadness in his eyes.

"Lord Jim was one of the finest men I've ever known. He was my first real friend since...since Henri Mouhot."

Martin did the math. "Over eighty years."

"Yes. Lord Jim reopened the Oriental after the war. I managed to secure a position with the—"

"The Bamboo Bar. Yes...I know most of that. Thompson was still in the OSS, and got involved in a case involving the Black Dragons. How did that end?"

"Badly, I'm afraid. Lord Jim and the others were led into an ambush. I took it upon myself to rescue Jim and execute the gang's leader, along with a nefarious police officer. This proved awkward, as I was now exposed. I chose to fake my own demise and left Jim to clean up the mess."

As the vampire continued his tale, the vehicle inched forward. "Since there were no witnesses to what finally transpired at the Mahakan Fort, I concocted a tale that Jim played his part in. We flagged down a truck and were dropped at the emergency entrance of Chulalongkorn Hospital. Jim told them that I'd apparently suffered a stroke. They treated me so. It took only a slight bit of acting on my part to convince them I was dead."

"So you died."

"I died. Again. They slid me into a metal drawer with a tag on my toe. I rose before dawn, switched tags with the only other foreigner in the morgue, and that was the end of *that* Ramonne Delacroix."

"And Thompson?"

"He managed to account for most of the night's events—the massacre, my arrival and help, the necessity to get to the hospital that caused him to bolt the scene. He cleaned up nearly everything but the lack of blood in Colonel Natiwat's corpse."

"That would seem a fairly difficult obstacle."

"Yes it would. However, the authorities here are most inventive when it comes to rewriting history...if the right palms are greased. Slowly, surely, the questions stopped and the incident became history."

Eventually they got through the intersection and made a right turn.

"And you?" Martin asked.

"I went back to my solitary ways. I greatly regretted the loss of the Bamboo Bar. I was quite at home there. But most of all I regretted the loss of my friend Jim."

"Did you see him again?"

Ramonne had gone back to gazing at the street. He reflected on Martin's question and then slowly turned to face him.

"Yes. But not for another twenty years."

Martin waited.

"That is another story, for another time."

The traffic was moving now and it wasn't long before the professor made another right turn onto Rama IV. Again they were stopped by a red light and the professor took the opportunity to study a hard, glossy map.

Eventually they came to the Sathorn intersection and the professor was forced to make a left. Martin smiled to himself.

Ten minutes later, he was able to make another right, this time onto Naradhiwas Rajanagarindra Road—a name so difficult to pronounce that most people referred to it as simply New Road. They were under the shelter of the skytrain again, and followed its path as they made yet another right turn onto Silom Road.

As they made the turn, Ramonne's gaze strayed to the site of the cemetery—Hernando's 'church' as it had been known forever. Behind the heavy steel gates and concrete walls, he knew that little remained of what had been, for over sixty years, his own personal morgue. He had greased generation after generation of police palms to make his victims' bodies disappear. All he had to do was make the deposit and the cops cleaned up after him. It was the discovery of this killing field that had led Martin Larue to believe he'd discovered the trail of a serial killer. The subsequent front-page article he penned for the *Bangkok Times* led Ramonne Delacroix to his doorstep and into his life.

But the boom years after the turn of the millennium brought an endless procession of construction cranes and Burmese workers to Bangkok. Initially they marched east on Sukhumvit and south on Sathorn, working twenty-four seven behind enormous metal nets that inched higher and higher amid the endless noise and dust until soon they were ready to march down Silom Road to the river. The two-block plot of land that the cemetery occupied was worth a king's ransom, and eventually the unthinkable happened and the ancient Chinese, Portuguese and Thai graves were disrupted, their contents moved to a newly ordained bit of hallowed ground in Sam Phran in Nakhon Pathom, fifty kilometers away. No doubt the skies had been filled with shrieking ghosts. Any Thai or Chinese with any sense at all would know that construction on such a sacrosanct site would be doomed to failure. It was blasphemy. But enormous sums of money were involved, and the property's former denizens were almost all relocated by now.

Traffic slowed to a crawl again as they neared the neon

jungle of Patpong Road. Martin's anxiety was increasing. Soon they would be at their destination.

"This place we're going to…do you know it?" he asked.

"I used to. A long time ago. I'm surprised it's still here."

"What is it?"

"It *was*, of course, a brothel. One of the first to cater to the Japanese after the war."

They inched past Patpong. Dozens of taxis and *tuk-tuks* double parked and squeezed the traffic. Their drivers smoked, drank, ate and harassed the tourists coming and going from the crowded night bazaar of human flesh and brand-name knock-offs.

"There was *nothing* here, Martin. Just a canal, grassy meadows and a lone teakwood house."

For a moment, Martin *saw* the street as it was 150 years before. Candles and torches lit the stately wooden house. The tall grass on either side waved in the night breeze and a single *sampan* poled by a tall man, glided silently down the canal. He blinked and the image was gone, replaced by the urban blight of the twenty-first century. They crawled past Patpong's little sister street, where gay men strolled arm in arm and an entirely different brand of sex was being touted.

Finally they arrived at their destination. Soi Thaniya. Patpong for the Japanese. Located between Surawong and Silom roads, just north of Patpong, it was full of bars, restaurants, massage parlors and karaoke clubs. As in Roppongi or Shinjuku in Tokyo, most of the clubs and karaoke bars weren't on the street level, but upstairs, hidden from view. Also known as Little Tokyo, but the difference being that in Tokyo foreigners were welcome. On Soi Thaniya, they were not. The signs for the clubs, restaurants and bars were almost entirely Japanese, with English names alongside—Club Marco Polo, Miláno, Club Sahara, Kiara.

As well as luring Japanese tourists, the area also attracted a criminal element, and by 1990, at the height of the bubble economy, more than 200 Yakuza and their associates were believed to be active in Thailand, mainly in Soi Thaniya. To the Thai police, who count on pay-offs to supplement their meager salaries, the Yakuza were seen as stepping on their toes. In 1992 the Crime Suppression Division, working with Interpol, busted all the gangs and ringleaders running the street. Now the brothels, massage parlors and karaoke bars were called 'member clubs,' with only Japanese members authorized for entrance.

The professor eased the van into the *soi's* entrance and stopped. Martin took out his wallet. He waved two 1,000-baht notes at a security guard.

"I need to keep this van here for one hour. The driver will stay with it." He spoke in perfect Thai.

The guard took the two bills, his eyes wide in disbelief at his good fortune, and then blew a shrill blast on his whistle. Loitering *tuk-tuks* moved and a parking space materialized.

"We'll be back," Ramonne could not resist saying as he and Martin exited the vehicle.

24

Bangkok, Present Day

They were immediately conspicuous.

Both of them were taller than most of the men jammed into the fairly wide pedestrian street. And they were Caucasian. The girls that stood in the polished chrome and glass doorways wore kimonos and had their hair and makeup done, apparently by the same 'artist,' to reflect a Japanese sense of beauty. Their large farmer's feet were squeezed into Jimmy Choo Plexiglas stiletto knock-offs or fuzzy bunny-rabbit slippers. In each case the tarted-up farm girls blatantly ignored the two white men as they passed. A few touts got in their faces and tried to convince them about the merits of the foreigner-friendly massage parlors or go-go bars further on. A single glance from Ramonne and they slunk away to harass other targets.

They reached the place. A large white sign proclaimed: 'Kasanova—Members Club 3rd Fl.' It was an old building. Four stories. The windows on the street were filled with meter-wide painted signs for the other establishments crammed into the rotting structure. Noah's Arc, Amore, Asaka, Shark's Tooth. A tattered striped curtain was stretched across the half-glass on the front door. Ramonne stood on the dirty curb and looked up at the façade. Ancient air-conditioning units filled the street windows in a line ascending to the roof. Narrow wooden slats covered all the other windows on every floor, giving it a prison feel. A very dodgy-looking fire escape ladder came from the roof but stopped two floors from the street. A jungle of neon signs projected out from the façade and fought their way to the roof.

Unlike every other venue they had passed, there were no kimono-clad girls to either greet or ignore them. There was no tout or security guard to give them dirty looks. There was no one.

They entered the dimly lit reception area. It was a mishmash of styles, with cheap Thai wall hangings and filthy paper lanterns. A granite table-and-seat ensemble looked like it belonged outside. As there was no one to usher them, they walked to the small elevator and pressed the button. The indicator showed that it was on the third floor. After a half-minute of gears winding, it started to descend.

The doors opened and two men stood in the car, pointing pistols.

Ramonne smiled as he and Martin raised their hands. "Good evening to you, too."

The two were young, Asian and dressed alike in sharkskin suits that showed off their muscular builds. They stepped forward.

The first man out of the car went to Ramonne. The second went to Martin. They proceeded to frisk them. Ramonne had nothing but a slim leather billfold with a dozen 1,000-baht notes and a sterling silver Dunhill cigarette lighter. Martin had the usual—keys, money, credit cards, ID, iPhone, reading glasses and his leather shoulder bag. The man glanced in the bag. It contained only the wrapped Picasso. He closed it.

"They're clean," Number Two said to Number One.

Number One motioned with his gun. "Upstairs."

Ramonne got into the car first. Number One moved next to him. Martin and Number Two got in last.

They had hit the maximum capacity for the little elevator, and it groaned and shuddered as the doors creaked closed. There was no air-conditioning or ventilation, and the air was thick with the odors of sweat and cologne.

Number One stared at Ramonne and Number Two stared at Martin. Martin and Ramonne stared straight ahead. The elevator seemed not to be moving at all, but the vibrations and the occasional light through the door's edges said it was.

In the yellow glare of the bare bulb overhead, the two men appeared to be twins. They even had identical scars on their eyebrows. Number One's on his left, Number Two's on his right.

"Brothers?" Ramonne said the word in Japanese, and Number One nodded. "After all these years, it's still a family business," Ramonne commented.

Martin arched an eyebrow.

"Black Dragons," Ramonne loudly whispered. He smiled at the expected reaction he got from the two men.

At last the elevator shuddered to a halt and the door opened.

The second floor of the Kasanova was no classier than the lobby. It had a reception desk with a huge fish tank behind it. The water was filthy, which didn't seem to matter as there weren't any fish. In front of the faded velvet desk was a small group of chairs and a couch. Seated amid this tattered finery was Toshiro Muraki.

"Mr. Larue." He looked at his watch. "Right on time."

He made no indication that he was getting up.

"Mr. Delacroix." He looked at Ramonne, who had Number One's pistol held in his back. "This is indeed a pleasure. You look remarkably well for a man over a century and a half old."

"Where is my wife?" Martin demanded.

"She is just through that door." Muraki nodded to a metal door to the left of the reception desk.

"And the boy?"

"The boy is with her. I assure you they are unharmed." He motioned to the leather bag. "I assume you have brought the Picasso?"

Martin took the bag off his shoulder and held it out. Muraki motioned and Number Two took it and brought it to him, all the while keeping his pistol trained on Martin.

Muraki took out the package and carefully unwrapped it. He held the framed sketch with both hands and smiled. "Exquisite."

"My wife and son."

"Of course…I am a man of my word." He stood and went behind the reception desk. There was a small safe, its door open. Muraki put the Picasso in the safe, closed the door and spun the tumbler.

"Please follow me." He led them through the metal door.

The narrow hall inside had faded cranberry carpeting. The walls were paneled in a cheap veneer and hung with tacky paintings of all manner of subjects. A half-dozen framed photos of young Thai girls hung under a hand-painted sign that proclaimed them 'Employees of the Month.'

The doors were all on the left side of the corridor. They were open and the rooms were identical—gaudy lights, a plasma TV, a huge stereo system, a couch and a dirty window with a heavy screen and an old air-conditioner.

Muraki led them past six empty rooms, Ramonne and Martin followed by One and Two, their pistols extended before them.

"Where is everyone?" Ramonne asked.

"This whole building is a family affair. You, my friend, are such an important guest that the entire staff has been dismissed tonight so that you may have our undivided attention."

"You flatter me."

They reached the last door. It was set back from the end of the corridor a lot further than the other doors, indicating a much larger room. A window was at the end of the hall, and through the grime the glare of Thaniya's neon was visible. Unlike the other doors, this one was closed.

Muraki took a key from his pocket and unlocked it. As it swung inward, Martin saw his wife.

"Areeya."

She was seated on the couch. Hon was next to her. Martin rushed through the door. Number Two tried to stop him, but Muraki motioned to let him go. She rushed into his arms. He crushed her to him. With his right hand he pulled little Hon to his knee. The boy squeezed him.

"Are you all right?" Martin held her and looked into her beautiful face.

"Yes."

He thanked God and leaned down to pick up the boy. As he did, he saw the look in his eyes. He was no longer scared. And he was no longer looking at daddy, his savior. He was looking at...

Ramonne.

Hon was staring at the vampire.

Martin held the boy close. He was convinced that if he let the boy down...he would run to Ramonne.

Martin turned to Muraki. "Now what?"

"Now you go."

Martin stared in disbelief. "We leave?"

"Yes."

"That's it?"

Muraki shrugged. "You gave me something of value, I returned to you something of value. We're finished."

Martin looked at Ramonne. "What about him?"

Muraki thought a moment. "He's a different story. He stays."

Ramonne stared at Martin, a slight smile on his lips. Without speaking, Martin felt the vampire order him to leave. He had no fear, and neither should Martin. *'Take your family and go. Be safe.'*

Martin took Areeya's hand and lifted Hon onto his shoulder and started for the door. One and Two made way for them. As they passed the vampire, Hon reached out his little hand. Ramonne smiled at him and the boy suddenly grew very calm. Martin could feel him relax on his shoulder. Before he knew they had left the room, they were in the corridor. The door shut behind them.

———

Professor Kaestle saw the young master and his wife and boy walking through the crowd. He got out of the van and opened the rear door.

Martin stopped. "He's still in there."

The professor smiled. "I know. He said he'd be delayed. I'm to drive you home."

Martin could see that the professor had no fear for Ramonne either, and so he helped Areeya and Hon to get into the back of the van.

———

Ramonne looked Toshiro Muraki in the eye. "How does it feel?

"Excuse me?"

"Death…How does it feel?"

"What are you talking about?"

"You're about to die…all of you. How does it feel?"

Muraki now felt a chill. He realized that he might have made a big mistake.

"There is no need for threats, my friend. All I want is that which belongs to my family."

"But it has been mine for a long, long time," Ramonne answered.

"And you have benefited from it. You prove its merit. You are living proof that the Oracle does offer the secret to immortality. Now it is time for you to return it to us."

"Why…? Why should I do this?"

"Because I am your friend. I let your friends live. I could have easily held them here and forced you to give it to me. I could have killed them one at a time. But I didn't. I wanted you to see me as your friend. I want you to share your knowledge of the Oracle. You alone know its secrets. You are the proof we've sought."

Ramonne held an accusatory finger at Muraki. "You really have no idea who I am, do you?"

Muraki raised his hands in prayer. "Show me."

Show you? "Show you what?"

"Immortality."

Ramonne thought for a moment. Then he went to Number One and pulled the man's pistol to his own chest, directly where his heart should be.

The explosion echoed in the hallway. The gun was a .44 magnum Smith & Wesson revolver. There was a gaping hole ten centimeters wide in the vampire's chest. Bits of gore and chunks of flesh were splattered across a black velvet and Day-Glo Elvis behind him. Smoke rolled off Ramonne's chest like miniature cumulus clouds. He turned to Muraki, his arms at his side, and turned the palms of both hands to him.

"Is this what you want to see?"

The astonished Japanese watched the jagged hole in Ramonne's chest fill in, viscous and wax-like at first, but within minutes it was bone, tendons and flesh.

"You are the proof."

"No. You fool." Ramonne smiled. "I destroyed your precious Oracle."

Muraki's eyes widened in horror.

Ramonne opened his hands. "I am not the proof you seek…I

was immortal before you hid your sacred vessel in the Oriental."

Muraki sank to his knees, bowing from the waist.

"*Goshujin-sama*. Master…it's true."

"It?"

Muraki continued bowing, his head touching the floor each time. One and Two stood frozen, their guns pointed at Ramonne but their eyes on Muraki.

"You are the one. The *chosen* one…I am the unholy one. The forgotten one. The demon son." Muraki was now prostrate on the floor. Number One and Two stared vacantly at these two madmen. They wanted to shoot Ramonne. They wanted to shoot someone—anyone, but they were waiting for the word from their boss. But the boss was now praying—*bowing and praying* to this *gaijin* devil. They had no idea what to do, so they kept their guns pointed at him and watched.

"You're a fool," Ramonne repeated.

Muraki raised up onto his knees. "Yes…it is true."

Ramonne grabbed his head by the hair and yanked viciously. "No. No. It is not. I am not who you think I am. I am not who you want me to be."

"But…you have the gift."

"I have the *curse*."

Ramonne turned to Number One. The man was standing frozen, the still-smoking gun now dangling at his side. Ramonne attacked him furiously, sinking his fangs into his throat, ripping, shredding—and sapping the life from him in a matter of moments.

He dropped the corpse and reverted his gaze to Muraki. Blood had splattered his silk suit and pooled at his feet.

"You seek immortality. You seek immunity. You seek wealth. Power. World domination."

He bent down and lifted the man's head with one finger under his chin. "I *have* immortality. But I seek only anonymity. Tranquility. Invisibility."

Muraki pointed a finger at Ramonne. "You lie! You took *our* secret. You used it and now you refuse to share it."

"Share it?"

Ramonne moved to Number Two. He was petrified, his gun shaking in his grasp.

"What exactly is it you think I should share with you?"

"The power. You have it. You showed me...share it with me."

Ramonne laughed. "You think I have *the power*? Because you can't kill me?"

He turned his attention to Number Two. In an instant the man raised the pistol and shot himself in the head.

"That's a little different, isn't it? Not only can you not kill me, but I can *will* you to kill yourself."

Muraki's eyes were now as wide as a barn owl's. He slowly rose to his feet. He grinned maniacally.

"Yes."

"Yes?" Ramonne was puzzled.

"Yes...You have shown me the way. Now I understand."

"You are truly insane." Ramonne stared long and hard at the man. This one was unique. He could not read him.

Muraki removed his jacket. He began unbuttoning his shirt. As he did, he revealed twin dragon heads—one on each breast. He pulled the shirt down until it was draped about his waist. His torso was covered in intricate tattoos. He crossed the room and took a long, narrow wooden box off a shelf. As he turned, Ramonne saw that the designs on his back were dominated by a large rendering of a tiger.

Muraki knelt before the table and opened the box. It contained a sword with a blade approximately a half-meter long, and a bone-handled knife no more than thirty centimeters in length.

Seppuku. Ramonne had knowledge of this method of departing the mortal plane. He knew that it was a death sought by men who were considered warriors but had somehow been dishonored. The act would prove the warrior's worth and restore him to grace.

Muraki handed the sword to Ramonne, who knew what was expected of him. He took the blade without comment.

Muraki then took a small white cloth and wrapped it midway on the blade of the bone-handled knife. He held it poised over his abdomen and looked up at Ramonne. He smiled. "You will give me what I seek. This is but the first step to immortality."

With those final words he plunged the blade into his stomach and made a left to right incision. And in one swift movement, Ramonne decapitated the Black Dragon.

May you find that which you seek.

———

Ramonne strolled through the thinning crowd of late-night revelers along Soi Thaniya. The professor had returned, and the van was waiting. Just as he approached the end of the *soi*, there was an explosion and a fireball erupted from the cluster of buildings at the far end of the street. The four-story Kasanova building burned with the eagerness of a torch that needed igniting a long time ago. People raced about and scrambled for safety as Ramonne climbed into the passenger seat of the van. The professor was guided by a *tuk-tuk* tout into the traffic on Silom Road and the van merged with the never-ending flow of vehicles. As the van headed off, a distant fire siren could be heard.

25

Bangkok, Present Day

Martin counted his blessings. His pregnant wife was back, safely tucked under a pile of duvets in their sleigh bed. She had been asleep for twenty minutes while Martin made himself a drink. Hon was also asleep, curled up with the despicable Small Talk. Both boy and cat were snoring.

Martin took the glass with the ice-cold Grey Goose vodka and settled into the couch on the patio balcony. The windows were open and a slight early morning breeze was blowing. The city was not yet awake, and he savored the relative quiet.

"You could use the elevator, if you'd like. I could even give you a key." Martin knew the vampire was in the apartment when he was in the kitchen making his drink. He just wasn't sure where until now. A light had come on by the entry. Martin watched as Ramonne carefully re-hung the Picasso on its old hook. He adjusted it until he was satisfied it was straight.

"Thank you," Martin said as the vampire sat opposite him.

Ramonne shrugged. "It belongs here."

"Thank you for getting back my wife and boy."

"They belong here, too."

"The Black Dragons...I assume they are all dead?"

Ramonne didn't answer immediately. He looked to the park and studied the trees moving in the light wind.

"Yes."

"That should put an end to this, then?"

Ramonne shrugged again. "Perhaps." He bore a great burden that Martin saw glimpses of when he allowed him to.

Martin *saw* the Oracle when Ramonne uncovered it in the basement of the Oriental Hotel, so many decades ago. And Martin *saw* a few glimpses of the bloodbath in the Kasanova. The last image was of Ramonne studying the severed Japanese head. For a few moments the mouth desperately tried to speak, and the eyes stared in fear. Then the head grew still and Martin was returned to the present.

Martin drained his glass in an attempt to erase the violent imagery.

"I realize now that I must dispose of the Oracle," Ramonne informed him. "It cannot be allowed to fall into a mortal's hands. It is too powerful."

"Can you do that? Destroy it?"

"I'm not sure. But I can hide it where it will never be found."

———

The next day found Martin sleeping in. He was exhausted and realized he hadn't slept in two days. The electric shades were drawn. A note had been left for the maid to take care of Hon when he awoke, but to let them sleep undisturbed until then.

For the first time in a very long time, Martin dreamed. He dreamed he was skiing—something else he hadn't done in a long, long time. He was a good skier. Better than good. There was a time when he was spending every winter in Zermatt, that he could easily have turned pro. He was hanging out with a group of freestyle champions and enjoying the nirvana rush of flying on snow and ice at ninety-degree angles and speeds of up to fifty miles an hour as he raced down one of the world's loftiest mountains—the Matterhorn. Crystals would form in his beard and the freshest, cleanest air on the planet would be disbursed through his system in extremely thin doses, causing a high that was unlike anything he'd experienced before or since. Combine that with the decadent nightlife and Martin was never sure why he had come down from the mountain. The answer of course was the weather. Spring came and the thrill was gone.

In Martin's dream he was flying over an endless landscape of moguls, valleys, jumps and jibs, using the sharp edges of his carbon-kevlar skis to carve out his trail. The powder exploding before him coated his face. He didn't wear a hat, only goggles and a headband that covered his ears. He shook the snow from his blond locks as he pushed on harder, faster, flying over jumps and landing moments later near the edge of the mountain.

Faster and faster...Flying down the mountain...Snow exploding before him, the 15,000-foot chasm constantly to his left as he raced closer and closer to the precipice.

"Martin."

Faster...Closer...Faster...

"Martin."

He jolted awake. Areeya was shaking him.

"What...? What is it?"

"I'm sick, Martin."

He sat up. The room was dark but he could see that she was covered in sweat. Her hair clung to her scalp and face in ringlets. He reached out a hand for her forehead.

"Jesus. You're burning up." He reached into the bedstead drawer and found the remote for the blinds. He cracked them a bit, and light flooded into the room. He looked at the clock. It was two in the afternoon. He could have easily slept through the whole day.

"How long have you been like this?"

Areeya started to shake. "For a couple of hours."

"A couple of hours?"

"I didn't want to wake you. You were sleeping so well."

He pulled her to him. As he did, he could feel her body temperature dropping. "What the hell!" He grabbed her hand. It was as cold as ice. She began shivering uncontrollably.

Martin picked up the telephone and was immediately connected to the security station downstairs. He told them he needed an ambulance.

———

> "Deck the halls with boughs of holly,
> Fa la la la la
> La la la la."

The little girls were all dressed in red sweaters and black tights, and each had a Santa hat perched over shining black hair. They sang the standard carols with Thai accents and made valiant attempts at harmony. They were in the center courtyard of Bangkok Nursing Hospital under a giant artificial Christmas tree, singing for an attentive group of hospital staff. But their most appreciative audience were the patients on the four floors of rooms that encircled the courtyard. If they were well enough, they stood at the window and smiled. If not, nurses had opened the window and the joyous sound brought a smile to them in their beds.

Martin looked down from a suite.

Christmas? How did it get to be Christmas? Wasn't it Halloween just last week? He realized that his preoccupation with Areeya's attempts, and then success, at pregnancy had taken over his entire life and he had been paying absolutely no attention to the calendar. Halloween had indeed been just a few weeks ago, but in Bangkok, like everywhere else, it was immediately followed by Christmas.

Behind him Areeya lay in an induced sleep. An intravenous tube ran into her right arm and a steady drip was being administered. Her right index finger had a metal contact attached, and she was hooked up to a machine that monitored her vital signs. The room was spacious, minimally furnished. There was a couch that could unfold into a bed for Martin, and a kitchenette with a table and two chairs. An easy chair alongside Areeya's bed faced the wall-mounted plasma TV. The decor was muted tones and the lighting was recessed and dimmed. An alcove led to the bathroom and front door. It was more like a four-star hotel suite…with a hospital bed wheeled in.

There was a very short ring of a low-volume door bell and a quick tap on the door. It opened and two women came in. One wore a light-gray lab coat over a coral blouse and charcoal skirt. She was the doctor. The younger woman in the skin-tight white uniform and cute little cap was the nurse.

"Doctor Irene. Good of you to see us." Martin shook hands with the doctor, who smiled warmly at him.

"Of course, Martin. You are one of my favorite patients. It's about time I met your wife."

"How is she?"

Dr. Irene looked at the chart that was in a file folder at the end of the bed.

"Stable." She continued reading…"But fluctuating body temperature. Body pain, nausea." She shut the file and went to Areeya. She opened Areeya's gown and looked at the center of her chest. She rolled her over.

"It's not Lyme disease. That's all we know so far…until the blood work comes back."

"What about the baby?"

"We haven't done an ultrasound yet. We've been concentrating on getting her stable. I'll do the scan as soon as she wakes, and we'll take it from there. Please try and relax, Martin. She needs you to be calm and strong for her."

The doctor listened to Areeya's heartbeat with her stethoscope, felt on each side of her throat and her temples. Then she moved to the foot of the bed and lifted the sheet and felt each of her toes.

She turned to Martin. "She should wake up in an hour or so. Call the nurse when she does."

"Thank you, Doctor."

The woman put her hand on Martin's back for a moment and then left the room. The nurse stayed behind and refitted a new bottle onto the IV stand. When she left, Martin went back to the window. Santa's little helpers had finished their show and the tree lights were about to be formally switched on. The sky beyond was a brilliant deep-maroon and there was applause from the gathering when the tree lit up with hundreds of pale-blue bulbs.

Martin closed the window and sat in the lounge chair and waited for her to wake up.

———

The goal of the Great Work of Alchemy, called also the Art, is the "Philosopher's Stone." The Stone was viewed as a magical touchstone that could immediately perfect any substance or situation. The Philosopher's Stone has been associated with the Salt of the World, the Astral Body, the Elixir, and even Jesus Christ. When applied to the human body, the Elixir cures diseases and restores youth.

Ramonne's library had been shipped from Roluos and assembled in what had been a private dining room of the old restaurant on Sukhumvit Soi 8. An ornate writing desk, lamps, cabinets and other furnishings had been retrieved from his storage locker and the vampire was now quite comfortably ensconced in his lair. He was perusing ancient manuscripts that he hadn't studied in a half-century or more. They were what he had been able to obtain at the time to satisfy his curiosity about the Oracle. At the time he had been merely curious.

He had rarely thought of them since the night when he had

used them as a lure to destroy Takashi and the other Kempeitai or Black Dragon agents at the old Mahakan Fort in 1949.

Now, with the intricately carved golden box set before him, he poured once more through the volumes of text and scriptures relating to alchemy, necromancy, demonology, magical amulets, astral magic and sorcery that had come into his possession.

Initially he used his great wealth to acquire the rarest of the rare: *The Book Of Eldon*, *The Book Of Iod* and the *Unaussprechichen Kulten*. These books, known as the Mythos Tomes, provided enlightenment into the occult world that surely was the genesis of the Oracle, but he never found a specific mention of the relic.

In recent times he had acquired an astonishing library from the blind shaman Charoen. The bulk of the texts were in Braille, which—to Ramonne's own amazement—he had absolutely no trouble in reading. He simply passed his hands over the pages and the meaning appeared in his mind. He had read all he could about vampires, a subject which had been of great concern to the little fortune-teller. Charoen had indeed been instrumental in restoring the vampire after his incineration at the Temple of Dawn. For this the vampire rewarded the shaman with a swift and relatively painless death.

Ramonne soon gained heretofore unheard of knowledge of his powers and the strength to command them. He expanded this knowledge to include centuries of folklore, mythology and hypothesis. His time in Cambodia had seen his library grow yet again with the addition of sacred texts and scriptures that related to the temples and mythology of Angkor. These, coupled with his latest papers on Oriental theology acquired from L'Ecole Française d'Extrême Orient in Paris, meant that Ramonne had a specific library that rivaled any within the halls of academia in Europe or the Americas.

And yet, the Oracle eluded him.

He stood and stretched. He had been holed up with his tomes since parting company with Martin two nights before. He had slept through the days, and except for a quick hunt early this evening, he had been poring over the volumes, scriptures and scrolls for the entirety of his waking hours. He was tired. Restless. Bored.

His frustration at not being able to solve the mystery of the golden vessel had run its course. It was time to bury the thing, to dispose of it. He took the golden box from the table and, as he picked it up, a book fell to the floor. He noticed a perceptible glow emanate from within the box, and he set it back in its place. He retrieved the book and studied its cracked and broken leather cover.

The Eleusinian Mysteries And Other Pagan Rituals.

It was sealed with hinges and a lock of rust-eaten iron, in the manner of books printed in Europe in the seventeenth century. He opened it gingerly. He was instantly appalled at the noxious odor of decay that rose up from the withered, stained and yellowed pages.

Where did this come from?

He didn't recall ever having seen the tome before. He took it to the heavy chair that he retreated to from time to time in his endless studying. He started to go through the ancient document. Its early pages were devoted to translations and illustrations of the initiation rites and ceremonies of a Greek cult formed in the seventh century BC. Fascinating as this was, Ramonne knew it could hardly pertain to that which he sought, and he quickly thumbed through the pages. The book soon described the Celtic rituals of the Druids, which he also chose to ignore. He flicked through the latter pages and was about to place the book back onto the pile from which it had fallen when his hand stopped. There, in a section on Indo paganism, he saw ancient texts written in Vattezhuttu—a Tamil script used in southern India in the third century BC. It was identical in style to the symbols carved on the Oracle.

Outside, an unseasonal lightning bolt snapped, and within a

few seconds a tremendous clap of thunder exploded. Ramonne took this as an omen and turned the page.

He read throughout the night, until it was time to return to his steel-bolted crypt and shut out the light.

When he returned to his den that evening, a window had been forced open…

And the ancient book was gone.

26

Bangkok, Present Day

The lightning seemed to be focused on Sukhumvit Road to the north, and judging by the time between the flashes and the thunder, it wasn't very close, but still it was a spectacular storm.

Martin was trying to read, but the storm and his concern for Areeya in the bed beside him made it impossible. He closed the book and got up and stretched.

He walked to his wife and felt her forehead. It was warm—not hot—but warm. She was still asleep. She had been asleep, if that was what you would call it, for over thirty hours now. From the time she'd arrived at the hospital and the nurses had administered a combination of pain-killers and anesthetics, she had mercifully been asleep.

But when does sleep become a coma?

Martin trusted his doctor. She had saved his life years ago when he had suffered a concussion in a foolish bicycle accident. He had thought he was fine, even though he had been knocked unconscious for more than two hours when a car side-swiped him as he exited Lumpini Park. This was back when he wore a helmet only on road trips. He had been run through the emergency room, given an MRI and installed in a room in the intensive care unit. He'd met Dr. Irene when he awoke. He told her he was leaving, and started to get up. She told him he was staying, and crossed her arms. There was something in the woman that Martin immediately trusted. He told her he'd stay for twelve hours. She said she wanted to observe him for 72. They compromised on 48 and Martin had convulsed within eighteen and was in surgery by midnight.

If he had left the hospital, the hairline fracture that ruptured would have killed him.

The doctor had now done a sonogram on Areeya, even though the patient remained unconscious. The baby was fine.

But Areeya was not.

Her stats were borderline. Dr. Irene was uncertain what was wrong. She was waiting, again, for blood work. Cultures were growing to rule out—or in—various cancers, and would take another 24 hours for results.

Meanwhile, she lay there. His beautiful, pregnant wife, the love of his life, the mother of his child to be. She lay silent with tubes running into her, plugged into machines that monitored her.

Between life and death.

He kissed her forehead. Lightning cracked. The thunderclap followed quickly. Closer now. It shook the window pane.

The door bell made its quiet announcement. Martin turned and watched the door slowly swing open. A male nurse dressed all in white entered first, while another, dressed in green, wheeled a gurney into the room.

"Excuse me, sir. We need to take the patient to the OR."

Martin stared in surprise. He checked his watch. It was almost 2:00 a.m. "Doctor Irene didn't tell me that my wife would be having any medical procedure tonight."

"I don't know about that, sir. We only provide the transportation."

The nurse in green was unhooking the IV bottles and transferring them to the gurney. He unplugged the monitor. The line on the screen flattened out and the machine hummed a moment before he turned it off. The nurse in white flipped down the safety bars on the bed, and then the two men gently lifted Areeya onto the gurney.

A shaft of lightning cracked outside the window, followed immediately by a tremendous peal of thunder. The room shook with the blow and the electricity in the room flickered for a moment.

When the lights were restored, Martin saw the door closing.

He looked to the empty bed, sighed, and sat back in the chair and picked up his book.

———

The girl was beautiful. Her hair tumbled in auburn waves as she shook her round face. The water didn't seem to bother her at all. She wore the little inflatable water wings Areeya insisted she put on any time she went onto the deck and would be near the swimming pool. But this was the first time she had actually gone into the water. Martin had taken her tiny hand into his and they had slowly walked down the steps at the shallow end together. She shrieked and giggled with delight as the cooling water caressed her flawless porcelain skin.

She was the most beautiful thing he had ever seen. He gently put his hand under her little belly and lifted her off her feet, and for the first time she felt the sensation of floating.

She shrieked with delight…

The wind woke him. That, and the lightning and thunder.

The window was wide open. Forced open, Martin assumed, by the storm. He got to his feet, and that's when he saw him.

"Jesus…can't you ever use the door?"

"Where is she?"

The vampire was standing between the open window and the empty bed.

"They took her." Martin looked at his watch. "A half-hour ago. To the OR. Probably more tests."

"Who took her?"

The vampire was soaked. Great puddles formed at his feet. He'd obviously been traveling in the storm.

"Two nurses. Why are you here?"

Ramonne didn't answer. He crossed the room and opened the door. He went into the hall. Martin followed.

The vampire stopped in the hallway. He put one hand on the steel rail that was at waist level and ran the length of the hallway. Instantly he *saw the two men wheeling the gurney down the hall to the elevator.*

Martin *saw* it, too. The vampire moved to the elevator, Martin on his heels. Ramonne pressed the down button and the car appeared in moments. They entered the car. The vampire paused for a moment, his hand over the floor indicators. Then he pressed number three. They rode for a moment—the silence punctuated by a short *vision of the two men and the unconscious Areeya riding in the same elevator.*

The door opened on the third floor. It was identical to the other floors. Soft, sensible lighting, with Plexiglas running along each side just above the floor and shining light onto the polished walkway. Ramonne got out and again put his hand on the rail. He walked to the first door to the right. He opened it. The room was small and empty. A nurses' prep room. A counter, a sink, some cabinets, a phone and a covered metal wastebasket.

Ramonne *saw the two men wheel the gurney in and close the door. They unfolded a wheelchair that was resting against the wall, and lifted Areeya off the gurney. They seated her in the chair. They disconnected her IV from her arm, and tossed the bottle and tube into the trash. The man in white took a blanket from a cabinet and covered her with it. The man in green wheeled the chair back into the hallway.*

Martin gasped as this last vision played out in his mind.

"My God…they've kidnapped her again!"

Ramonne strode swiftly back to the elevator, Martin in tow, and they descended to the lobby. The high-ceilinged foyer was virtually empty except for nurses and the reception staff and the massive Christmas tree.

They crossed the polished marble floor and headed for the entry. Ramonne's *vision showed Areeya wheeled by the two 'nurses' to the sliding glass doors. The doors were opened by two uniformed men who bowed respectfully.*

Immediately a black SUV pulled up to the porte-cochère and Areeya was lifted into the rear seat. The man in white climbed in next to her while the man in green got in front. The vehicle pulled out, windshield wipers slapping at the rain.

A lightning bolt instantly removed the image and Martin found himself alone in the lobby with Ramonne. Terrified, he grasped the front of the vampire's sopping jacket.

"What the hell is going on?"

Ramonne gently removed Martin's hand.

"It's a little hard to explain."

"Try…please."

Ramonne sighed and smoothed the front of his wrinkled jacket. "It seems we've been pawns in a very complex game. And now, I fear your wife is about to play a role."

"What are you talking about?"

At that moment the van with Professor Kaestle at the wheel pulled up to the entry.

"Martin. We don't have time for this." The glass doors were open and the vampire went to the van.

Martin hurried after him. "Do you know where they're going?"

Ramonne was already in the passenger seat.

"I know what they're planning to do. And I know where I'd do it."

Martin slid into the rear and the van lurched into the storm.

27

———————

Bangkok, Present Day

Hernando's Cemetery.

Or what was left of it.

The thunder and lightning cast menacing shadows among the remaining crypts and tombs. The Chinese and Portuguese who were the original inhabitants seemed to be the last to leave. Their massive tombs rose a meter or more above the ground. Stone crosses and carved headstones and statuary of all description stood guard atop them. They were unattended and the grass and weeds enveloped them.

Hernando's 'church,' the large vaulted mausoleum, now stood alone to the side of the remaining tombs. The bulldozers that worked daily to remove the hundreds of remains from the four blocks the cemetery formally occupied, stood an eerie silent vigil on this last remaining plot, just behind the wall onto Silom Road.

The massive gate was unlocked, the rusty padlock lying on the ground. It had been forced. As Ramonne pushed the solid metal barrier, it creaked loudly. The sound was as familiar to Martin as his own door bell. This was his fourth foray through this portal to 'hallowed ground.' Each time, his life had changed irrevocably. He doubted tonight would be any different.

Martin reached into his pocket. He brought out a gun. A snub-nosed .38 revolver.

Ramonne stared in amazement. "What are you planning to do with that?"

"They kidnapped my family—twice. They're not going to kill my wife or my daughter."

"Your *daughter*?"

"It's a girl."

"Oh…Put it away, Martin. It's of no use here."

There was a split-second tearing sound in the sky, and a bolt of lightning was followed almost simultaneously by a gigantic thunderclap. The bolt slammed into the top of a forty-story building a few blocks away and caused it to lose power. The whole building went black. Within a few seconds emergency lights flickered to life in a straight row from top to bottom.

Martin reluctantly put the pistol in his pocket and turned up his collar in a vain attempt to thwart the pounding rain. The ground was a swirling soup of mud and debris, and walking in the darkness was dangerous and difficult. They followed the wall that led to the graveyard. Its height virtually blacked out any ambient light, and it was pitch black except for the constant flashes of lightning.

The trip from the hospital had been less than ten minutes. The professor turned right onto Sarasin, right again onto New Road, and then a reluctant left onto Silom and they were there.

In the van, Ramonne gave a brief explanation of his theory.

"This thing—the Oracle—has been in my possession since the end of the war. Except for my initial curiosity that was roused by the appearance of the original Black Dragons and their battles with Jim Thompson and the OSS agents, I've ignored it. I thought as long as I possessed it, it was harmless.

"I was very wrong. The Oracle is cursed."

Martin saw for the first time that there was a leather satchel on the seat next to him.

"Is that it?"

"Yes. Don't touch it."

"Jesus." Martin moved as close to the window as he could.

"Don't worry; the curse isn't exactly like those on mummy's tombs...you touch it, you're cursed." Ramonne smiled. "It's more complex than that. The one who first procured the Oracle for the Japanese had limited knowledge—just enough to activate the curse."

"And what exactly is the curse?"

"Immortality...what else?"

Ramonne shifted in his seat and faced Martin. "I have been killing the same man over and over for more than half a century without knowing it." He used his walking stick to move the leather bag away from Martin and into the opposite corner.

"The chain of brothers that I've dealt with—I thought they were twins at first, and then ancestors. They have all been the same man. But with subtle changes...long hair, short hair, put weight on, take it off, beards, mustaches, goatees...It wasn't until I saw the full body tattoos on the man I beheaded in Thaniya—"

"You *beheaded*?"

"Technically he was already dead. *Seppuku.* I was just completing the act."

Martin wasn't sure why this surprised him. The first time he'd met Ramonne, the vampire had just beheaded the man who had been Martin's bodyguard.

"His tattoos were exactly the same as the Black Dragons I dispatched in 1949. Exactly. And the fingers. Always two missing on the left hand. Yoshiro Nakimira, the first of this Japanese dynasty that I encountered, always wore gloves. He was portly—pudgy. His reincarnation was stronger. The next was stronger still, and this last one proudly displayed his tattoos."

Martin was puzzled. "I don't understand. They are immortal. So why do they keep searching for the Oracle?"

"They don't know they're immortal. They are reincarnated without any memory of the past life."

"They're reincarnated as adults."

"Yes. With fully formed memories of everything except their previous life...and death. Each time, the reincarnation is faster, and each time the supplicant is stronger."

"Why do they need Areeya?"

"In their mad quest, they are going to try and summon the force that controls the Oracle."

Ramonne hesitated.

"They require a sacrifice...a *human* sacrifice."

"Areeya!" Martin gasped.

"Actually, no. She will undoubtedly be sacrificed, as well. But what they need...is your unborn child."

"Jesus. But you can stop them?"

Ramonne said nothing.

"You can...yes?"

"Muraki, or whatever his name is now, knows what I know, Martin. The possession of the unborn gives him enormous power. I can no longer kill him."

———

A fire blazed. A sacrificial fire. In the midst of the storm. Seemingly it burned because it had been built directly in the entry to Hernando's crypt—the massive stone roof providing shelter for the roaring flames.

The blaze cast its shimmering light over a grisly tableau. Areeya was splayed across the marble sarcophagus, her arms and feet bound with rope and tethered to the stone.

Ramonne stopped Martin from rushing to her.

Lightning cracked, thunder pealed, rain pounded and the wind howled and whipped the flames. The fire swirled around a towering figure that stood poised over the woman. The man was naked except for a linen loincloth. His body was covered in tattoos. His massive deltoids rippled and caused the tiger illustrated on his back to move menacingly.

"Stop," he commanded without turning to face them. "Stop. Or I will gut her like a pig."

He turned. It was Toshiro Muraki. The man that Ramonne had beheaded in the Kasanova. He was attended by the two 'nurses,' now also stripped naked, their bodies tattooed—not as extensively as Muraki, but impressive nonetheless.

The unborn child—she is the key.

The dagger was poised over Areeya's swollen belly.

Martin pulled the pistol and aimed it.

"You cannot kill him." Ramonne put his hand on the barrel of the gun.

Martin held the gun with two shaky hands as the rain ran into his eyes. "You killed him before."

"He died, yes. And he rose again…stronger. But you can't kill him now." He looked into Martin's eyes.

"It's begun." Ramonne slowly lowered the gun.

Martin released his left hand and wiped the water from his eyes.

"He's protected." Ramonne put his hands on Martin's shoulder. "Trust me."

Martin's hand and the gun now hung limply at his side. Ramonne turned back to the tattooed man, who no longer seemed aware of their existence.

"*O Fire, hear our call. We offer thee the sacrificant of the rite.*" Muraki raised the dagger as to the heavens and chanted.

Ramonne stepped forward, into the glare of the fire.

"*He who gives to thee with the fuel, to the knower of the births, holds the hero-energy…he ever grows.*"

To Muraki's surprise, Ramonne joined the chant.

"*Bring forward, O Fire, the vast and supreme word. Bring forward the lights of illuminations.*"

Lightning crashed and struck one of few remaining trees in the graveyard. It split and crashed to the ground with the boom of thunder.

Muraki's face glistened with the rain, and the fire danced about the rivulets of water that ran off it. He turned and addressed Ramonne.

"My brothers were sacrificed to you time and again in a vain search for the blessing you have received."

"I have not been blessed, I've told you. I've been cursed."

"We've sought the answer for so long. We believed we knew the answer. We thought we knew the location of the vessel…but it was never true—because you."

Muraki pointed the dagger at Ramonne.

"You…you *destroyed* it."

"I lied." Ramonne removed the satchel he had slung over his back. He opened it and revealed the carved golden box.

It glowed.

"I have the vessel. You don't need the child."

"The Oracle!" Muraki's eyes grew wide as saucers. The knife trembled in his grip.

"Put the knife down."

The blade remained poised over Areeya's belly.

"You seek immortality. The vessel does not offer that."

Muraki glared at Ramonne. The fire danced in his eyes. "You lie."

"You know I tell the truth. The vessel offers not eternal life, but eternal *death*. The pain. The coldness of death. Over and over again."

Ramonne chanted, "*May our words make the Fire to grow. The Fire that carries the vision.*"

He held the Oracle before him and the fire grew taller— becoming a column of flame rather than an inferno. The wind howled and the rain lashed like needles. The lightning and thunder continued their dazzling dance in the background.

Muraki's blade remained over Areeya but his eyes were

fixed on Ramonne. *"That is not dead which can eternal lie. Fire, the Son of Force, who hears the things that are eternal, this bringer of delights would reach and possess the purifying light."*

Ramonne's eyes were on the dagger as he spoke. "I know you know the truth. You sacrificed your life to find out the truth. Committed *seppuku*. An honorable death. You sought peace. Only to be wrenched back to life again within hours. Your only memory—that of all the times you've died before."

Muraki's eyes were moist. The insane passion of the ritual had overtaken his senses, but Ramonne had hit a nerve.

"What you seek now is release. Release from the curse…I can offer you that."

Muraki stared at the vampire. His hand trembled with the knife remained poised over Areeya. He spoke in a voice just above a whisper.

"It gets worse. I am nothing now."

He held his out his empty hand. The light of the fire glowed through the skin of his arm. His flesh was translucent, the bones seen as shadows within.

"All I have is death…no life."

"I can release you."

Slowly the knife came down. Muraki took one step back and nodded. "Do it."

Ramonne held the Oracle up to the fire and chanted. *"Protect us, O Fire, from the abhorred Rakshasa."*

At the mention of the name Rakshasa, the fire whipped towards Ramonne. It curled and wound slowly around him, like the coils of a serpent.

"Rakshasa, who would war against us." The fire never touched Ramonne but writhed bare inches from his hair, his clothes, his body. Martin was astonished, as he knew that they were on hallowed ground, and that this made the vampire vulnerable. Fire was the one thing that could destroy him now, and yet Ramonne seemed to be beckoning the flames, toying with them as he chanted the satanic verse.

"Rakshasa, who would do us evil, hear me…"

The flames held everyone captivated. Muraki and his tattooed henchmen were as speechless as Martin at what they were witnessing. The fire now took the shape of a dragon. It grew to a height of ten meters above Ramonne, all the while its flames encircled and coiled around him, giving a wide berth only to where he held out the Oracle.

Ramonne continued his chant. *"O Fire, I seek the truth of knowledge. Hear me, for I am the Priest of the Call."*

At this, the great vacant eyes in the fiery head were as holes in the flames, staring down at Ramonne. The great beast stooped and passed over the inert body of Areeya. It studied her. It paid rapt attention to her belly. It hesitated slightly as it, no doubt, became aware of the unborn life force within her. It then reared up to its full height. As it did, a lightning bolt crashed and split the very ground that they stood upon. The sonic blast was enormous, and all except Ramonne were moved off their footing.

Martin desperately looked to the vampire. In his head he heard a sigh of desperation:

'It's not working.'

'What? What's not working?'

Ramonne looked to Martin. He was entwined in coils of fire from toe to head—the tail of an enormous serpent-dragon demon that did not appear pleasant. He shook his head and rolled his eyes.

'Nothing's working.'

'What do you mean nothing's working?'

'I thought I knew how to do this but…it isn't working.'

'And?'

'And I don't know what to do. Doesn't that happen to you?'

'Of course…but I'm not immortal with inhuman powers— conjuring a spell to save the life of my wife and child!'

The fiery beast cut a wide path around the vessel, then slithered seductively over the apparent corpse of Areeya. The demon head looked back to the vampire and through the flames that constituted its body. It smiled. The most malicious smile imaginable.

Ramonne knew that the demon meant to take the unborn child. To rip it from its mother's womb. Sacrifice it. *Send it to hell.*

He could not allow this to happen. *"Rakshasa. I summon thee forth…heed the call of thy son."*

The demon turned. The flames roared. Its hideous, vacant gap of a mouth opened wide and a blast of heated vapor washed over Ramonne.

The effect was immediate. The vampire began to wither and age. Slowly, but undeniably—time was catching up with him.

"Rakshasa. Heed thy son…restore the infidel." Ramonne supplicated himself in front of the demon, the Oracle thrust out before him and pointing directly at Muraki.

"I approach thee with outstretched hands and with obeisance."

Gray-haired now and infirm, the vampire continued to age.

"With a mind strong for sacrifice, I beseech thee…"

Ramonne raised his head and locked eyes with the beast.

"Take me."

Martin understood the meaning of the words the vampire spoke. Ramonne was offering himself as sacrifice.

"Take me," he repeated.

The fire-beast bent again to study the vampire. Then the monster tightened the flames about the feeble body of the vampire and he started to burn. The Oracle also burst into flames. It burned with a white fire that was blinding to the eye. Ramonne continued to hold it in a death grip as they were both consumed by flames.

Martin, shielding his eyes from the phosphorescent glare, was horrified, knowing there was nothing that could be done.

The decision had been made. The sacrifice was offered. And accepted.

The Oracle burned out and disappeared, while the fire

consumed the form of the vampire for what seemed an eternity to Martin. Then slowly the flames subsided, spiraling earthward as the column of ash that formerly was Ramonne Delacroix started to crumble. The fire changed color to a cold azure as it flickered and faded.

The pile of ash unceremoniously tumbled to the ground.

No one moved.

The skies, Martin realized, had gone quiet. The thunder and lightning had abated. The rainstorm was now just drizzle. He went to his wife's side. She was starting to wake.

"Areeya."

"Martin…" She clutched him to her. "Where am I?"

He smiled. "Nowhere…But you'll be home soon."

He helped her to sit up. She sat holding a hand to her head, bewildered as she glanced around at the creepy surroundings.

Dr. Kaestle appeared. Martin looked into his sad eyes and knew there was nothing to be said.

He knew.

The professor helped Martin get Areeya to her feet.

"Take her to the van, please."

Areeya looked back at Martin as the professor helped her walk. "Martin?"

"I'll be there in a moment."

He turned to Muraki, who also seemed to be in a daze.

"Are you mortal now?"

Muraki ran a hand over his hair, still plastered to his skull from the rain that was now letting up. He held the hand in front of him and flexed the fingers.

"Yes. I believe I am."

"You can die now…and you won't be reborn?"

"Yes, finally."

"Good."

Martin shot him in the heart.

Twice.

Muraki clutched his chest and gaped at Martin.

"No one will ever threaten my family again."

He pointed the gun towards the other tattooed henchmen. They were in shock as Muraki tumbled to the ground. Slowly they raised their hands and started backing up. Martin felt assured that they would not cause any further trouble.

No one will ever threaten my family again.
He tapped the gun to widen the other. A burst from inside
they went in ...

28

Bangkok, Present Day

The fish were enormous. Unless you knew that the murky Chao Phraya was home to massive catfish, some reaching two or three meters in length, you'd think it was some bizarre Thai myth. But not only are there giant fish visible in the river, there are hundreds of them.

As Martin looked over the rail of the Oriental Hotel pier, they seemed so numerous that you could almost imagine walking on them. They were in a frenzy, like in the videos he'd seen of salmon spawning, only these fish weren't spawning. They were feeding. On anything. They had learned the spots to congregate. Around the piers and patios of the luxury hotels, where tourists would drop chunks of bread and rice into the water. They were like animals in a zoo—the zoo being the river.

Martin dropped the pistol right in the middle of three or four dozen thrashing catfish. It disappeared forever.

He'd come to the river for a number of reasons, not the least of which was to get rid of the gun.

The 'River of Life'—murky, polluted and crowded. With its tributaries the Ping and Nam rivers, the Chao Phraya formed a network that traversed the length of the country, emptying into the Gulf of Thailand in the south. Its watershed covered over a quarter of the country and provided the means for an intricate irrigation network of life-giving water for the nation's rice paddies. Its canals had once snaked through the capital city, giving it its once well-deserved title—the 'Venice of the East.' But there were few canals left now.

It was here on the river that Martin had gotten to know the vampire. A first meeting was held at the Oriental, in the Author's Lounge, amidst the photographic history of kings past and present. And it was on the opposite bank of the river, at the Temple of Dawn, where the vampire allowed himself to be destroyed.

He said he had grown weary of the struggle to survive.

Had he grown weary again? Did he now have a suicidal tendency that caused him to yearn again for his demise, as it seemed Muraki did?

No, Martin was confidant. The vampire was at peace with himself. There was no reason for him to become a sacrifice other than to save the lives of Areeya and her unborn daughter. A sacrifice that Martin would be eternally grateful for.

It was dusk. Christmas Eve. The patio of the Oriental always looked like Christmas Eve when the sun went down. Thousands of little white lights sparkled amid the trees.

For the holiday the patio was decorated with potted poinsettia plants. They formed a red border that outlined the paths from the riverside back to the hotel. A huge white and silver Christmas tree glowed in the lobby of the Author's Wing.

Martin left the railing and walked slowly, lost in thought. Areeya was at home. There was now a security guard stationed outside Martin's door. Twenty-four seven.

His wife was fine. Healthy and strong. Their baby was fine. Healthy. Strong. He had much to be thankful for.

Martin headed for what was still referred to some fifty years after its construction as the new wing of the hotel. He passed through the Verandah restaurant and into the corridor. Ahead, on his left, the Bamboo Bar had just opened its doors. He studied the warm, inviting room through the open door. Not much had changed, he supposed, since 1947. He imagined Ramonne, resplendent in his tuxedo, greeting the guests.

A lone guitarist was setting up his equipment. He would serenade the early guests until the band came to the stage later in the evening. His hair was long and tumbled into his eye as he tuned his instrument.

Martin thought about having a drink. He decided he would.

Just one.

As a tribute to an old and dear friend.

Bangkok, 1967

The boat slid silently along the canal. Equipped with a six-cylinder engine mounted ingeniously on a gimble that allowed the driver to raise and lower the entire engine shaft and propeller, and thus navigate any depth of water, it had glided without power for the past three or four hundred meters at the vampire's instruction. The *klong* here passed through Ban Krua, a neighborhood in every sense of the word. The wooden homes on each side were occupied by silk-weavers, entire families dedicated to spinning the splendid material that the whole world now associated with the Kingdom of Thailand. All due to the diligence and foresight of one great man.

Jim Thompson.

It had been nearly twenty years since Ramonne had seen his old friend. Ramonne had not aged a day. His long hair was tied back tonight in deference to the slight breeze that was blowing, despite the heat that signaled the arrival of the dry season.

He motioned to the boat's driver, who used a long paddle to slow the craft as two graceful wooden spires appeared on the south bank of the canal. Through a verdant grove of trees, the distinct outline of a traditional Thai house on stilts could be seen. Warm light cascaded through its large open windows. The rich lacquer on the wood siding and paneling glowed in the lamplight and the leaves of the dense foliage played in the moonlight. The boat came to a halt directly opposite a large double window. In the window's frame, a white-haired man could be seen. Ramonne held his breath lest he call out to his old friend.

Jim Thompson was 61 and his face bore the lines of a life well-lived. Ramonne was pleased to see his old friend looking so fit. He watched as Thompson meticulously studied columns of figures in a business ledger. *Business.* Even at this late hour, it was business that was on Jim Thompson's mind. It was business that occupied his life now. The adventures of the past were just that, it seemed. *The past.*

As they should be. Ramonne smiled to himself.

Live long and prosper, my friend.

He motioned to the boatman and the craft was slowly and silently turned around. They headed back up the canal.

Cameron Highlands, Malaysia, March 26, 1967

Jim Thompson was restless. He'd tried a siesta but hadn't actually closed his eyes. The trip from Bangkok had been particularly exhausting.

He had just turned 61. He had a slight paunch but was still within ten pounds of the weight he'd maintained his entire adult life. He drank sparingly and he was trying to quit smoking. He felt good for his age and regretted very little of the rich and full life he'd led. He was known far and wide as the 'Thai Silk King' and he had come to the picturesque Cameron Highlands for a well-deserved vacation. He had recently moved his business into a handsome new building, a reconstruction of an eighteenth-century Siamese structure. The two days in the Highlands were meant to be a rest before he traveled down to Singapore and more business meetings.

He'd left Bangkok in a hurry with an old friend, Connie Mangskau, owner of one of Bangkok's finest antique shops. At the airport it was found that he'd neglected to get a mandatory cholera vaccination, and to get a stamp showing that his Thai taxes had been cleared. The former was taken care of by an official at the Customs office, and the latter was waived when Mrs. Mangskau agreed to sign as his guarantor for any outstanding taxes.

They flew to Penang. Neither of them had been to the 'Pearl of the Orient' before, and after checking in to their hotel, they made a taxi tour of the old colonial island. The next day, they crossed to the mainland at Butterworth and drove to the Cameron Highlands in a hired car. Throughout the journey, Thompson was aware of a big dark car that seemingly followed them after they had got off the ferry. The car stayed with them for about an hour and then was gone. Thompson didn't give it another thought until their driver said he was having engine trouble and needed to stop at Tapah, the last town before the road began to climb steeply up to the Highlands. Thompson and Mrs. Mangskau took an early lunch in the town. When they returned to the garage, there was not only a new vehicle, but a new driver and two large Asian men. The new driver told Thompson that the two men had also paid for the trip to the Highlands and would be sharing the car with them.

Thompson, by now, was not only tired but his military training had aroused his suspicions, and he said that the car wasn't big enough for them all to travel comfortably. He insisted that he had paid for a private car. Reluctantly the driver transferred their baggage and they departed for the hills, leaving the two men to wait for another ride.

The house was called Moonlight Cottage, and it was fairly

isolated. The road from the golf course below narrowed to one lane, bordered by thick jungle, before ending abruptly at the house. The two-story cottage was quite comfortable—three bedrooms, each with its own bath; a large living room with a fireplace; servants quarters; and a well-tended garden. It was owned by a Chinese doctor and his American wife, Mr. and Mrs. T.G. Ling. Thompson had enjoyed many long weekends here as their guest. He was an ardent hiker and loved the jungled hills.

On Easter Sunday the occupants of Moonlight Cottage got up early for church service, then enjoyed a lazy picnic on a broad plateau a short drive from the cottage. They returned to the cottage mid-afternoon, and all retired to their rooms for a nap.

After a while everyone was asleep. Everyone but Thompson. He lay on the bed, but sleep wasn't what he wanted. He wanted a hike. He put on his shoes, grabbed his walking stick with the elaborate silver handle, and very quietly, so as not to disturb his sleeping hosts and companion, slipped out the door.

The weather was mild. Much cooler than Bangkok. Twenty plus years of living in Southeast Asia had made him quite immune to thoughts about the heat. It was an ever-present factor of daily life, and one dealt with it without comment. But he appreciated the lure of the cooler climate that also brought his friends up to the Cameron Highlands.

Thompson kept to a trail that he knew. It took him downhill through thick jungle, and the cottage quickly disappeared from view. He used his cane to steady himself in the sometimes treacherous terrain.

He felt the most at ease and relaxed that he had in days. The small talk of the picnic had put him off. He was, if anything, extremely sociable, but the group encounters he preferred were usually of his own design. He regularly threw elaborate dinner parties in his beautiful old Thai house on the *klong* in Bangkok, so that he wouldn't suffer eating alone.

There, the conversation was tailored to his taste, as were his guests.

As he continued his descent, he thought about the remarkable journey he had been on since his odd arrival in Thailand 22 years earlier. On August 15, 1945 he was ready to parachute into the Cambodian jungle and assist the Thai resistance on a march to liberate Bangkok, when they received word on the plane that the war was over. They landed instead in full view of the Japanese, and calmly proceeded to disarm them.

Those years had seemed so full of adventure. The end of the war and the reorganization of Southeast Asia. The renovation of the Oriental Hotel. The espionage that his continued involvement with the OSS lured him into…

He shook his head and smiled as he thought of Delacroix, the remarkable Frenchman.

The man had claimed to be immortal. He most certainly was in possession of amazing, abnormal powers. Thompson still had dreams about their night 'flight' across the rooftops of Bangkok. He was sad he never saw the man again. He was also sad when he learned of the untimely fate of Lady Jane—she had perished when a Pan Am Clipper on a short flight across West Africa had crashed in Liberia in June, 1950. All forty on board had died.

Thompson's subsequent journey into the glitzy world of international fashion paled in comparison to those early forays into international intrigue. He actually missed the danger. He definitely missed the adventure.

But life was good. Life was full. He had no regrets.

The track grew slightly wider as he approached a narrow asphalt-and-packed earth road that bisected the track and snaked down to the golf course.

The sun was descending and Thompson thought he would rest a while on the road before turning around and climbing back to the cottage. He was surprised to see a big dark car parked beside the road. The passenger door was facing the track, and it swung open as Thompson approached. A man in a dark-gray suit smiled at him.

"Mr. Thompson, how are you?"

Curious, Thompson walked forward onto the asphalt and packed earth.

"Do I know you, sir?"

The man continued to smile as the rear doors of the car opened and two large men stepped out. He recognized them as the two he'd encountered at the garage in Tapah.

Thompson stopped in the middle of the narrow road.

"What is this?"

"Merely a meeting…between old friends."

Thompson stared at another man who sat stoically in the front seat of the car. He was a big man. Muscular. His hair was wavy and slicked back. He wore a neatly trimmed goatee. He was oddly familiar to Thompson.

"You're Japanese."

"I am…Excuse me, I seem to have forgotten my manners. My name is Nakimira. Koichi Nakimira."

Nakimira. A name Thompson hadn't heard in almost twenty years.

"What do you want?"

"You feel you know me. I sense that." The smile would have been at home on a Cheshire cat. "I feel I know you, as well. We have a history, you and I. One that I would like to explore…here in this leafy glade. It is a most pleasant spot, don't you think?" He made a token gesture to the forested hillside. In doing so, Thompson saw that the man was missing two fingers on his left hand.

Thompson hadn't taken another step since the two men had gotten out from the rear. They stood immobile, side by side, leaning against the car—watching him. Back at the garage he had paid only the slightest attention to them. They were unwanted, and that was all. Now that they represented an imminent threat, he studied them. They were Japanese, too.

Identical in stature. Brothers. Twins perhaps. They were armed, no doubt.

"Mr. Thompson. Please." Nakimira motioned for Thompson to come to the car. "Talking like this is becoming awkward."

The only thing that Thompson had working in his favor at the moment was his freedom. He could bolt and dash to the brush that led down to the golf course. He'd never make it back up the steep hill to the house, but he could possibly make it to the clubhouse.

"Mr. Thompson...I'm getting tired." Nakimira was now holding a pistol. Thompson felt the air go out of his lungs. The two men stepped away from the car and walked slowly to his side. They each placed a firm grip on his arms and led him towards the pistol. As he got close, Thompson recognized it.

A Walther PPK. Now an antique.

"It's a shame, Mr. Thompson, that we can't just have a civil discussion without having to resort to these..."

He turned the pistol in his hands. "These nasty toys."

Nakimira's smile faded and he turned the gun back on Thompson, who was now standing in the open door of the car. He had one goon on his immediate right, but due to the swing of the open passenger door, the other one was separated from him and watched from the front, where he leaned against the car's hood.

Thompson's chances of surviving whatever this encounter was all about, had just plummeted.

"Do you know who we are, Mr. Thompson?"

"No. Who are you?"

"We are patriots, Mr. Thompson. Much the same as you."

"I'm a businessman."

"Yes. The Silk King. A very good cover."

"I don't know what you're talking about."

"Please. Do not insult me. You were OSS in 1945, you are CIA today. A tiger does not change his stripes."

"That was a long time ago. The past should stay the past."

"We never get our property back."

"I never had your *property*. As far as I know, it was never recovered."

"And yet, your country got rich from what you did recover."

"What are you talking about?"

"The gold. Yamashita's treasure."

"Those were ill-gotten gains. Stolen from the countries you raped and pillaged."

Nakimira leaned forward. "Was the wealth returned to those countries? Was it redistributed?"

"You are talking of affairs that I have not been involved in for twenty years."

"I don't believe you."

"I don't care...Now, if you'll excuse me, I really must be getting back." Thompson turned to leave.

The man to his right moved forward and the other stepped from behind the door. They stood side by side, blocking his way.

"Mr. Thompson, our mission is the same as twenty years ago. Our question is the same."

Thompson turned back. He planted the walking stick on his right side and subtly adjusted his stance.

"Don't bother to ask. The answer is still the same. I don't know where your precious *Oracle* is...I never did."

Thompson was well aware of his predicament. He was alone. Against three armed men. Men who, no doubt, meant to kill him.

He had but one chance.

"Mr. Thompson, I'll ask you just once."

One chance. *Strike first.*

Thompson gripped his walking stick firmly with his left hand, and in one swift move he yanked the knife free with his right and drove it straight forward into the heart of Koichi Nakimira.

The Japanese's face registered the shock as he clutched for

his chest. Thompson yanked the blade free and thrust it upward at the man on his right. The blow managed to slice a deep gash in the hand that was reaching for the gun.

Thompson spun to his left and swung the stick out and back. It caught the other man on the knee and caused him to yell. It was merely a glancing blow, and by the time Thompson was able to move forward, the man had his gun out and shot Thompson in his right side.

Thompson used his stick to brace himself. The pain was nothing compared to the adrenaline that was rushing through him.

The will to live. It forced Thompson to take another step. A step toward freedom. A step towards the woods. A chance. That was all he needed. *Just a chance—*

Another shot rang out. This one was aimed. Carefully. It caught Thompson behind the right ear.

He was dead before he hit the ground.

29

Bangkok, Present Day

A child is born.

It is always a miracle. *That this child was born at all was truly miraculous.* Martin felt truly blessed.

Nina Simone Larue was born at 7:07 on New Year's Eve.

Martin had proposed to Areeya on New Year's Eve, two years before.

Martin's parents had been married on New Year's Eve. It was an auspicious date.

She weighed seven pounds, seven ounces. She was an auspicious baby. Seven was a very lucky number in Thailand. The nursing staff was delighted. They called her their lucky little rainbow.

Martin lay in bed beside Areeya. He held her to him and gazed through the window as the fireworks lit up the sky. Little Hon had been brought to the hospital by the maid to meet his little sister, and Martin could see his wide almond-shaped eyes reflected in the glass as he watched the explosions.

Martin pulled Areeya closer and kissed her beautiful hair. He knew that this was undoubtedly the happiest time of his life.

And the saddest.

————

"The master is a complex man."

Professor Kaestle refused to speak of the vampire in the past tense.

"The knowledge I've gained in just a few short years with him would equal a lifetime in the finest universities."

A bit overstated. But Martin understood the professor's attachment and loyalty. It was all part of the enigma that had been Ramonne Delacroix. Enchantment, seduction, repulsion and envy had all been emotions that Martin had felt in the vampire's presence.

It was early evening. A beautiful January day in Bangkok. The breeze blew uninterrupted down lazy Soi 8 as Martin approached the old building nestled in the grove of stately trees. The little *soi* was where he'd first resided when he arrived back in 1988. The old Indian hotel was still standing, where he'd lived for a month while he got his bearings and waited for the trust to be set up for him.

Those had been good days. One of the only times in his life that he had actually been forced to live on a budget. Twenty years ago there had been no skytrain, no subway, few condos, few high-rises at all. The very first condominium had been built on Soi 8, right next to the old French restaurant. It seemed very quaint and unassuming today.

How rapidly the city had transformed itself into the *Blade Runner* aspect it had today. The skytrain took forever to complete. Sukhumvit Road was a nightmare of construction for ten years, but once it was complete, it changed everything.

Martin remembered riding the virgin train on the evening it opened, on the King's birthday in 1999. Suddenly you could go almost anywhere you wanted, whenever you wanted. It was a miracle. He and his friends rode to Victory Monument, got out and admired the lights, then got back on and rode down to the river. Prior to this transformative event, you had to plan your journeys in the city carefully. You could not, for instance, go from Sukhumvit to join friends for drinks at the Oriental anytime from 4:00 to 9:00 p.m. Impossible. Traffic was completely frozen.

But the skytrain and the subsequent link to the new subway made those journeys not only possible, but rapid.

But Martin rarely rode the public transportation, preferring to use his driver, and he still planned his social engagements around the daily traffic. But he was not averse to having his driver drop him off at the nearest station, should the need arise.

These were the changes Martin had seen in two decades. The city that Ramonne sailed into in 1858 had been marvelous. He knew because Ramonne had *shown* him. He'd used his powers of thought transference to put Martin in his memories. It had all been magical. The tall ships filling the river, the graceful royal barges and the thousands of *sampans* plying the numerous canals, the city's golden temple spires shimmering by torchlight. He had experienced it all. Yet, he had no real knowledge of the Bangkok Ramonne had known after the Second World War.

Ramonne had spoken very little of it, and then only recently. Martin's knowledge of the era came mainly from the talk he'd had with the secret agent Babe, and that story didn't come with pictures. The one image he had was the newspaper photo of Ramonne and Jim Thompson in the Oriental.

He was staring at that photograph now, only it wasn't a faded newspaper clipping. He was looking at a sepia-toned print in an ornate silver frame.

They sat in the front room of the old two-story house. There were numerous large windows, all of which had previously been heavily shuttered and locked by Ramonne. They were now open, and the view of the garden was as Martin remembered it on the occasions he had dined here. Several times he thought he had missed the restaurant as he got deeper into the little street, and then suddenly, nestled amongst the trees, the warm glow of its elegant interior would beckon him.

The professor had called and invited Martin to visit. It was the first time Martin had been away from Areeya's side since Nina's birth, and he felt a bit nervous about entering the vampire's domain. He had been in his former lair, beneath the Lumpini Stadium, only once—and that was after the vampire's demise. It had been a fascinating treasure trove. Antique furnishings, hundreds of bottles of fine wine resting in a golden rack, fabulous daguerreotype photos of Angkor. And in the center of the room, a richly polished mahogany coffin.

After his rebirth, the vampire had chosen for his new 'pied-à-terre' a rooftop apartment deep in the bowels of Patpong.

Martin had never actually set foot inside Oiseaux, the villa the vampire occupied in Roluos near the temples of Angkor. He had wanted to keep his life with Areeya and the orphanage as far removed from the vampire's as he could. But he had driven by the villa and noticed the slow transformation that took place there. He had even hallucinated, seeing the vampire in the daylight, sipping wine in the shade of a huge tree. Tricks of the light and his mind, no doubt, but they convinced him to keep far away from Roluos and the vampire's châteaux.

The professor brought tea in blue-and-white china on a silver tray. "It was the cross, you know. He was cursed by the cross."

"I don't understand." The tea was strong, and Martin added some milk to his to temper it.

"Ramonne Delacroix. Of the cross. The family name. It cursed him for eternity." Professor Kaestle poured a shot of brandy into his tea. He offered the decanter to Martin, who declined.

"I still don't understand."

"He told me things. Things he never told anyone else."

"Yes?"

"Like the time he and Henri Mouhot traveled the Mekong into Cambodia and were shrouded in fog. The very first sight of Cambodia was this enormous cross breaking through the mist. The missionaries were there before them. Long before them. For over 200 years the Jesuits were instructing and inducting the natives. Mouhot was a staunch Catholic and sought them out wherever they traveled."

"Ramonne, no doubt, was born a Catholic."

"Ramonne was a *failed* Catholic. His uncle, Gustave, was a famous Jesuit. Thousands followed the coffin of the 'Apostle of Paris' through the streets when he died in 1858. Ramonne had turned his back on the Church at a young age."

He refilled Martin's cup.

"He despised the missionaries. He felt wounded that his own kind would seek to change what had been in effect for thousands of years."

Professor Kaestle sipped his brandy-laced tea. "Indigenous. You are familiar with the term?"

"Yes. Of course. It means the original."

"The Stens in Cambodia. The Akha and Karen of Thailand and Burma. The Hmong. These were the indigenous tribes that Ramonne encountered. He respected their traditions. Their legends, their lore. He felt as one with them. He could not understand the zealots' mission to introduce Christianity to these so-called savages. To save their souls. Ramonne believed their souls were quite safe as they were. Unmolested."

The setting sun cast long shafts of light through the trees in the garden and onto the bookshelves that housed Ramonne's library. Below the hundreds of rare volumes sat the stereo. The finely-balanced tone arm of the Bang & Olufsen turntable sat silent in its cradle, the stacks of classical and jazz LPs in a rack beside it. Martin smiled at the memory of his discovery of the remote-controller for the machine, lying in the silk folds of the coffin. When he had pushed 'play' the tone arm set gently into the groove and Chet Baker's magic horn filled the room below the old boxing arena.

"All the devils that plague the world are the product of the elimination of the indigenous peoples," Professor Kaestle continued. "Their connection to Nature and the gods kept the balance. Ramonne was not evil. He was a force of Nature. He personified the energy of Nature in plant and animal life. The energy that manifests itself in people, in music and dance. Intoxication and ecstasy. In lovemaking."

And bloodletting Martin thought as he sipped his tea.

"When he was *turned*…bitten…he related even more to the indigenous, in all its forms. Because now *he* was frozen in time. He did not age. He was indelibly tied to a world that would come and go. As the world progressed, he withdrew deeper into himself. He chose to ignore the modern world. He abandoned it, as it abandoned him."

The professor helped himself to more tea and the brandy decanter. "You were aware of his wealth?"

"I was. Although in the beginning he led me to believe he needed my money. In truth he wanted a friend."

"Do you know what my main function was?"

"I assumed you were more than just a driver."

The professor smiled. "He entrusted his fortune to me. The only stipulations were that it maintained a certain balance, and that the funds were never associated or affiliated with organized religion of any type. In that sense he had a non-denominational bias."

The professor opened a slim file and extracted a single sheet of paper. He handed the sheet to Martin. It was a typed list. A short list.

Martin scanned the sheet. "This is what you did with his money?"

The professor nodded.

"Endowing charities that have no religious affiliations isn't an easy task."

There were a few names on the list that Martin recognized. An organization that purified water in developing countries; another that provided food and shelter to victims of drought and pestilence. Midway down the list were two more names Martin recognized. One was Enfants Sans Refuge, the French group that he had worked with in rescuing children from the stinking rubbish dumps outside of Phnom Penh, where they scratched through the fetid waste for their daily sustenance.

Directly below the French group was a name that brought tears to his eyes. École Des Orphelins d'Angkor. The orphanage that Martin had founded in Siem Reap five years before. Initially to serve as school and home for a dozen hand-picked orphans, it had grown to house over four dozen today.

Grown with the help of an anonymous French philanthropist's trust. The Ennomar Foundation.

———

Martin went home. Home to his wife. Home to his miraculous newborn daughter. Home to his son.

Home to his family.

Home.

He treasured his life. He had had amazing journeys. Amazing adventures. His life had been mysterious, serendipitous and fascinating. He knew now that he was truly blessed. He could have continued to go on those journeys alone. But now he had the blessing of companionship.

He had been lost. Ramonne found him.

He had been unloved. Areeya loved him.

He had no family. Now he had a wife and children.

Life was splendiferous.

He wished his friend were here to share his immense joy. He was in the Ethan Allen living room, baby Nina on his lap. Areeya was asleep on the couch, and little Hon was torturing

Small Talk. The window was open. It was a very mild evening and the air-con was switched off.

Something brushed against Martin's shoulder. Little Nina smiled in recognition of something in the room.

Hon let go of the cat, and his face lit up.

"Da da," he blurted.

Martin just smiled.

Finis.

ABOUT THE AUTHOR

Jim Newport is a writer and Emmy-nominated production designer of both film and television. His film credits include *Bangkok Dangerous, Brokedown Palace, The Stepfather* and *Heart Like A Wheel*. In television he has set the "look" for many series by designing the pilot episodes of *The Lyon's Den, The Shield, The Education Of Max Bickford* and *China Beach*. His work on *The Piano Lesson* for the Hallmark Hall Of Fame was nominated for an Emmy in art direction. He was the production designer of season four of the worldwide hit TV series *Lost*. When not writing books or designing films, Newport performs as his alter-ego Jimmy Fame—a blues shouter, known to haunt the saloons and annual Blues Festival of his adopted home, Phuket, Thailand.

Please visit the author's website: www.vampireofsiam.com.

THE VAMPIRE OF SIAM SERIES

"These books are rich in cinematic imagery… and fascinating details of Thai history."

— THAILAND TATLER

The Vampire of Siam series is an epic tale that spans half the globe and a course of 150 years.

In *The Vampire of Siam* (Book 1) a nineteenth-century explorer, Ramonne Delacroix, encounters an ancient Chinese demon in the temples of Angkor Wat. His subsequent nocturnal transformation leads him to the capital of Siam, where he witnesses the coronation of kings and the city's metamorphosis into the modern day sin-city of Bangkok.

Living the life of the lone hunter for the first 145 years of his incarnation as a night stalker, the vampire is reborn in *Ramonne* (Book 2) and eventually seeks to know the true extent of his powers. As he learns, he evolves. By the second book's end, the vampire's strength is enormous and he has control of the true magic he has been vested with.

In *The Reckoning* (Book 3) Ramonne, armed with newfound knowledge, seeks the source of his powers. He journeys back to Cambodia and the ancient temples to a fateful encounter with Zhoupeng—the mighty devil who "turned him" so many years before. Ramonne vows to put an end to Zhoupeng's reign of evil over the poor land.

Throughout the three books, Ramonne's fate is inextricably entwined with that of Martin Larue—wealthy American expat. Drawn to each other by mutual admiration and fascination, they eventually end up relying on each other to sort out the twisted path they find themselves thrust upon.

Together they face vampire-hunters, corrupt cops, opium dens, bordellos, blind fortune-tellers, jealous lovers, terrorists, suicide-bombers, smugglers, warlords and soul-sucking demons.

The Siamese Connection (Book 4) begins in 1948 Bangkok, shortly after the end of WWII and the Japanese occupation of Siam. The vampire, Ramonne Delacroix becomes involved in a quest for a mysterious artifact—The Oracle—hidden during the war by the Japanese. He joins forces with the famous American Expat Jim Thompson, (before he was the Silk King he was an OSS agent) and together they do battle with the nefarious Japanese Black Dragons.

The tale continues in the present day picking up where *The Reckoning* left off. Martin Larue and his pregnant wife Areeya cross paths again with the vampire and soon they too are involved in a deadly game of cat and mouse with the descendants of the Black Dragons, who are still in search of the mysterious Oracle.

A fast-paced blend of fact and fiction, *The Siamese Connection* finally solves the mysterious disappearance of Jim Thompson.

"Newport artfully shapes the vampire legend into a Mekong cocktail of surprises." Christopher G. Moore.

CHASING JIMI

Chasing Jimi is a rock 'n' roll period piece. It spans one year - the summer of 1966 to the summer of 1967. From New York's Greenwich Village to swinging London to the stage of the Monterey Pop Festival. It follows the ascension of one Jimmy James, a struggling back-up guitar player, to the exalted throne of rock-god superstardom.

On the road through merry-old England with the re-named Jimi Hendrix we meet the madcap royalty of the British pop scene. Jimi forms an endearing friendship with Rolling Stones founding member Brian Jones, whose battles with numerous personal demons and plunge from the top mirror Jimi's rise and fascination with the drug culture.

As the Jimi Hendrix Experience gains recognition, Jimi's past associations throw their own stumbling blocks in his path. Contracts signed by him as a hungry studio session musician surface. Jimi's management team are able to put out most of these fires, but one particularly sleazy New York record producer refuses to be bought out, and even goes so far as to send a couple of Brooklyn wiseguys to London to bring back his artist.

Chasing Jimi is "The Sopranos" meets The Beatles. The author's intense admiration for Jimi Hendrix, his own magical experiences as a hippy in the great Summer of Love and a stint as a touring rock 'n' roll photographer in the 70s served as inspiration for Chasing Jimi.

Knowing the scrutiny he would be under for daring to write a fictional piece about Jimi, the author strived to be as accurate as possible in the timeframe of events. Liberties were taken, but they were taken in order to craft what hopefully is an amusing and entertaining tale that transports the reader back to a better time.

"Did you miss the 1960s? This funny, yet loving and respectful adventure mystery about the decade's electric sugar stud will take you back."

— JERRY HOPKINS, AUTHOR OF *THE DOORS: NO ONE HERE GETS OUT ALIVE.*

TINSEL TOWN: ANOTHER ROTTEN DAY IN PARADISE

"Tinsel Town is the best introduction-to-Hollywood novel I've ever read."

— DAVID GILER, PRODUCER/WRITER *ALIEN,*
UNDISPUTED, MYRA BRECKINRIDGE AND
MANY MORE.

A Hollywood novel by an author who has been there - done that. Jim Newport is an Emmy-nominated production designer of both film and television. His experiences in the early years of his career served as the inspiration for Tinsel Town.

Memoirs from those in the film trade are nothing new. The bookshelves are crowded with star biographies—directors, writers and producers offering to show how difficult and arduous it is to either direct, write or produce a movie. But Tinsel Town is no simple straightforward autobiography. Like Chasing Jimi, it is a work of 'faction' - combining fact and fiction. Tinsel Town doesn't gloss over the cracks in the scenery —the grit, the stench, the plain old-fashioned blood and sweat that making movies was really about in the wild and woolly Easy Rider days of independent filmmaking. A non-stop party.

Art student Joey Morton arrives in Hollywood in 1968 and stumbles onto a sound stage. It was everything a young New Yorker could possibly hope to find—sex, drugs, gorgeous women, backstage passes, access to movie stars, rock 'n' roll... and more sex and drugs.

The author not only gives the reader a glimpse into what it

was like to enter this privileged profession in arguably its most exciting time (when movies played out in front of your own star-struck eyes, rather than against a green screen to be digitally composited later), but he also spins a tale, unravels a mystery, and takes the reader on an adventure.

"Newport's novels succeed in their purpose ... they entertain."

— THE NATION.

"It moves like a runaway asteroid." Tim Hallinan, bestselling author of the Poke Rafferty series (set in Bangkok).

— TIM HALLINAN, BESTSELLING AUTHOR OF
THE POKE RAFFERTY SERIES (SET IN
BANGKOK).